Hounds
of the
Underworld

Hounds
of the
Underworld

The Path of Ra Book 1

Dan Rabarts   Lee Murray

RAW DOG SCREAMING PRESS

Hounds of the Underworld © 2017
by Dan Rabarts and Lee Murray

Published by Raw Dog Screaming Press
Bowie, MD

First Edition

Cover Image: Daniele Serra
Book Design: Jennifer Barnes

Printed in the United States of America

ISBN: 978-1-935738-96-1

Library of Congress Control Number: 2017938638

www.RawDogScreaming.com

Acknowledgements

Lee: Jennifer's asking for our acknowledgements.

Dan: You'll have to do it. I broke my wrist.

Lee: We should probably say something about how this isn't our first collaboration.

Dan: So you want me to thank the Baby Teeth contributors? This book is all their fault: if Baby Teeth hadn't been so fun, Hounds of the Underworld would still be lurking in a parallel universe somewhere.

Lee: When we thank them, can we get in this quote by American scholar Brené Brown? The one that says, "if you're not in the arena getting your arse kicked then I'm not interested in your feedback."

Dan: We did get some great feedback, and from some of the best in the arena: Debbie Cowens, Sandra Dusconi, JC Hart, and Grant Stone. Simon Fogarty.

Lee: Don't forget Jake Bible, Phillip Mann, Paul Mannering, and Jeff Strand. We should thank Raw Dog Screaming Press, too, Jennifer Barnes, John Lawson and J.L. Gribble for taking a chance on a couple of unknowns from down-under. When we set out to find a home for this quirky story, I didn't expect we'd feel quite so at home. I'm going to go first and thank my family, okay? To my children, Céline and Robbie, who understand Mum's need to write, and my soul-mate, David, who doesn't really, but always supports me anyway.

Dan: Damn, you did the family thing first. Now it'll sound like I'm copying. Never mind. To Chrissy, for letting me spend countless hours with my head in the clouds, because she prefers that to watching me rock back and forth in the corner, slowly gnawing my knuckles to the bone, which is what I do when I'm not writing. To Mum and Dad and Tony and Jan, who have always encouraged me in their own ways, despite never having witnessed the trauma of the knuckle-gnawing. To Isaac and Annabelle, for giving me all the right reasons.

Lee: And Dan, I want to thank you for agreeing to work with me. For all those long emails, the unexpected explosions, and beautiful sentences using the word 'spooling'. For being the Matiu to my Penny. Writing this book with you has been a challenge and a joy. (Next time, warn me about the explosions, okay?)

Dan: Likewise, thanks for having me along for the ride, and for the talking fridge. I quite literally couldn't have done this on my own. But I can't make any promises about explosions. They just happen.

Publisher's Note

Because the region this novel takes place in is so much a part of the story we have chosen to retain the British spelling conventions that are the standard in New Zealand. This work also incorporates New Zealand phrases and words from the indigenous Māori people so we have included a brief glossary in the back for anyone not familiar with these terms.

CHAPTER 1

- Matiu -

The place smells wrong. Not even bad, nothing Matiu can put his finger on. Just plain *wrong*, yet also, inexplicably, quite perfect. Spread out before him in shades of blood and bone he can see the shape of human history to come. Gradual decay and violent collapse all rolled into one brutal augury which he, for all his cursed vision, is too blind to comprehend. Like rot and sand and despair, and this stink of death just a distraction. An afterthought.

Moving away from the babble of voices—his sister, the detective, the uniform, the real estate agent who found the remains—Matiu walks a long, slow arc around the mess in the middle of the room, hemmed in by its sagging border of yellow crime scene tape. In some places, the tape droops into the muck, the edges turning up in the draught. Like something out of a B-grade horror flick.

It's not his business, nothing the fuck to *do* with him. He's just a driver, the moody Māori with the ink on his cheek, his nose, his chin, drawing those mildly suspicious glances from the cops. Wouldn't even be allowed in here if Penny wasn't the consult, if he wasn't her de facto bodyguard.

But he can't look away. They're convinced someone died here, because there's a puddle like someone dumped a barrel of offal and rotten vegetables soaked in red wine across the floor. But try as he might, Matiu just can't see a *body* in the muck. The only thing in there he can recognise is the bowl. It's one of those carved wooden pieces of junk they sell at the Pasifika markets over in Manukau, soft light wood with figures carved on the sides and detailed in black ink, trying to make itself look all authentic as if it actually came from the islands and wasn't just churned out in some South Auckland garage by kids whose parents should be sending them to school but are sweatshopping them instead. The bowl sits there in the muck, soaked in red, rivulets of dried blood clinging to its sides like spider webs. Like some fool thought they could catch all that mess in a goddamned fruit bowl.

"Bet they got a shock," Matiu mutters. He kneels near the crime tape, drags a finger through the congealed blood, sniffs it. Wrinkles his nose. He doesn't know what a dead body should smell like; meat and shit and stale blood, probably. This is all that, and something else. Something sweet, fruity. Almond? Something he really doesn't want to put his nose into any further, in any sense of the word. He rubs his fingers together, feels grit on his skin. Dirt, maybe, or sand, in the old blood.

He stands, wiping his hand on his coat, looks about. The rest of the building was pretty clean, swept and vacuumed and ready for potential buyers. Until the real estate agent had forced the locked door, thinking it was stuck. She'd entered the room and found the pool of gore; stepped into the scene of a murder, maybe, or something worse.

Interesting shit.

But it's not any of his fucking business.

His eyes fall on the bowl. It's inside the tape, not far, but further than he can reach. He'll have to step over if he wants to touch it.

None of your fucking business.

That would really piss off his sister. Penny gets funny about shit like disturbing the scene of a crime. But the bowl *knows*. It's the thing that doesn't belong. Hell, none of it belongs, not the cold spill of mortal remains, not the blood-spattered crime tape, not the creeping sense that something happened here, something more than just someone dying, someone being blended to a sludge, something rank and corrupt. It's the bowl.

"Go get it."

"Piss off," he replies to the shadows, to the voice at his shoulder.

But he knows he will.

- Pandora -

Penny can hardly wait to get inside. Hitching up her satchel, she nods to the uniform on the door. It's all she can do not to grin, although that would hardly be professional. Nothing for months, and now she's offered lead researcher on a case? Not just an assist either, but lead researcher. And in her own right, for her *very own* company. Instead, she gives her ponytail a cheery tug. Maybe things are finally picking up. Then she remembers Matiu.

Yeah, things are just peachy.

Penny can't understand why her parents insist on treating her like a twelve-year-old. She'd called for a driver, not a damned babysitter. The last thing she needs is Matiu tagging along like a piece of soggy toilet paper stuck to her shoe. She clamps her lips shut and glances back. And just look at him: head down, shoulders slumped, hands stuffed in the pockets of his leather jacket. *He's* the one behaving like a sulky teen. Why does he have to go talking to himself when they're out in public, anyway? Mumbling under his breath to his imaginary friend…

She steps through the doorway, noting its splintered frame, and is confronted by a human wookie. Two metres plus, with oversized hands, and long overdue for a haircut.

"Who the fuck are you?" it bellows.

Penny jumps, startled. "I was called…"

Get a grip, Penny. You're not here to audition for Miss Muffet. You have a right to be here…

"You the lab girl? The one that Noah Cordell recommended? Pandora somebody? Cordell swore you were reliable; I expected you half an hour ago."

Penny tries not to bristle at the slight. After all, this is *work*. And apart from a few tests—some simple DNA analyses to resolve a private paternity suit and routine monitoring of the blooms stinking up the city's beaches—there hasn't been much cause to turn on the fumehood since she left LysisCo. She squares her shoulders, extends her hand.

Suck it up, girl.

"Yes, I'm from Yee Scientific Consultancy. Although, I prefer to be called Penny, if you don't mind. You must be Detective Tanner."

No handshake. Instead, the behemoth raises two gloved hands. "Yeah, and in an ideal world, I prefer His Lordship, but hey, I can't have everything. That over there is Senior Constable Toeva Clark," he says, indicating an officer with a backwards jerk of his head. Behind him, Clark is taking the statement of an expensively dressed woman in her forties. He acknowledges Penny with a wave of his tablet. "You'll work with Clark; he's the uniform on this case, and your liaison with the department. Anything you need to tell me, you tell him."

"This isn't the first time I've worked a crime, Detective."

"Yeah, that's what Cordell said. He also said you were cheap, and with this latest round of frickin' budget cuts and seventeen serious crimes to solve—"

Penny cuts him off. "I get it. You need a result. So what do we have?"

"You tell me, because I'm stumped." Tanner sweeps a meaty arm about the room. "Firstly, we've got this storeroom painted top to bottom in black, which, if you ask me, looks more like the inside of a nightclub than an office block. We've got a guy's clothes, a pool of blood, a cereal bowl, and not much else. The real estate agent, Patisepa Tayler—that's her with Clark—turned up with a client this morning, found the door jammed, and it wouldn't open with her so-called 'master key'. So she crossed the road and got a construction worker to come over and prise it open with a crowbar. We already interviewed him. Said it was bolted from the *inside*."

She glances at the sludge of gore on the floor. Messy. "No body?"

Tanner stares at her. "Do you see a body, Ms Pandora?"

Penny's cheeks burn, but luckily, the detective's phone rings and he turns away to answer it. While Tanner is barking at the poor sod on the other end of the line, Penny moves away to survey the scene. Now, the important thing here is to ignore the gore. She's made that mistake before, getting dragged in by the horror. And in some cases, there can be enough blood and offal to make a meat worker blanch. Head, not heart, is the key here. Separating out the emotional. Making objective observations.

Vaguely aware of Matiu's dark form hovering near Clark, Penny pulls out her phone to record her observations and, trying not to feel too self-conscious, makes a tour of the room. "November 4, 2045, 10:12 am. Vacant industrial premises owned by Fletcher Enterprises, second floor, crime scene. It's large for a storeroom: I estimate forty metres square. A couple of cabinets along the northern wall. Windowless. Cool, stop." And relatively clean, if you exclude the *jus*. Environmentally controlled? She presses record again. "Suspect the black paint on the walls and ceiling is recent: the smell of volatised organic compounds still noticeable, stop." If she had a portable flame ionisation detector, she could measure the concentration of aerosolised solvent particles still in the air, and then extrapolate back to determine the date the room was painted. Penny almost snorts. Chance would be a fine thing! Even if she could stretch to a piece of equipment that pricey, those things are dangerous. And judging from the way Tanner's people are traipsing in and out of the room, the result wouldn't be accurate anyway. Penny rejects the idea, but it's OK: she's just warming up, and there are other clues. Like this slight bubble in the floor. Bringing the device closer to her face, Penny minutes her observations: "Irregularities in floor, stop. Question possibility of a false floor, stop." Penny steps on the bubble and lets it bounce back. Perhaps this room used to house an old data centre? Back in the late 2020s, a lot of companies put in their own after the big US data SNAFU. They drilled it into her at university, even though she never studied a single IT paper. One-oh-one grand fuck-ups. Caused a huge backlash against the use of public clouds and people—companies—figured it would be safer to operate their own data storage hardware locally—like they used to in the old days. That could explain the lack of windows here. And a false floor, because a large data centre would require a cooling system, somewhere to run the ducting, cables. Well, there's an easy way to determine whether it's hollow. Dropping the phone into her satchel, Penny pulls out a pair of gloves and snaps them on. Then, still outside the sagging yellow tape, she crouches, rapping her knuckles on the floor. It would help if Tanner wasn't still bellowing, she might be able to hear. Instead, she lowers her ear to the floor.

Low frequency sound.

Yup, sounds like it could be hollow. So, if her hunch is correct, the original under-floor grid cavity has been covered by a false floor allowing the room to be used as a basic storage area. It doesn't look like the false floor has been removed, so there's little chance a body—if there was a body—could've been stowed there, but Penny makes a record to have Clark pull up the floorboards later, after the scene is cleared away. Actually, come to think of it, she'll have him check the overhead vents, too. If a body was taken out that way, she'd expect to see a disturbance in the dust.

Tanner is still yabbering, his face is reddening. At least *she* isn't getting the brunt of it. Should she wait for him? No. Best not to bother him. He's already made it clear that where she's concerned, efficiency is the key criterion. Penny pockets her phone, steps over the tape, and almost ruins her shoes in the congealing pool of blood and gristle, a macabre version of Bunol's *La Tomatina*. Lucky she's not squeamish. Stepping around the pool, Penny doesn't bother to calculate the likely volume of liquid. There's a lot; certainly enough to have been fatal, although, to be fair, a little bit of blood can go a long way.

From the looks of the blood spatter, a major vessel was involved. But unless the victim was a child, surely there'd be some drag marks? Even then, it's unlikely an offender could remove the body without leaving some kind of trail. And these clothes are adult sizes. A polo shirt and pants. She flips the collar out. Size L.

Then there's the little bowl. It's odd. Why would a bowl be here? And how did it come to have blood in it? Do these things belong to the murderer, or the victim? Tanner probably already had Clark search for identification, but Penny rechecks the pants' pockets anyway. She can't risk getting egg on her face for not being sufficiently thorough.

Nothing.

A stray wisp of hair has escaped from her ponytail. She brushes it back awkwardly with the inside of her arm. Careful. Don't want to contaminate the scene.

Or myself.

The offending strand out of the way, Penny rests her satchel on her knee and flips it open. She'll need to bag up the bigger items later, but for the moment, she takes out some adhesive specimen tape and begins her sampling.

Working again. Penny almost hums, but stops herself in time. Not that she's ashamed or anything. There's no rule that says a person shouldn't enjoy their work, but it wouldn't be appropriate here. Most people think crime scenes are sad, wretched places, and they'll do whatever they can to avoid them. The suit on his way to the office. Students meeting outside a coffee shop. Call it superstition, but most will look away, cross the road, take another route, afraid the victim's misery might somehow settle on them. It's as if where there's betrayal, Misfortune lingers, conveying Her despair on the passing breeze. Even a wallet, snatched at random in the street, can leave a sense of loss that will haunt passers-by long after the offender has pocketed the plastic and gone on his way. But Penny loves crime scenes. Not the suffering, of course. Or the ugliness. Only a psychopath could take pleasure in that. No, Penny loves their matter-of-factness; the way they reveal themselves in logical yet exquisite patterns, like the interlinking of bases in a DNA polymer. And when a crime scene is chaotic like this one, then Penny loves it all the more. The thrill of teasing out the tangled bundles, each newly uncovered node leading into the next. It's like a dance, a beautiful dance of discovery.

"Hang on, who's that guy?"

Miss Muffet caught out again, Penny leaps up and just manages to avoid compromising her sample. *Matiu.* What the hell does he think he's doing, lurking at the edge of the tape, poking his nose in where it doesn't belong? She told him to keep out of the way. Penny throws him a dirty look, to back off. Not that he's looking at her. "Him?"

"Yeah," says Tanner, "him with the tats. He's not one of ours."

Damn. She knew she should've made Matiu wait outside.

Like you could ever make Matiu do something he didn't want to.

"Um, he's my driver."

"Driver, eh?" Tanner lifts an eyebrow.

"Yes."

"You two married?"

"No!"

"Really? Because the look you just threw him was like the one my wife gave me this morning when I took the three-day-old sweats out of my gym bag."

Penny stifles a grimace. "It's just…he's my brother."

"Really?" That eyebrow again. Good one. Consultant brings baby brother to crime scene. Penny can just imagine how that will go down in the department lunchroom. "He doesn't look like your brother."

"Same mother, different father." Not exactly true, but Penny isn't about to give a genealogy lecture at a crime scene. Tanner scrutinises them with his detective gaze, first Penny, then Matiu, then he shrugs. "That figures…" he says. "Yeah, what is it, Clark?"

"Sorry to interrupt, Sir, but Ms Taylor was wondering when she might be able to leave? She says she has to meet a client. She's getting quite agitated. I told her that you wouldn't be long, but that was before you got on the phone…"

Tanner heaves a sigh. "OK, let's go talk to her."

Originally, Penny had thought the woman was in her forties, but on closer inspection, she revises her estimate up a decade. It looks as if a good percentage of the agent's sales commissions have been spent—along with her lunch hours—in one of Auckland's drop-in enhancement salons. With her mustard pantsuit and over-teased mane, Patisepa is vaguely leonine. Not to mention roaring mad.

"Detective, I'd like to help you, but I really must go."

"Just a few more questions, if you don't mind, Ms Taylor." Tanner's tone is smooth. "You say, you found the room locked?"

"That's right. I already told Officer Clark everything."

"It was locked, you say?"

The agent rolls her eyes. "I keyed in the code and it wouldn't let me in."

"Did you consider that someone might have changed the code?"

Now Patisepa folds her arms across her chest. "Why does it matter how I got in? If you must know, I have the master code. It's supposed to override any other code, and this *is* just a storeroom, after all. When it didn't, I assumed it was jammed, so I got someone and we broke in. And that's what we found. Over there. All that blood! And my vendor, Mr Fletcher's clothes sitting in a pile right there!" She exhales pointedly, through flared nostrils, like a highly strung race-horse.

Tanner isn't intimidated. "How do you know they're his clothes?"

"It's his polo shirt."

"This is an Auckland Blues Super Soy polo. Thousands of people must own this shirt."

Taylor shrugs. "I don't know. It looks like his polo. He was wearing one just like that the last time I saw him."

"And when was that?"

"Four days ago, I think. I'd have to check my diary. I dropped in at his office to set up today's viewing."

"Sir?"

Penny and Tanner turn to look at Clark.

"Well?"

"I've had the department trying to track down the building owner—this Darius Fletcher that Ms Taylor refers to—and it turns out he was reported missing by his sister..." Clark consults his notepad. "...a Miss Rose Fletcher on the first of November. Seems Darius planned a late supper with his sister on Halloween but he never showed up."

"Why didn't I know this?" Tanner storms. Penny has to admire the way Clark doesn't wince.

"Sir, the person in question was an adult. Uniforms on the desk figured Fletcher got a better offer than dinner with his sister. And maybe that better offer extended to more than one evening. The Desk didn't think there was anything to investigate, so they...they filed it."

Tanner's stare fixes his junior. "So, at this point what we have is enough blood to fill a small aquifer but what we don't have, is any idea of whether Fletcher is missing, or dead?"

Patisepa taps a patent court shoe. "What's the difference? All that blood? I imagine my client will be put off buying now."

- Matiu -

"You stay out of it."

Matiu talks into his collar. He doesn't need to speak loud for Makere to hear him. Sure as hell doesn't need anyone hearing him talking to himself. They already think he's *pōrangi*. No point giving them any more reason to believe it.

"I'm not getting into this. Nothing to do with me."

Matiu stares at the bowl, biting his lip as the voice drifts at him from the shadows of empty cabinets at his back. The stick figures carved on the bowl's skin shiver a little, as if trying to free spindly limbs from their wooden prison, from their etched fishing poles and canoes, like they want to step away from that time-frozen sea, flee whatever lurks beneath the black ink.

"But you want to know what happened, don't you?"

Matiu glances at the others, all talking, taking notes, buried in their thoughts and assumptions. Surely they won't notice if he has a look.

He steps over the tape, reaches for the bowl.

A quick step here, a stretch, and it's in his hands. A long string of black and red gore clings to it as he steps back.

The walls scream at him.

He drops the bowl with a clatter, and from the shouts he knows that Penny is screaming at him too, and the cop is yelling. He barely hears, the white noise ringing in his ears. Matiu staggers, skids in the muck, goes down on one knee. Then Penny's there, dragging him back, the yellow tape tangling his shins.

"What do you think you're doing?" she hisses. "You can't go touching the evidence. Now we have to eliminate you as a suspect, you moron."

But Matiu doesn't hear her. The bowl rolls long lazy circles on the clean floor, catching in the sticky blood. He sees its sides coated in red. Remembers, without remembering, the hot spill. Remembers the hunger.

"Why did I ever let you come down here?" Penny grumbles, hoisting him to his feet. For a techie, she's surprisingly strong. Or maybe it's just that Matiu's bones feel suddenly thin, light as a ghost. Some days he feels like the air can just pass straight through him. Some days, he's sure it does.

"Go wait in the car," Penny growls. "I can't afford for you to screw this up for me."

Matiu shakes her off, casting a look over her shoulder at the cop, his thunderstorm brow. If he wasn't her brother, and a driver, he'd be locking him up, Matiu knows. He gives him a cold grin. Can't be worse than where he's already been. "You don't want to take this on, sis," he says, keeping his voice low so the cop won't hear. "It's uglier than it looks."

Penny glares at him. "Why don't you just leave the science to the experts? I'll be down once I've got what we need to take back to the lab. Now get out of here."

Matiu shrugs, walks away without another word, leaving Pandora and the cops to their work. The warehouse echoes around him, and he holds his hands to his ears to keep out the hollow ringing of his own footsteps, of the screams that resonate back up from the brief moment when he touched the bowl. Felt the rush of life, death, intermingling.

It's his blessing, his curse, to feel the veil that lies between the worlds, to touch it as it slips and slides in his grasp, rasps along his senses, teases at his dreams. Not that Penny, with her blinkered commitment to scientific process and logical explanations, has ever been willing to accept that. She is her father's daughter after all, just like he is his mother's son.

"Aren't you glad you did it?"

He doesn't bother looking for Makere; knows that if he does all he'll see is a hunched form turned away from him, long raven hair falling over his shoulders, more figment than form, a hint of someone glanced in a crowd, never quite where you expect him to be. But there, no less. Not that anyone else can see or hear him. Makere is Matiu's other curse, his other blessing, though some days he doesn't think of him as either of those. Sometimes he's just a right royal pain in the arse. Has been, ever since they were kids.

Outside, the sky is as hard a blue as ever, the temperature quickly climbing as the sun gets up. It'll be another hot one, and it's not even December. The bloom in the harbour will start to stink fairly soon, and the wind off the Hauraki Gulf will spread it over Auckland's hills and suburbs. But the stink of death seems to hang on Matiu, the stink of everything that's so wrong about this scene, hanging around and refusing to leave him alone, just like Makere. Crossing to the car, he leans against the door and runs his hands through his thick dark hair, lank around his neck, sweating in the sun beneath his leather coat. The tainted factory looms against the perfect sky, its face cast in shadow and quietly mocking him.

Something happened here, something dark and deadly that crept up from the earth and crawled among the shadows. Maybe murder, maybe not. Maybe something Penny shouldn't be getting caught up in. For all that she's a pedantic pain in the arse, her worldview hemmed in by their parents' expectations of her and her own misconceptions of reality, she's still his sister. He has to keep her from this shit as best he can, and if she's too stubborn to walk away, then he'll have to hang on her like a bad smell so that when it all turns sour, he might be near enough to do something. That's what family's for, right?

Yeah, right.

CHAPTER 2

- Pandora -

Penny wishes she didn't have to come straight back to the lab. Grubbing around in the detritus at Fletcher Enterprises has left her feeling grimy. Crime scenes always do this to her. A shower would've been nice: a good scrub using a shower brush and a decent dose of 4-chloro-3,5-dimethylphenol soap, with its antibacterial properties and distinctive pine smell. She sighs as she pushes open the door to the lab with the back of her hand. She'll just have to make do with a box of antiseptic wipes instead. Inside, she deposits her satchel and the bagged samples on the bench, taking care that the little bowl doesn't roll off onto the floor. Just a glimpse of the bowl's crudely carved rim reminds her of Matiu, and instantly her hackles rise. That idiot. What did he have to go and touch it for? Penny could've throttled him. She'd said stay out of the way.

Stay. Out. Of. The. Way.

What's not to understand? But no, Matiu can't even get that simple instruction right. And what was the deal with his ridiculous paranoia over this little bowl...?

Penny stomps to the cupboard and takes a lab coat off the hook. Too big. This must be Beaker's spare one. Jeepers. What is it with guys today? How many times has she told him to hang his lab coats on the *right*? Replacing the lab coat on the correct hook, she slips on her own, just as the coat-hook culprit comes out of the chemical store.

"Hey, you're back."

"You know, Beaker, some days you astound me with your powers of observation," she says, laying it on, but they both know there's no malice in her words. Why berate poor Beaker for her problems? Truth be told, it's lovely to come home to the lab and find him here, like a loyal sheep dog, waiting on the porch. And Beaker *is* loyal: the only one who really supported her when the shit hit the fan. She knows that kind of devotion shouldn't be exploited: it could come back to bite her. Besides, Beaker deserves more. It's not his real name, of course. A scientist called Beaker? Hardly original. Grant Deaker is the name on the payslips, but Beaker's passion for bench-work, together with a striking resemblance to the century-old cult figure, made freshly famous by the animated show that ran on MTV in the 2030s, means no one calls him anything else, not even his mother.

"So, how'd it go? Did we get the contract?"

Penny can almost see his tail wag. Pulling her lab stool over to the bench, she sits down and leans on her elbows. "Seems like it."

"No way. How?"

"Gee, Beaker," she says wryly. "Thanks for the confidence."

"I didn't mean it like that. You know I didn't. I meant how did they—"

"Find us? Cordell, apparently."

Beaker's eyes widen. "You're kidding me."

Penny shakes her head. "Nope."

A frown. "You sure there isn't a catch? There's got to be a catch. Cordell doesn't do anything for nothing. He's so…calculating. I can't believe that you—" Beaker breaks off, his blush as red as his hair.

Pretending not to hear his last comment, Penny makes a show of sorting through the labelled samples on the bench. "I don't think Cordell was doing us any favours. It's more about taking some heat off LysisCo. Apparently, the department has seventeen—no, make that eighteen—cases on at the moment. And that's just on the southern side of the city. The way the police super told it, there's an epidemic of brutality going down, and only his department to hold back the floodgates of hell."

"In conclusion, there's too much work on so Cordell's thrown us his dregs."

"Probably, but beggars can't be choosers, Beaks."

Ain't that the truth? The last time Penny checked it—just this morning after breakfast—her bank account was running precariously low. She figures she has enough of her savings to last maybe another month. After that she'll have to let Beaker go. Sell off the equipment. Admit defeat. She doesn't want to have to do that.

And give Cordell the satisfaction? *Like hell.*

"Pand—" Her head snaps up. "Sorry—Penny—what exactly are we working on?"

"Oh, yes. We haven't got much time. It'd be helpful to have some information before I interview the victim's…" Is Fletcher a victim? Is he even missing? Penny doesn't know. She trails off. Instead, she removes the adhesive samples from her satchel. "There's this blood…"

Beaker cocks his head.

"You're certain it's blood?"

"Uh-huh," says Penny. "I did a presumptive test at the site: took a swab and tested it with TMB and peroxidase. Lovely blue-green colour indicating the presence of a haem group. So, at least we know it's blood."

Beaker cocks his head again. Penny smiles. That consistency is one of the things she likes about him. He may not be able to tell his coat hooks apart, but Beaker is a stickler for method. There's always a chance of false positives with indicator tests, which means the substance sampled might not be blood at all.

Beaker is cheery. "Want me to do a crystal confirmation?" he asks.

Slipping off the lab stool, Penny shakes her head. "Microscope's quicker." She lifts off the dust cover and turns on the apparatus, then sets about preparing a blood slide, chatting to Beaker as she works. "It was like something out of a TV show. Locked room. Blood—" She pops the slide on the stage and sets the clips, then corrects herself. "Possibly blood everywhere. And the weirdest thing, there was no body. I thought it was creepy, but it completely freaked Matiu out. And I didn't think anything shocked him much." She twists the objective into place, then fiddles with the fine focus. "Well, it's definitely blood because we have erythrocytes, leukocytes—quite a few of them are neutrophils... Hey, Beak, look at this." She moves aside to allow her colleague a peek down the eyepiece. "Check out the erythrocytes."

He steps back. "I'm not sure I know what I'm looking for."

Penny leans in again, adjusting the magnification up for sharper focus. "I don't know. I guess I'm out of practice using these old light microscopes, but I thought I saw a central pallor in these red blood cells."

"You think the sample might not be human?" Beaker edges her out of the way. "The size looks OK. Biconcave. $7\mu m$."

"Possibly a dog? Their red cells are comparable to ours." Although how a dog might be involved, Penny couldn't say. Still, it seems the case might not be as sinister as they first thought. If the blood found at the scene is all of canine origin— and they won't know that until they've checked all the samples—then it's possible that the only victim could be someone's pooch. Horrible enough, although in that case, it would mean that Fletcher is only missing, and not murdered, and Tanner has one less case to worry about.

But Beaker is already off after a stick, heading towards the chemical store, delighted to have something to chase. "No sweat, Penny, I'll check for dog erythrocyte antigen. That way we can rule it out."

"I'll make a start on the clothes, then."

He waves his hand in agreement. "Put some tunes on, will you?"

A minute later, the two of them have their heads down working, Gen Zedders' latest remix blasting through the lab.

"Penny?" Beaker says, an hour and a half later. Penny can hardly hear him over the grumbling of her stomach. Damn, she's missed lunch and Matiu should be here soon. Meanwhile, all she's managed to do is eliminate his dirty great thumbprint from the bowl. Although, to be fair, it wasn't particularly hard. There were only two sets, and Penny would bet her flailing bank account the other set belongs to Darius Fletcher.

"This sample is definitely canine blood." Penny cocks her head. "There's no question. It tested positive for DEA, and I ran a DNA fingerprint, too."

"The new machine run OK?"

"Yeah, great. Did the job."

That's a relief. The Breadmaker™ bench-top DNA typing machine had been the biggest single capital outlay Penny had had to fork out to set up her little lab, but these days, with so much analysis dependent on DNA typing, she was banking on the purchase being a good one. Investment on a price per use basis: it's the same way she justifies spending money on decent jeans, and the reason there's only cheap FirstWorld supermarket make-up rolling around in the bottom of her bathroom drawer. It also explains why her bank account is emptier than a beer keg at a high school leavers' party.

"But you should have a gander at this," Beaker says. Penny turns off the light-box and follows Beaker to his workstation where he pulls up a screen. He steps back and gestures at her to take a look.

- Matiu -

The Commodore speeds across Auckland Harbour Bridge. A freight truck crawls past in the opposite direction, sickly sweet biodiesel fumes funnelling into Matiu's nostrils as they pass. Apart from that, there are few cars to be seen. Aside from logistics carriers, public transport operators, cops, the unusually wealthy and drivers like Matiu working for companies with lucrative government courier contracts, most people don't have the means to burn up fuel jaunting around. If you can't bill for it at the other end, you probably don't take the car but a biodiesel bus, or a solar-powered train. One of the benefits of family. Even with his past, he still has a solid job doing something many now consider a luxury.

The motorway slides by, typically quiet. Matiu tries not to think about the pool of blood, and the voices that swarmed him when he touched the bowl, but he suspects it will continue to haunt him. For how long, he doesn't know. Until he can forget it? Or until he's put whatever was in that sucking pool of darkness, screaming his name - screaming every name - to rest, somehow?

Further thoughts are put on hold as his tablet pips on the passenger seat.

"Yo," he answers, and the tablet opens the call in speaker mode. Matiu has never liked that neural implant shit the rich kids have been getting injected between their ears. He could afford it—Mum and Dad could afford it for him, anyway—but he has enough voices in his head already without adding any more.

"Matiu, it's Erica. Did you forget our appointment?"

Fuck, Matiu mouths silently. Erica frowns on him swearing. "I've had work on. Didn't I message you? Sorry."

"I suppose the work logs will back you up?"

Matiu smiles. She doesn't miss a trick, Erica, and she's kinda hot for a white chick, but this time his alibi will hold water. Today has all been about bona fide work engagements, and nothing more. No need to blackmail Penny into hacking the logs and making them say what he wants them to. Not this time. "Sure will. Been at a murder scene this morning."

That shuts her up, for a second anyway. "I'll make a note to follow that up, you know I will. Where are you now? I've got a slot open this afternoon."

"No can do, I'm afraid." Matiu shakes his head as he eases onto the Manukau off-ramp. "Got an important pickup from the airport to drive up to Auckland Council HQ. Then I'm back on call for the murder investigation."

"Well, don't you just have the exciting day job?"

More exciting than a probation officer's, he wants to say, but he's learned it's best not to wind Erica up. For all his freedoms, she still has the chops to make his life hell if she wants to. "Look, can we say tomorrow, eleven-ish? I'm heading over your way to see Ma—" He cuts himself off mid-stream, remembering who he's talking to. He fakes a cough. "Tomorrow. I can come by tomorrow. That OK?"

"Be here."

"I will."

The call cuts off, and Matiu takes a deep breath as he swings down towards the airport. A couple of dark blips bob through the sky, at the end of the runway that used to be for the international jets, back in the day when jet fuel was affordable. Probably experimental photovoltaic aircraft. The near end of the airport is cordoned off for government operations, and the rest operates as an aero club for mad scientists trying to reinvent the wheel, so to speak, without the luxury of gasoline. Poor deluded sods. All that hope and enthusiasm, chasing a fool's dream. The Golden Age of cheap oil is over, man. The sooner some people get that into their heads, the better.

Matiu's early. He parks on the hill outside the security zone. No point being the Māori boy hanging around the airport, the bored rent-a-cops watching him sidelong, any longer than necessary. So he gets to watch the Chinese naval helicopter thunder in, its rotors throwing a hundred-meter-wide shadow across the grass and water around the landing zone. Somewhere, maybe five miles offshore, Matiu imagines the PLA warship that's steamed down here at great expense to transport this diplomat to Aotearoa. What else will it be doing while it crawls up and down the coast? Sure as shit won't be idly waiting for their VIP to come back from his meetings and diplomatic receptions.

But, once again, it's none of Matiu's business. Spying on other nations still happens, maybe now more than ever; it's just harder to move people around than it used to be. Matiu sees it, like a fly on the wall, but paying attention to shit like that is asking for trouble. Or to get yourself disappeared.

As the bird settles on the tarmac, Matiu pulls the Commodore onto the road. Fuck the politics, he's just doing his job and keeping his nose clean. As he drives through the checkpoints, he tries not to think about the bowl, the voice. The rage that flowed up out of the darkness, the hunger.

The way the dark had *looked at* him. Like it wanted him to look *back*.

CHAPTER 3

- Pandora -

OK, so where the hell is Matiu? She'd said to come back after lunch today, not sometime next week. It's already after three. Checking her watch, Penny goes to the window and looks along the street for the Commodore in case she missed him arriving and he's parked out there waiting. Nada. Rien. Zip. Just a row of overflowing dumpsters and a kid spraying pink graffiti on the fence opposite. Heaving a sigh, Penny comes away from the window and dumps her satchel on the bench. Thrums her fingers on the hardtop surface. Taps her toe. Geez, if she'd known he was going to be this late, she would've run a few more tests, rather than clearing up. Like she's got nothing better to do than waste time waiting. She would've liked to have made some progress on the clothes found at the site—tested for hair and skin—instead of handing the responsibility over to Beaker. She shakes her head. Of course, what would Matiu know about responsibility?

"Matiu still not here, then?" Beaker asks. Penny almost chews him out for stating the obvious yet again, but she holds herself back because she can see him nibbling his bottom lip, nervous. Is she really that scary or is Beaker just projecting her anxiety back at her? Poor guy. Only half a day in the lab with Penny and he runs the whole emotional gamut.

"Did you call despatch? Maybe they can give you an idea how far away he is."

Penny treats him to an over-wide smile and throws up her hands. *Yeah, good idea, Beaks.* Except, she can't call despatch because she's already called twice and a third time would surely bring the wrath of the gods down on Matiu. Well, the wrath of Mum and Dad, which is bad enough. When sufficiently provoked, Dad does a pretty good impersonation of Vesuvius, spouting black ash, rock, and molten lava. Penny wouldn't wish that on her worst enemy, let alone her brother, even if he is a monumental pain in the arse. Penny can't fathom how Matiu faces it every day, working for them, being under their noses all the time, on the clock. She sure as hell wouldn't want to walk that particular tight-rope, thank you very much. She's much happier working for herself, even if that means grovelling before an overworked police detective for Cordell's lousy cast-offs. And hardly enough funds in her wallet to buy a round of drinks. Reaching up with both hands, Penny tightens the elastic band of her ponytail, yanking the tresses outwards and pushing the band back hard against her head.

Come on Matiu!

"What about his cell?"

"Already tried it. Turned off."

Beaker pulls a face. "Guess you just have to wait, then."

"Yeah, I guess."

Was that a car? Penny makes another trip to the window. Cranes her neck. But it's just another graffiti artist, this one with a can of silver paint. Looks like they're working on a political slogan to replace the one the Council painted over a few days ago. Penny can make out the word: BASTARD. Furtive, the kids turn often, checking the street for witnesses, unaware of Penny watching through the tinted glass. She gets the need for anonymity when you're vandalising someone's property with revolutionary propaganda, but how can they wear those hoodies in this heat? It's got to be 35°C down there on the footpath, the heat rising off the concrete in translucent wavy ripples, the kind you see on the opening credits of a vintage western. They must be cooking. Mind you, the way they've spelled 'GOVERMENT' she'd probably cover her head, too. A black speck passes in front of the sun, and Penny squints as her eyes follow the movement. Looks like another experimental aircraft out of Manukau. Now those guys are really something: trying to maximise biofuel output on minimal research funding: that takes guts. Not that they've got much chance of pulling it off—at least, her parents better hope they don't; or their stock would hit the bottom faster than a faulty elevator. With a final glance at the street artists—currently halfway through the word ARSEHOLES—Penny turns away.

"Still nothing, huh?"

"Not yet."

Where is he? He'd better be lying dead in a ditch: forty minutes, she's been waiting. Forty minutes. He's going to wish he *was* lying dead in a ditch when he gets here. Maybe she should set up a test anyway? But what would be the point? As soon as she gets underway, Matiu will stroll in touting his lame excuse, and she'll have to clear up again. Still, she can't just stand around. There are other ways to make herself useful. Lifting her satchel off the bench, she hangs it back on its designated hook. Then she fills the sink with soapy water, snaps on her gloves, and scrubs the lab glassware:

two beakers, two Erlenmyer flasks, a glass pipette, a volumetric flask, and a Büchner funnel. She gives them a decent scrub: pushing the bottle brush into corners, the coiled wire handle imprinting its pattern on her palm. Then she holds the glassware up to the light to check for blemishes, the sun throwing rainbowed prisms into the soapy angles.

If she could drive she wouldn't be so dependent on her parents—and Matiu— for transport. Well, yes, she would, because she can't afford a vehicle, but presuming they would lend her one—which is doubtful. She sighs. It's a pity public transport is out of the question. Too dangerous. And so…dirty. Imagine if she didn't have to phone up her parents and beg them to send a car every time she needed to get somewhere. Imagine the freedom. The independence. God, she misses that.

There's still some hard water residue in the flask. She's going to have to have a word with Beaker about soaking the glassware after he uses it. She does some more scrubbing, then holds the flask up to the light again. Better.

Tap water rinse.

Distilled water rinse.

Distilled rinse again.

Acetone.

Right, all done. She sets the glassware in the rack to air dry, and looks around for something else to do. Naturally, it's a big joke to everyone that she can't drive, especially given her parents own what is probably the largest fleet of hire vehicles in the country. Hilariously funny, that. She doesn't tell people that she used to drive once upon a time. Once upon a fairy tale. That turned into a nightmare. She should probably clean the worktop too, since she's at it. Taking a bottle of Decon from a shelf over the sink, Penny sprays it liberally over the epoxy resin work surface, paying attention to the awkward corners and cracks where micro-organisms and other contaminants like to congregate.

"Uhm…Penny?" says Beaker from behind the bench, where he's working on the polo shirt.

"Hmm?"

"You know, you don't have to do that. I did the worktops yesterday, when there wasn't much on—"

Penny doesn't bother to look up. "That's OK, Beak. It doesn't hurt to do them again. Gives me something to do." With a disposable cloth, Penny sets to, rubbing down the laboratory's hard surfaces: the bench-tops, the sink, the stools. While she's waiting, she may as well give everything a decent rub.

Right through the bloody stainless steel coating.

- Matiu -

Matiu cruises to a stop and hits the horn, once. That'll wind her up, for sure, and given how many of her calls he's missed, she'll be pretty wound up already. But what could he do? The Chinese are prickly about people taking photos of them without their knowledge, so out of courtesy he'd been obliged to turn his phone and tablet off while they were in the vehicle. And after he'd delivered them? Well, sometimes a guy just enjoys a bit of quiet time, to himself.

Makere doesn't bother him when he's driving, another reason Matiu likes the job, and why he sometimes takes the long way round, observing a healthy respect for speed limits. The sooner he gets places, the sooner someone is pestering him— be it Penny or Makere or a client, it doesn't matter. They're all just white noise most the time anyway.

Pandora practically flies out the door at him, her brow creased in that curious imitation she has of a furious glare. Matiu stares out the window as she loads her kit into the back seat and climbs in.

"You took your time," she growls, slamming the door.

Matiu pulls back out into the street as she fastens her belt. "Work's work," he says, and that's *all* he should say. She can't argue. If she could afford her own courier service instead of relying on the family to drive her around, she could get herself where she needed to go, when she needed to get there. Or she could drive herself, if she could bring herself to get behind the wheel again. But she can't drive, *won't* drive. Not anymore. He should probably let it go, but he can't resist another jab. She's just so easy to wind up. "Tough on the breadline, eh?"

He can see her, out of the corner of his eye, her jaw clenched tight and the colour rising in her cheeks. Pissed, man. She's hilarious when she's angry.

"Just drive." She pulls out her tablet and swipes the screen, bumping the address up to the onboard nav.

Matiu drops his shades over his eyes as they swerve around potholes and wind-blown debris. Penny is stubbornly focused on her tablet, and since the car will do most of the work of finding their way to the Devonport address, he can let his mind wander again. Every time he does, all he can see is the bowl, the damned bowl and the blood that fills it, spills over its sides, the echoing chill that burned through him for that long dark moment when he held it in his hand.

Like the blood hadn't poured *into* the bowl, but *through* it.

He could tell Pandora about this, but what's the point? She has about as much of a care for his gut feelings as he has for her anal retentive method. No matter that Matiu feels, *knows*, that he walks with one foot in the shadow; that to him, a bad feeling is never just a bad feeling, but a fucking *resonance* of what lies beyond the curtain separating this world from the next. Penny can't take that and assemble a code for it to run through her processors, or fit it into a spreadsheet, or express it as a chemical formula or an algorithm, so therefore it has no relevance to her work.

So too bad for her.

Matiu curls his lip at the thought, and shakes his head. It's spiteful, and it won't help to think that way. Mārama would be disappointed in him.

"It's that attitude that got you in trouble in the first place," she would say, and he can hear the scolding in her tone. He must be imagining one of her lucid moments. He's never quite sure which he fears more; her lucid times, when she can see through him like he's made of glass, or the other times—the *rest* of the time—when she seems to be in another place altogether. A far darker place. Both are terrifying, and both leave him powerless to help her. But she's his Mārama. They have that much, at least. He looks forward to seeing her tomorrow. And dreads it.

The harbour bridge looms before them, a desolate rusting thing. They'd paid the Japanese some extraordinary amount back in the 1960s to build the "Nippon clip-ons", to cope with all that extra traffic. Now it stands mostly empty. That's some crazy shit. A city of roads, with hardly any cars. Like a city walking with one foot in the shadow. One foot in the grave.

Waitemata Harbour spools out beneath them, green and sickly in the heat that rolls off Waitakere.

"You should drop this case," Matiu says at last, spying the Devonport off-ramp. He broaches the subject because they're almost there, and any argument can only last until they reach their destination. "There's something totes wrong about the whole fucking thing."

"You do your job, and I'll do mine," Penny huffs.

"My job isn't just to drive you around, sis. I'm expected to make sure nothing happens to you as well. You're safe enough back in the lab, but out here? This is a nasty world. Bad shit happens. This shit? This is bad."

"I need the work."

"Find another case."

"Matiu…"

Matiu throws up his hands, letting the nav steer them off the bridge. "I'm just saying."

"Steer the car!" Penny screeches, reaching for the wheel.

Matiu grips the steering wheel again, as the Commodore slows to take the bend. "I'm just saying, is all. You can't say I didn't warn you."

Chicks, man. Chicks.

- Pandora -

No doubt Patisepa Taylor would describe Rose Fletcher's north shore suburb as a desirable enclave of colourful two-hundred-year-old rimu villas, renovated to today's modern standard, conveniently located close to the city, and surrounded by nature. And it's true that the occasional picturesque villa still exists, money pits for misguided preservation enthusiasts. But mostly the outlying suburb is run-down and tired, a cornucopia of flaking paint and rotting lintels, populated by retirees with no need to make the daily trip into town, and whose sense of smell has dulled so much they're no longer offended by the pong rising off the green sludge of the ocean. Although, to be fair, Rose Fletcher's building isn't without its charm: an old high-rise of sixteen stories, its shared entrance lined with a grid of little red mailboxes. With mechanical keyholes. Talk about a blast from the past. That delightful little touch of kitsch almost makes up for Matiu's tardiness in picking her up, trying to talk her out of the only paying job she's had in weeks and then, when she didn't agree, almost driving her off the bloody road. Actually, no. It's going to take a lot more than a row of little letterboxes to make up for the crap she's put up with from him today. Only minutes ago, when she'd leaned in to grab her satchel from the back seat of the Commodore, she'd told him to wait outside until she'd finished her interview. She'd only made it this far—the building's external glass door—before the stubborn shhlrrrp of the car door announced his plan to completely ignore her instructions. Again.

She whirls to face him as he starts up the painted concrete steps. "And just where the hell do you think you're going?"

"Inside. With you."

Penny puts her arms akimbo, blocking his path, Matiu's eyes level with hers even though he's standing two steps down. "No, you're not. I won't have you

coming in and sticking your mitts where they're not needed. This is *my* case."
Matiu lifts his chin defiantly and pushes his lips out. It's a classic James Dean
look, sans cigarette. Penny still has girlfriends who would go weak at the knees
if Matiu were to throw that look in their direction, but it doesn't work on Penny.
She's seen him wearing dinosaur pyjamas. "I haven't got time to play games,
Matiu. You're not coming in."

His dark eyes smoulder. "I have to, Penny," he says. Now he calls her Penny?
Because he wants her to listen to his hocus pocus? "Believe me, this isn't a game. I
wasn't kidding before. This case, there's something not right about it. It's—"

"Yeah, I heard you before: it's shit. I tell you what, Matiu…" She bats her
eyelashes, exaggerating the movement, a Betty Boop caricature. "If you don't like
it, maybe you should do what I ask, and stay in the car." Turning her back on him,
she makes a point of daintily stepping up the remaining steps to the intercom.

She presses the button.

It's another piece of olde-worlde kitsch. After the harsh tone—the same one you
get if you give the wrong answer on a game show—a crackle of static escapes, and
then, almost immediately, a woman's voice asks, "Darius? Is that you?"

Penny hates to let her down. "No, it's Penny Yee, Ms Fletcher. We talked earlier."

"Who?"

Penny takes a step closer. "Penny Yee. I'm the scientific consultant to the police:
here to talk to you about your missing brother." Matiu is suddenly at her shoulder.
He leans in, pressing against her back to get closer to the intercom. What's he doing?
Is he sniffing it? Penny jabs at him with her elbow, forcing him to back off.

The internal entry door buzzes and Penny and Matiu both rush to get to it
before the mechanism clicks off. Unfortunately, Matiu does a text book front row
fend and gets there first. All boyish charm, he holds the door open, sweeping his
hand across his body and inviting her into the corridor where the lift awaits. And
then he follows her in.

Penny pushes the button to go up, but by the time the doors open Matiu is there,
stepping into the lift first, muscling his way to the control panel. He raises an eyebrow.

"Twelfth floor," she huffs.

As the lift ascends, Penny gives it one more go: "Just stay out of the way,
OK?" She reads his answer in his scowl, reflected in the elevator's mirror. He
turns to face her, placing one hand above him on the wall, in a blatant attempt to
make her feel small.

"Look, Pandora—"

Penny shows him her palm. "Talk to the hand, Matiu," she says wearily as the elevator doors ping open.

Rose Fletcher has the appearance of a weed grown in the dark, spindly and white and scared to breathe lest anyone notice her and pull her out at the roots. She jumps at the sight of Matiu, overlarge in the cramped apartment, like a giant come to a little girl's tea party. The ink on his face doesn't help either. It isn't the first time someone's found it intimidating. Penny motions for him to sit down. Can't he see he's making her witness nervous?

Rose Fletcher has already made the tea. Unlike her hands, which are limp and white, the tea is black and strong. And lukewarm. Definitely less than 60°C. Assuming it was 85°C at the moment of pouring, and then kept in a stainless steel teapot at ambient temperature, if she considers the volume, calculates for heat loss... it was probably made twenty minutes ago, when Penny had phoned from the lab.

"You said you had news of Darius?"

Penny replaces the teacup on its matching saucer. "Not exactly, Ms Fletcher. We're here to follow up on the call you made to the station." What could they tell her? For the moment, they had no concrete evidence to go on, just supposition and hearsay.

"You've taken a long time to get back to me."

"Yes, well..."

"Five days." So, clearly she's not as frail as she appears. Penny supposes even weeds can be tenacious.

"It was Halloween, Ms Fletcher," Matiu says in the charming voice he reserves for hostesses at tea parties. The kind of reassuring voice that gets middle-aged spinsters eating out ot the palm of his hand. The voice that turns the tattoos on his cheek from frightening to alluring. "As you would expect, there were a few calls to follow up from that night—a bit of trouble in town, some street fires—so we've had to prioritise."

Penny hesitates. They can't tell Rose the police didn't believe Darius could be missing until today, or that even now it's not certain, with no body to speak of, and only the real estate agent's word that the clothes were his, until her analysis of samples from the scene bear out the facts. "Yes, that's right," she says, glowering at Matiu with her best 'butt out' face. "Our colleagues at the station have had some backlog. They...they..."

"What makes you think your brother is missing?" Matiu interrupts, smooth as satin.

Turning to offer Matiu a piece of almond slice on violet sprigged crockery, Rose Fletcher directs her answer at him. "Darius didn't come for dinner."

Quick.

While the witness' back is turned, Penny whips out her adhesive sample tape and pats it on a strand of dark blonde hair she's spied on the arm of the chair. It's probably Rose's, but a close enough genetic match to the DNA on the blue polo shirt could support her suspicion that the clothes were her brother's, potentially placing him at the scene.

"Could he have had another engagement, perhaps?" says Matiu, observing Penny's rapid sampling manoeuvre and keeping Rose's attention away from his sister.

"He didn't mention anything else, and he *always* has dinner with me on a Tuesday."

"Even Halloween?"

"Of course. Where else would he go?"

Penny stuffs the sample into her satchel, smoothing down the flap. "No girlfriend then?" she asks.

Rose Fletcher flaps her hands like a chicken. "No, Darius didn't have time for all *that*. He was too driven. There was a girl, Sandra someone, but that was almost a year ago. It wasn't anything serious."

"So, on the date he's alleged to have gone missing, you'd seen him earlier that day?"

"I didn't allege at all, Ms Yee. Darius is missing," she says frostily. Clearly, Rose Fletcher would like to cast Penny in the role of bad cop with Matiu as the darling golden boy. Penny tries to shrug it off. Rose Fletcher doesn't know her. Doesn't know anything about her. Anyway, as roles go, playing second fiddle to Matiu's first is one Penny doesn't have to rehearse: she's played it all her life.

Rose Fletcher adjusts the platter on the coffee table, then pushes a tiny crumb into the corner of her mouth with her finger. She goes on, "Darius dropped in briefly on his way to work that morning. He often does. We were both in our teens when we lost our parents, and we don't have any other family." She taps the surface of the coffee table and brings up an old holographic photograph of a young family, pushing the platter to the edge of the table to reveal the entire image. "That's all of us. Before." Penny and Matiu lean in obediently, but hardly waiting for them to study it, Rose swipes her hand over the table and brings up a second image. "And this is Darius here. That one was taken last year at a work function."

Forty-ish, with a square jaw and dazzling blue eyes, Darius Fletcher had won the genetic lottery over his sister, although he'd had a few plastic enhancements done. The decent head of hair could be cosmetic too, were it not for his resemblance to his dead pater.

"He's a very good-looking man."

Rose Fletcher reaches across to swipe at the table-screen. "And this one was taken just a few weeks ago."

Penny examines the image. "He's lost a lot of weight in this second photo," she remarks.

"Yes, seven kilos. It didn't take him long either," the woman gushes, Penny's compliments about her brother causing her to warm. Penny, however, has nothing nice to say about her own. Matiu has moved from the couch and is roaming the apartment, touching things. And more sniffing. What does he think he is? A bloodhound? He needs to sit down. If he keeps that up Rose Fletcher might throw them out. They're only here by proxy. Penny tries to distract the woman from Matiu's poking about. Why's he going into the kitchen?

Luckily, the woman is more interested in telling Penny about her brother's dieting success. "I've never lost a kilo my entire life," she's saying. "I really should ask Darius how he did it. It was his talent agent who suggested he go on a diet. She said at his age he needed to be careful or he could find himself out of a job. It's a cutthroat business. He's in broadcasting, you see: the presenter on Dish-It. Do you know it?"

Penny shakes her head. "Sorry, no."

"It's a daily gossip U-View show. Not the calibre of the *Antiques Roadshow*, of course—that's show's been going for nearly a century—but very funny and extremely successful. The ratings go up practically every week, Darius tells me."

Where is Matiu?

Penny tries to note down the name of Darius' show without moving her eyes from Rose Fletcher. It'll probably be illegible.

"I did wonder if work was the problem—"

"Oh?"

"Well, yes, because some people can't see the funny side of things. I thought perhaps he'd ruffled the feathers of someone he shouldn't have. One time, he got offside with two of the Prime Minister's secret service guys: outing both of them as plushophiles. He said it was just too good a story to miss. A fluff piece, he called it. Secret agents with a thing for soft toys. Who wouldn't want to run a story about that? Darius didn't mean anything by it, you understand. For him, it was just business, but the secret service men didn't see it that way and since those guys carry guns, Darius went underground for a bit. They knew where he was—they were in the Prime Minister's secret service, so they had *means*—but so long as Darius was off the air, it allowed the rumours to die down and they were satisfied. He was gone for ten days. After that, he was more careful about what he broadcast."

"Do you have any idea where he went that last time?"

"We own a few buildings, Darius and I—our inheritance. They're mostly rented but at the time one of them was between tenants so Darius camped there."

Penny nods again, desperate to prevent Rose from noticing Matiu doing God-Knows-What in the rest of the apartment. "Uhm, you don't think something like that has happened again? Perhaps he's gone to hole up in one of your rental buildings."

"No. Darius would've told me."

"Would you mind if I kept a copy of this photo?"

"Go ahead."

Penny touches her tablet to the table to effect the transfer.

"When he dropped in that day, do you remember what he was wearing, by any chance?"

"No. I don't recall." Rose looks into the space to her right, searching her memory for an answer. "Can't think. Look, it's all very well you people asking me these questions, but when are you going to look for him? I know he's a grown man, but I've called his office and they say he hasn't been there either. They're not very happy. He didn't call in sick and they've been forced to play pre-recorded material. I'm getting quite frantic with worry."

"Try not to be too concerned. A lot of people are reported missing and most of them turn up eventually."

"But I've been up and checked and he hasn't been home."

"Been up?"

"It's up one floor, on level thirteen. I have the entry code. It's another reason I'm positive something has happened to him. He wouldn't have left without making arrangements for Cerberus."

"And Cerberus would be…?"

"Darius' dog."

A dog…

"I've been going up there to feed him. Well, obviously I can't have him down here. My apartment's not suitable: he'd wreck everything. Although, the neighbours are going to get tetchy soon. He keeps yowling for Darius."

Suddenly Matiu is there, standing over them. "We need you to take us to Darius' apartment, Ms Fletcher. We need to see it."

"The apartment? Or the dog?" she asks, puzzled.

"Yes," Matiu says, his broken grin smothering any further questions she might have as she melts into a befuddled smile.

Penny rolls her eyes.

CHAPTER 4

- Matiu -

"What the fuck are you, Mister Detective now?"

In Matiu's periphery, Makere's shadow slides along the wall. Footsteps that aren't there thump in the back of his skull, like an echoing heartbeat. "Stay out of this," he hisses under his breath. He'd ignore Makere if he could, but that just makes him more insistent. Makere getting more insistent tends to give Matiu a headache, which can drive him to violence. It's easier just to shut him up early, rather than suffer the consequences.

Like ending up in prison.

"What?" Penny asks, her voice just as low so that Rose won't hear.

Matiu waves her off, ignoring her sullen glare. Just edgy, slightly crazy Matiu muttering to himself again. Nothing new to see here, sister. Rose presses the button for the elevator. The shaft hums and creaks as the car drops to meet them.

"You're going to love it when you find it," Makere snickers, which winds Matiu's guts even tighter. He can't help feeling there's nothing Makere knows that he himself doesn't know already. And if Matiu knows, it means he's involved somehow. He only knows Darius Fletcher from the streams, but the dogs...

Thinking about dogs turns his stomach. Too many late nights walking the shadows on the fringes of abandoned factories and warehouses, listening to the screaming crowds, the growling and the tearing, the smell of money tainted with blood. Too many still or twitching bodies dragged by their collars from the barbed wire rings with spiked gaffs. Too many teeth, gleaming red and white under halogen floodlights.

The doors slide open with an artificial 'ding', synthesised to replicate an old-school elevator, but not quite achieving the authenticity the designer was going for. It's not the tone that doesn't ring true. It's the resonance. It's missing the vibration that runs through your spine when a bell tolls, the unheard notes which distinguish the real from the illusory. Telling these two apart is something Matiu has to do constantly. It's a skill he's grown very practiced at.

Matiu steps into the car. Real or not, with a swipe from Rose's access card the elevator takes them up.

Darius Fletcher is not a man who likes to share. As such, the lobby of his floor is just that—the lobby of *his* floor. When the doors whirr open with another faux tinkle, Matiu steps out into a small space sporting black leather couches flanked by tall brass flower pots. Their foliage is drooping, dried pollen scattered across the backs of the settees like a dusting of snow, or wind-driven sand. The blinds are pulled, thin slivers of afternoon sun cutting through the gloom as the motion-activated overhead lamps flicker on with a warm buzz. Across from the lift lurks the only other door on this floor, its muted timber grain smacking of too much money and nothing to spend it on. No doubt the door is real wood and, from the grain's golden-yellow glow, it's probably kauri—endangered, protected, centuries in the growing. Matiu doesn't have a lot of time for U-View gossip shows, but if Fletcher is some sort of B-Grade mini-celebrity trying to make an impression on his peers, then it's unlikely the wood is recycled. "Jerk," Matiu mutters over a fake cough, as Rose bustles past him to open the second door with her swipe card.

Penny follows their escort into the apartment beyond, firing Matiu a dark glance that unequivocally says *Don't you screw this up for me, brother*.

He grins, not really feeling it. The smile, as ever, is as much a sword as it is a shield. It keeps people out, cuts down their defences. Sometimes, it just cuts. But he wears it all the same. Ignoring the burble of chatter that flows from Rose Fletcher like effluent from a sewer pipe, he moves into the apartment. His first surprise is that the loyal Cerberus hasn't come bounding to the door to meet his newest best friend and to warn away the intruders. Even a sleeping dog should've roused at the sound of unfamiliar footsteps, the waft of new smells. Rose is turning on lights and calling for the dog as she goes, leaving Matiu to scan the penthouse's front hall. It's wide, sparsely furnished with an occasional table on one side, old-fashioned coatrack near the door and a bookshelf that looks like a kid's building-block experiment gone wrong fixed to the other wall. There are no books on it, just a random selection of junk that Matiu supposes is meant to be art. His lip curls. How much money does this guy have to blow, and what else does he waste it on? Even the dog's probably some docile pure breed with what little brains its massively inbred genes can scrape together. And seriously, what idiot calls a dog Cerberus? Do people have any idea what they're opening themselves up to with bullshit like that? Dude is missing, probably dead. The dog might as well be guarding his road to the underworld. Maybe that's why it hasn't roused, because it knows its master is dead. Gone, and the dog left behind to mark his passing.

He carries on down the hall, past a guest bathroom on his left and a spare bedroom on his right, the doors ajar but everything tidy, orderly, as if the cleaner had just been through. Less like a home, more like a hotel. Yet with every step, the air grows heavier. The oppressiveness settles on his shoulders. Nothing looks out of place (which in itself might be part of what crawls along Matiu's spine), nothing smells wrong, nor is there anything eerie about the sound in the building. No false bells chiming silently, like the calls of lost ghosts. Just a tickling, crawling sense of dread.

"You feel it now, don't you? It's here, bro. You know it."

Matiu casts his eyes both ways, avoiding the lights that throw their spidery shadows from the living room across the hallway. "If you're so smart, why don't you tell me what happened?"

"Where's the fun in that?"

"Then shut the fuck up. I don't need you on my case."

"Oh, you need me, bro. You need me now more than ever."

"Given that I've *never* needed you in the least, that's not saying much. Now get out of my headspace. I'm trying to concentrate."

Matiu stops at the door of what appears to be the master bedroom. The blinds are drawn, backlit bars of sunshine the only light, since Rose and Penny went the other way. Something rank flows through the open door, pressing against Matiu's chest, pushing the air from his lungs. His eyes water and there comes, in the back of his skull, a resonating thrum. Like the missing echoes from the fake bells at the elevator, a sound he can't hear but which wraps itself around his brain and *squeezes*.

Makere is at his back, looking over his shoulder. It isn't reassuring. He half-expects the apparition to push him into the room.

"What are you waiting for, bro? It's all there for you. Go take a look."

Matiu's chest is tight, almost too tight to breathe. The room, or its presence, or the awful withering spirit of whatever took place beyond this door sits on his shoulders, on his skull, threatening to drive him to his knees or to send him running from the apartment, screaming. But like hell will he give Makere that satisfaction.

He steps into the room.

- Pandora -

Penny follows Rose through Darius' cavernous penthouse reception room to an equally cavernous open-plan kitchen decked out like an operating theatre with stainless steel countertops, scalpel edged lines and a surgical light-head chandelier.

"Gorgeous apartment," Penny says.

Rose shrugs. "Darius sometimes entertains for work," she replies. "Now, where is that damned dog? It's typical, isn't it? The silly animal whines all hours of the day and the minute we turn up, it disappears. Cerberus! Where are you? Let me check the laundry."

"Go ahead. I'll just look around."

Penny clucks her tongue. The place is as sterile as its décor. Normally, kitchens are great places to get fingerprint samples. There'll be a smudge on a wine glass, a solid thumbprint on the taps, a complete set of prints on the handle of the fridge. Not this kitchen. Every surface gleams as if it's been swabbed with alcohol, the sleek lines and reflective materials making it more abattoir than kitchen. The only ornament on display is a surgical cotton ball holder in pride of place on the counter. Coffee? Sugar? Penny lifts the lid and peeks inside. She's rewarded with a waft of liver. Dog treats in a solid silver container? Darius must have money to burn. Broken down and incorporated into antibiotics, the ionic silver contained in that receptacle could treat a pandemic.

Penny replaces the lid and opens the fridge. There's a tub of tarasamalata and half a bottle of wine—a pricey Canterbury chardonnay—but otherwise the shelves are empty. Had Darius been deliberately emptying the fridge? Preparing to go away? But would he forget to make arrangements for his dog? A man who keeps his dog treats in a silver container? Penny's spine tingles. She ignores it. It isn't relevant. Scientists operate on fact, not feeling. Instead, she checks the use-by date on the pink fish paste. It expired two days ago.

"Come on you, out!" Rose trills.

Penny closes the fridge, turning as the dog bounds over, its nails clicking on Darius Fletcher's tiled floors.

"Hello, boy," Penny says, giving him a scratch under his chin. The dog's tail is a blur, wagging faster than an oscillating sifter. "Aren't you beautiful?"

"Spoiled more like," Rose says. "Cerberus is Darius' baby." She glances down the hall as she approaches Penny.

Stealing peeks at Matiu.

"Is your colleague okay?" Rose says, tilting her head in Matiu's direction. "I'm only asking because he looks kind of peaky. He isn't allergic to nuts, is he? Because there were almonds in my slice, and your colleague ate two."

Penny ducks her head around the corner, following Rose's gaze. Matiu's at the far end of the hall, his hand gripping a door frame. The muscles of his neck are bunched. Something has him uptight. What has he found?

Time to gather your samples and get out of here.

Looking back at Rose, Penny gives her a wide smile. "Oh, he's just a sucker for good home baking. The thing is, he's also gluten intolerant."

"Really?"

Penny hides her mouth with her hand and whispers conspiratorially in the spinster's ear. "I expect he's paying for it now he's gone and got himself a stomach ache."

Rose's eyes widen. "I could get him something," she says a little too quickly. "The bathroom's this way." Before Penny can stop her, she bustles away. Penny gives the dog a treat from the silver cotton ball container and hurries after her.

Off the hall, the bathroom's a marble masterpiece: a double shower across one wall, and twin vanities under a wall-to-wall mirror opposite. Rose is flicking through the left hand cupboard under the vanity. "There should be some paracetamol in here somewhere."

"Perhaps it's on this side," Penny says. Crouching, she opens the adjacent cupboard where she finds a purple toothbrush, a roll of dental floss and a dozen or so bottles of designer perfume for men: Yves St Laurent. Boss. Aztec. Zac. Samuel Jones…

Hang on, what's this one?

Snapping on her gloves, Penny lifts the bottle out by its cap.

Cerberus growls, a low grumble deep in his throat.

"Is your brother a fan of Felicity Jones, by any chance?" she asks. She holds the dewdrop bottle containing the pop singer's signature scent above the cupboard door so Rose can see it.

Rose snorts. "It'll be hers. That Sandi woman's. All bra-cup and no brains, that one. She tried very hard to weasel her way into Darius' affections. Had designs to move in here with him too, but Darius didn't come down in the last shower of rain. He saw her for what she was."

"And what was that?" Penny asks, using her other hand to slip the toothbrush into a sample bag.

"A manky, manipulative gold digging cow."

Oh.

"Did Darius say that?"

"Not in so many words, but I knew because he stopped bringing her here, didn't he?"

"Hmmm." Penny examines the dewdrop-shaped bottle, noticing a tiny smudge in the glass near its apex. She rummages in her satchel again, this time for her sampling tape. "Ms Fletcher—Rose—would you mind if I lifted a fingerprint off this bottle? If we can find this Sandi person, she might be able to tell us where Darius is."

Rose cackles. "Do the police keep a file of gold diggers, then?"

"Just a database of criminals and their associates."

Rose's eyes widened. "A criminal! Now, *that* wouldn't surprise me. If you find her on that database, do you think you could let me know?"

"Uuum…" Penny says, drawing out the word.

Rose sighs, sitting back on her haunches. "It's okay. I know you can't say anything. Confidentiality and all that. I doubt that trumped up floosie will be able to tell you anything, anyway. Like I said, Darius gave her the short shrift ages ago."

Penny presses her sampling tape to the smudge, drops it in a plastic sample bag, and returns the dewdrop to the cupboard. Cerberus growls again and she soothes him with a quick pet with her elbow.

Buried in the cupboard up to her waist now, Rose says, "I think I can see the paracetamol!"

"You know, Ms Fletcher, while I'm at it, perhaps I should take a sample from Darius' cologne, too."

"Darius isn't a criminal." Even coming from inside the cupboard, Rose's voice is indignant.

"Oh, I mean for the missing person file," Penny says, backtracking. "In case we find Darius and he isn't able to speak for himself."

Rose's gasp echoes inside the cabinet. "You mean if he's dead?"

"Well…"

"Yes!" Rose cries. She emerges from the cupboard clasping a crumpled box of tablets. "I found them!"

Rose said 'yes'. She'd definitely said yes.

Still hidden from view behind the cupboard door, Penny's hands are frantic: choosing a bottle of cologne, pressing the tape to the bottle, bagging it, and making a tear in the edge of the plastic bag so she can tell this sample from the dewdrop.

Not that there's any need. Penny had definitely heard her say 'yes'.

Getting to her feet, Penny closes the cupboard with her bottom. She peeks around the door into the hall. Matiu is no longer there. "Actually, come to think of it, Rose, perhaps we shouldn't say anything about my colleague's stomach ache," she says, giving the paracetamol box in Rose's hand a tap with her finger. "You know how sensitive men can be about their little flaws."

"Oh. I hadn't thought about that," Rose says.

Penny raises her shoulders, dropping them again in an overdramatic shrug. "You know how it is. It's the loss of face."

"No, no, you're right," Rose says, slipping the box onto the vanity. "We don't want to embarrass him."

Penny smiles. "I knew you'd understand."

- Matiu -

The room tastes of fear, pain, despair, and—perhaps worst of all—determination. There aren't many places that taste that way, though Matiu can think of a few. Prison, for one. The fight ring, for another. He imagines that's how the trenches must have tasted, back when wars were fought on the ground, with men and guns and mud and steel. Whatever had taken place within these walls, it had been a fight. Lives had been at stake. Something had won, and something had lost. Such is the way of all fights.

"Officer?"

Matiu jerks around, his heart thundering. Rose is there, her smile as gluey and vapid as before. Penny is beside her, her eyes blazing in silent warning. "Ah…" he stammers, more flustered by being ripped out of the moment than he'd like to be.

"This is Cerberus," Rose says, stepping aside so Matiu can see the dog.

It's a Golden Labrador, and looks about as unlikely a dog as any to bear a name as ominous as Cerberus. Matiu wonders if Darius Fletcher even knows what Cerberus was—or who the ancient Greeks were, for that matter. Smart guy, maybe, but his classical education is lacking. Taking a breath to calm his nerves, Matiu steps into the hallway and kneels by the dog, who lies prone on the carpet, paws folded one atop the other, muzzle settled on top of these, ears drooping. "Hey, boy." He reaches out to rub the top of the dog's head.

Something sharp lances into his hand, through his arm, cascades down his spine. If not for the two women watching him, he might've yelped in pain and snatched his hand away, might've crumpled as the wave slices down his legs, exploding anew as it hits his knees. As it is, he maintains his stance by sheer force of pride, only withdrawing his hand as the dog leaps back, suddenly animated, and starts to bark.

Matiu wants to get to his feet, get above Cerberus and make sure the dog knows who's in charge, but this pain won't allow it. Instead, he hunkers on one knee, eyes locked with the retriever as Rose calls shrilly for the dog to heel—the woman clearly knows nothing about dogs—and stretches his hand out again. This time, when he touches Cerberus' head, there's nothing, except, perhaps, the fading memory of a pain now buried. The dog quiets instantly, settles back onto his hind legs, and lifts a paw to Matiu.

"Oh my," Rose breathes behind him. "I didn't know it could do tricks."

"We need to take the dog," Matiu says, still focused on Cerberus' huge dark eyes, seeing in them a hint of what his master saw when he chose the name—a dark river, slow, deep and persistent. And calling the dog Styx would've just been stupid. *Right, I'm going to take Styx out and throw him a few sticks.* So maybe Darius isn't the douche Matiu put him down for.

"Oh, I'm not sure," Rose is saying, but Penny slips in smoothly with some pseudo-scientific mumbo-jumbo about evidence relevant to the ongoing investigation, and blah blah blah. Matiu tunes it out, getting to his feet now that the shock and pain have subsided. Cerberus holds his gaze. Matiu reaches down and rubs a hand across the dog's shoulders, through the thick pelt at his neck. Feels good to have a dog at his side again, one that isn't slated for a fighting pit. The dog walks past Matiu and settles at Penny's side. His sister looks from the dog to him in muted horror. Matiu flicks her a surreptitious thumbs-up, ignoring the animal's rebuff.

"He certainly seems to like you," Rose effuses, clearly sold on both Penny's reasoning and the dog's obvious affection for her.

"Maybe," Matiu agrees quietly, though he suspects that's not all there is to it. Cerberus is pining for a lost master, and Rose can never fill that role. Rose is below Cerberus in the pack, as far as the dog is concerned. She is a bringer of food, a cleaner of shit, and nothing more. Had Cerberus been left too much longer, she would no doubt have found this out the hard way. But it's not just about the pack, which is something Matiu knows only too well. Finding your place in the pack is a matter of life and death in some of the places he's been, which is perhaps why he so enjoys tormenting Penny about her own struggles to do so. He'll always be the pack leader, loner or not, and it's bred into him to keep things that way. So at least the dog thinks Penny belongs in the pack.

Whatever happened to Darius Fletcher at the warehouse is inextricably tied up with what happened in this bedroom, between the man and his dog, and Matiu might have an inkling of what that was. It wasn't a fight, at least not how he thought it might've been. There was no violence. This was a fight that took place *inside*.

A decision was made. Something to win, something to lose.

Matiu turns back to the master bedroom, its rotten presence leeching into the hall, the weight of sorrow clustered in the shadows. "We're going to need his laptop too," he says, gesturing to the computer satchel sitting on the side table in Darius' room. "For the investigation." He flicks a look at Penny who rolls her eyes, makes a throat-slashing motion behind Rose's back, then puts on her most professional face as the spinster turns to her, no doubt to quibble fruitlessly again. What Matiu wants, Matiu gets, but clearly the woman needs to give the impression of protecting her brother's interests to the bitter end.

Matiu ignores them both, hovering on the edge of the room, as if poised on a precipice. When he touched Cerberus, did he feel the final lingering traces of bad energy the dog still carried from that moment? It was a bitter triumph, a hollow victory of sorts, and not the dog's, but the man's. However, it wasn't without cost. A choice was made, and the resonance of that choice haunts this place. Darius Fletcher cut out a piece of his soul when he made that decision.

Matiu waits as Rose retrieves the laptop case, handing it to him with a fat-lipped grin which she might think is flirtatious, but which strikes him as merely salacious. He represses a shudder, and in return treats her to his winning smile. Then they head for the lift, Cerberus trotting at Penny's heels while she juggles a bag of dog biscuits and a blanket. The lift dings, and Matiu wishes everything could be as hollow as that false bell, as empty as the shaft beneath his feet. The lift drops, and he knows they are falling into hell.

CHAPTER 5

- Pandora -

Heading back into the city, the traffic is tediously slow. While only the privileged still have the means to run their vehicles, everyone who can has chosen this particular moment to be on the road. Impatience emanates from Matiu in waves, like heat rippling off the hot asphalt.

Actually, he's been acting weird all day. Even more weird than usual. All that muttering and scowling. And the pained looks. Anyone would think his appendix was about to burst.

The woman seemed to accept Penny's phoney explanation, but what was it in the apartment that had him so distressed? So *wounded*. And was whatever prompted his reaction—his over-reaction—the cause of his sudden flip flop? Because, on the way over here, Matiu was adamant she shouldn't take the case, insisting there was something eerie and untoward about it—it's a crime, for Christ's sake, there's always something shady—and then, when he got into Fletcher's apartment, he completely changed his mind. He even had them remove crucial evidence without proper authorisation. And Penny had gone along with it. Stealing Fletcher's computer. She'll have to do some fast talking to explain this to Tanner. Unlike the grieving sister, there's nothing vanilla about the police detective: Penny won't be able to fob *him* off with a hushed whisper. Penny takes a deep breath. She could lose the contract. Sighing, she hooks her fingers over Fletcher's laptop, preventing it from slipping off her lap into the foot well. Still, she has to admit it was a good call on Matiu's part: it might contain something useful. She peeps over her shoulder into the back seat.

God knows what use the dog will be,. though.

Penny looks towardsthe CBD, shielding her eyes from the glare. Dull sunlight reflects off the Sky Tower spire, making the skyline look lonely and dystopian, as if some calamity or other had caused the population to abandon it. Probably not the first time someone's had that thought on the motorway in rush hour. To make the most of the delay, Penny rummages in her satchel, pulls out her phone and dials the lab. Outside, heat from the road causes the car in front to haze in alternating shades of red and grey.

"Hey Beaks, we're on our way back to the lab now. Any updates?"

"Yeah. I ran our doggie DNA results into Zoogen—they keep an online database of canine SNPs—and a quick comparison of the DNA from our sample blood against their database suggests a high probability that the dog is a crossbreed."

Penny nods. It figures. The chances of it being a pure breed were low. Like people, dogs get around.

"The good news is that I can tell you the dog is predominantly American Pitbull, with a bit of Staffie—about 15 percent—thrown in."

Penny glances at Matiu, who remains focused on the road, then looks back at Cerberus in the back seat. "Hmm. Not Golden Labrador, or Retriever? OK, whatever. Pitbull-Staffie: that's an aggressive mix," she surmises out loud.

Beaker's reply is tinny as Matiu takes the car through an underpass that will allow them to avoid the city centre.

"I guess that all depends on what side you fall on in the nature-nurture debate," he says. "A lot of people would argue that the temperament of a dog says more about the handler than the breed—"

"Anything else?" Penny cuts her assistant off before he can go any further. The nature-nurture issue is probably not the best tangent to take when you're sitting alongside an adopted brother whose true parentage remains somewhat obscure.

"Not all of the blood samples were canine. At least one of them is human. I've run one through the new analyser so far, but I can't tell you who it is because I've no way of checking the results against any human DNA databases without security clearance."

"Thanks, Beaker. We'll ask Clark to run a comparison with the known criminal database tomorrow."

"You think Fletcher's DNA will be on a criminal database?"

"Probably not. We're more likely to find him through his medical records. In the meantime though, I pinched Darius' toothbrush from his apartment. It was purple, if that tells us anything. And it was the only one in his bathroom cabinet, so I think we can reasonably assume it was his."

"Well—" Beaker starts.

"I've got a sample from the sister, too," Penny says before he can go on. "A hair. A genetic near-match would suggest the clothes belonged to Darius."

Beaker says: "How can you be sure the sister's a blood relative? It's not a given these days. Family connections are complicated."

Penny steals a glance at Matiu. That's certainly true. "Matiu and I were allowed a look through the family album. There's quite a family resemblance."

"Such an accurate test, that," Beaker says, and Penny can hear the smile in his tone.

"Actually, Beak, it's not so silly," says Matiu, not taking his eyes off the road. "Take dogs, for example: it's pretty easy to tell a Doberman from a Daschund just by looking at them. And I once met a dwarf. I didn't need to see his DNA to know it would be different from mine."

"Those are extreme cases..."

"We'll know more when I bring the samples back, won't we?" Penny says, putting an end to the argument.

"Shall I get started examining the clothes, then?" Beaker says, the puppy dog eagerness already returning to his voice. "Or would you rather I waited for you?" If Beak had a tail, Penny imagines it would be going for it.

Matiu snorts loudly. Loud enough for Beaker to hear anyway. Penny swipes the speaker off. "No, Beaker, I can't ask you to do that. It's late and Matiu and I are still...maybe twenty minutes away... Yeah, exactly, it's worse than number crunching by hand. Look, why don't you head on home? Anything else can wait 'til tomorrow." She rings off.

Matiu gives her a lopsided grin. "That's not nice, Pandora. Taking advantage of that poor boy just because he's got the hots for you."

"He has *not*."

"Pandooora, he wants to kiiisss you," he teases.

In spite of herself, Penny feels her face turn as red as the car in front. "Shut up, Matiu."

At once, Matiu is all seriousness. "I'll bet you Mum's Christmas present that he stays late," he says.

"You're on."

A cackle of static breaks the conversation as Carlie from despatch comes over the VOIP-speaker. Matiu swipes the screen, accepting the transmission. Carlie's face pops up.

"Hey, Carlie."

"Hey, Matiu. Got another job for you."

"I'm just taking Pandora back to the lab now. I should be free in a half hour."

"Oh, you've got Pandora with you. Hi, Pandora." Carlie waves enthusiastically at the screen, even though with the camera angled at the driver, she can probably only see Penny's shoulder. "Actually, that's brilliant, Matiu. It'll save you a trip. That was the job. Mr Yee said you were to pick Pandora up."

"Done, then. Pandora had some business in Devonport. We're on our way back now."

"Yeah, I saw that. Well, I saw you were heading out that way before you turned the GPS tracking off. I didn't think you'd still be out there. You're not supposed to do that, you know, Matiu. Turn the tracking off and go walkabout. Mrs Yee doesn't like it—"

Matiu interrupts. "Was there more to the message, Carlie? Where I'm supposed to take Pandora, perhaps?"

"Oh. Sorry. Yes. Mr Yee said you're supposed to pick Pandora up for the family dinner tonight."

Family dinner?

Penny's heart sinks.

"I thought you knew about it. It's at your parents' place," Carlie says. "I'm sure you know where that is." Giggling. "Your dad said they'd expect to see you both at seven… Hey, is that a dog I can see in the back seat—"

Quickly, Penny pulls the screen about and leans close to the camera, blocking Cerberus from view. Feigning shock, she exclaims: "Did you say Mum and Dad were expecting us at seven? Shoot, it's nearly that now. We better not keep them waiting. Bye."

"Bu—"

Penny cuts the connection. "What if we don't go?"

Matiu throws her a withering look taken straight from Mum's repertoire. He does a pretty good job of it. It's a look to turn you to salt.

"Sure, Pandora. Let's not go. No sweat. All we need is an excuse that the olds will find acceptable."

Penny sighs. It's hopeless. They'd have to have been abducted by aliens and they'd probably still get a dressing down from their parents for being irresponsible. Matiu knows it too, because he's already changing lanes.

The kitchen is too bright. Too stark. All harsh white light reflecting off angled surfaces. Or maybe it just seems that way because, over the years, Penny's been the subject of numerous family interrogations here. Penny, the dissenter, sitting on one side of table, and the Yee Family Inquisition on the other. The list of Penny's crimes is long: unsuitable boyfriends, unacceptable behaviour, inappropriate choices in what she wore, what she read, who she hung out with, the way she talked, even her hair colour. The outcome of those little across-the-table discussions was always the same; her parents were very disappointed in her, they expected more, they would've thought by now that she should know better.

—No, we are not bigots, Pandora. It's just we don't know the young man's parents. We have absolutely no idea what kind of family he comes from.

—No, that is not the way we do things, Pandora. What sort of example is that to set for your brother? Yes, it might have been Matiu's idea, but you are the eldest so we expect you to demonstrate some responsibility.

—When you do that, you're representing our family. What kind of impression do you think your behaviour gives? How do you think that reflects on us? That kind of thing is just not acceptable, Pandora.

—No, we will not call-you-Penny-please. Why would you want to give yourself that everyday ordinary name? What's wrong with the lovely name we picked out for you? You know what this makes us think when you decide to call yourself something else? It makes us think you're ashamed of us, that you're ashamed to be part of this family. That's what happens when you decide not to use the name we gave you.

—You want to study what? Sweetheart, there's no money in that. How do you think you're going to keep us in our old age on what a scientist makes? (Penny recalls her mother's overarching smile). Anyway, what's wrong with Commerce? Would it really be so terrible to join the family business?

Under the hanging lights of the kitchen, Penny allows herself a pinch of satisfaction. At least she'd won that particular battle, enrolling in Economics, then secretly switching to Sciences in the second week of her first semester. By the time her parents discovered the subterfuge, halfway through the academic year, she was past the point of no return. And when they descended on the Faculty demanding Pandora be allowed to change, the Dean, a diplomat, had asked why Mr and Mrs Yee would request such a course of action when Science was so clearly a good career fit for their daughter. Penny had been making straight As.

"We're here," Matiu announces, stating the obvious. He throws the car swipe card onto the counter. At the opposite end of the kitchen island, their father is assisting Bituin, holding the pan as the housekeeper spoons steaming gravy over a dish of slivered beef and Chinese jelly ear mushrooms. Dad's business colleagues would probably consider it good practice that an employer work alongside his subordinates from time to time. To walk a mile in their shoes. But Penny suspects, in reality, their father is micromanaging Bituin, making sure none of her subversive

Filipino cooking practices slip into the preparation of his favourite dish: *fun see chow wan yee*. These days the mushrooms are hard to come by—expensive enough that even their parents balk at the price—so Penny realises this isn't just any family dinner. She crinkles the flowers' paper wrapping with her fingers, grateful now that Matiu had insisted they stop.

"Hello, Bituin. Dad." She shrugs off her satchel, dropping it on a chair, then, the flowers in hand, goes to the cupboard to look for a vase.

"You're late."

"Pandora's on a case," says Matiu, artfully managing to excuse himself and accuse Penny all in the same breath.

Their father grunts. "Your mother's waiting in the living room. You know she's not going to be happy…"

When is she ever happy?

"OK," Penny says. "I'll go right through, just as soon as I've put these flowers in water." Taking the flowers out of their wrapping, Penny crushes a pale green sepal with her fingers, hopeful its minty perfume might calm her. But there's none. Nothing detectable anyway. She shouldn't be surprised. Odorant molecules are tiny, typically less than 300 dalton, and these are in too low a concentration to be detected over 50,000 parts per million of braised beef.

Her father puts a bamboo chopstick into the serving dish, then takes it out and sucks the gravy from it. He closes his eyes. *To better appreciate the flavours, or to block out the view of his children?* Apparently, the dish comes up to standard because after a second or two, he opens his eyes and nods his approval to Bituin. His scrutinising complete, he slides the chopstick into the sink. "I wouldn't dally if I were you, Pandora. Your mother's been out there entertaining Craig Tong for the last half hour."

Craig Tong!

Penny stabs at the flower stems, pushing them around in the vase, trying to make the half-hearted bouquet look halfway decent. Penny thought she'd made herself clear the last time. Well, one thing's for sure; their father was right when he said Mum won't be happy. She'll be positively ecstatic. No doubt her makeup will have cracked from an excess of smiling. Did Matiu know about this? Penny swings to face her brother, but Matiu's eyes slide away from her gaze.

Et tu, Matiu?

Well, that's just typical, isn't it? He knew Craig would be here and didn't bother to tell her. She could bloody kill him. Instead, she gives a little cough. "I'm sorry we've kept everyone waiting." As soon as it's out, Penny wants to take it back. She's been in her parent's house a little over five minutes and already she's apologising for having a life. She ploughs on. "I picked up an important case today, Dad. A police contract. They're looking for a quick solve, so there were a couple of urgent tasks for me to attend to." She fills the vase with cold water from the tap, observing the way the bubbles, nucleating around particles on the stems, form a row of tiny diamantes.

"Nothing is more important than family, Pandora."

"Yes, of course. I know that."

"Then I suggest that you don't stand around fluffing with those flowers. Go out there and apologise to your mother." Penny bites her lip. This is why she drags her heels when her parents invite her to visit: they *always* have some ulterior motive and she *always* ends up apologising. And what about Matiu? He was as late as she was, and no one's taking him to task. No one's asking him to say sorry. Penny's about to say as much but what would be the point? She already knows she's a disappointment. It doesn't matter anyway. Dad has already turned away to open a bottle of wine.

Luckily—as Penny expected—the visitor has made her mother as squishy as the fondant centres of chocolates left to soften in the sun.

"Sweetheart, you're home. Did you have a nice day?" Still seated, Mum turns her cheek for Penny's kiss, while Craig Tong gets to his feet, his suit trousers barely creased after a day at work. "Isn't this a lovely surprise? Craig stopped by earlier to see your father on a business matter and it turns out he had no plans for dinner. Can you imagine that, Pandora?" Penny doesn't answer, suspecting her mother's question to be rhetorical. "An accomplished young man like Craig with no dinner date. What are the chances? Naturally, your father seized on the opportunity to have him join us, and Craig was kind enough to say yes."

"It was very kind of you to invite me at such short notice, Mrs Yee."

Puh-lease.

"Now Craig, we've been through this before." Mum's tone is flirtatious, bordering on obsequious.

"Kiri, then. There, I said it."

"That wasn't so hard, was it?"

For crying out loud.

Penny does her best not to vomit on the polished schist floor.

"Hello, Pandora." This time, it's Craig who leans in to give Penny a kiss on the cheek. He smells of too much cologne, and by a squillion parts per million, if Penny were to give an estimate.

"Hello, Craig."

"Your mother tells me you've gone out on your own, bought yourself a lab. I think that's fantastic, Pandora. Although, it's a gutsy call in these economic times. Your m... Kiri and I were just saying that you might've been better to wait out the recession, but then you've always been very independent...Kiri mentioned there being some sort of tussle with a co-worker...?"

Penny tenses her fingers. Does her mother have to tell people *everything* about her? And then they wonder why she doesn't want to share anything? Penny's about to ping upwards, like the switch on the kettle, but Matiu gets there first, saving their mother—and her guest—from a steaming.

"Hey, Craig. Good to see you, man." Stepping in, Matiu shakes Craig's hand and simultaneously slaps him on the shoulder in the traditional post-match ritual. "Been way too long. You must be coming close to running the country by now."

"Oh, I wouldn't say that," says Craig, beaming.

"Well, it won't be far off," Mum interrupts. "Craig was just telling me he got a promotion recently. He's reporting directly to the Transport Minister now."

"Really? That's great, man."

Craig waves his hand dismissively. "I'm a glorified coffee boy with a bit of extra paperwork, that's all."

"Nonsense. You'll be kissing babies before you know it," Mum insists.

Penny can imagine how pleased her mother is to have squeezed a mention of babies into the conversation. She fancies Craig for Penny. Or rather, she fancies him for the leg up he can give the family business, with Penny being served up as the sweetener. Bartered like a piece of common property. This isn't the Middle Ages. Penny doesn't appreciate her parents' assumption that she'll play along, even if all that's involved is a few hours of small talk over a family dinner. And she definitely will *not* be providing any sacrificial babies. Things like that don't have to run in generations. All Penny has to do is stop the cycle. Although convincing her mother of that may be harder than getting a rainfall reading in a hailstorm.

Craig, though, seems happy enough with the unspoken arrangement. Penny considers the man chatting with Matiu. Something about him makes her skin prickle. He looks well enough, but he has a slightly too-polished air about him, which has nothing to do with his plastic enhancements. Perhaps it's that his belt doesn't have a single over-stretched belt hole, or it's the flawless triangular symmetry of the Windsor knot in his shot silk tie, or the perfect rounded curve of his manicure. Whatever it is, it makes Penny want to go over there and muss up his hair—and not in a sexy way either. Craig throws back his head and laughs loudly at a comment of Matiu's, their mother chiming in with her tinkly treble notes. He might be full of good-natured bonhomie, here in a private setting among longtime friends, but Penny suspects in public it'd be another story. In any official capacity, Craig's the sort to put a judicious layer between himself and anyone who might tarnish his campaign image. Someone like Matiu would be shunted into the background by Craig's security entourage. In a photo, he'd be digitally removed, or at the very least another body be slipped in to buffer Penny's bad-boy brother from the political politeness of her suitor. But behind closed doors when the curtains are drawn and the lights dimmed? Who is he then? When that immaculate Windsor knot is loosened and the mask comes off? Stifling a shudder, Penny thinks of the tests waiting for her back at the lab. She heaves a sigh. It's going to be a long evening.

Throughout the meal, Craig is über-charming. Penny can't help but be flattered by the attention. She wonders if perhaps she's misjudged him; not bothering to look past the shiny packaging to see the product it contains. "So tell us a bit more about your new lab, Pandora," he's saying, dabbing at the corner of his lips with a napkin. "I must say, I think it's entrepreneurial of you to go out on your own. Kiri tells me you've been doing environmental analyses? That's valuable work."

"Yes, it is, isn't it? Pandora's always been a big proponent of the environment," says Mum.

Craig nods, his head bobbing, reminding Penny of her ecology studies and the ritualistic nod-swim ducks make when mating. "It's very commendable."

Penny's mother beams and nods back, making Penny feel slightly nauseous. Craig may be charming, but she wishes her mother wouldn't throw him at her. Does she really believe that if she presents the lost puppy enough times, eventually Penny will scoop him up and take him home? Penny's quite capable of choosing her own date. And her own husband for that matter. On this point, Penny holds to her mother's Māori heritage which allows a woman to choose with whom she sleeps. Or indeed, with whom she chooses *not* to sleep. Although, obviously, in Penny's case, a half titre of Māori doesn't count.

"Actually, Pandora's been contracted by the police," Matiu interrupts.

Immediately, their mother's antennae go up. "What's this about the police?"

Damn it, Matiu.

Mum raps her chopsticks impatiently against the side of her bowl, as if she's been using them all her life and not just since she married Dad, trying to prove that she's something, or someone, she's not. Because any Chinese child knows that rapping your chopsticks against your bowl is the height of bad manners.

Tap, tap, tap, tap.

Heaven help her if Penny dared to do the same. Yet another thing for her parents to reprove her for, but then, she's not the parent, and this isn't her house. "I don't like the sound of Pandora carrying out analyses for the police," Mum says "We don't know what she might be getting herself into. Hing, tell her. I don't want Pandora getting involved in anything untoward."

"It's not really that big a deal…"

"I wouldn't say that," Matiu says. The missile loosed, he scoops translucent vermicelli noodles into his mouth, his eyes on his bowl, waiting for the inevitable explosion.

Well, two can play at this game. Penny plasters on a smile. "Matiu, I know it's sweet of you to drive me, but I really don't think it's appropriate to be discussing a case…"

"So it *is* dangerous. Hing, please say something. I don't like this at all. And working with the police. It's so…so *sordid.*"

"Pandora?"

"I told you before, Daddy. It's just work. Matiu's exaggerating. Honestly, it's nothing to worry about."

"Pandora, when you asked us to give you some money to set up your lab, you led us to believe that you'd be taking on contracts the bigger laboratories didn't consider lucrative. You planned to create a niche, providing routine, low key work in a timely manner. I'm sure those were the words you used. There was no mention of crime work. It was going to be straight-forward medical analyses and environmental sampling. Not police work."

"I didn't say…the money was an *investment…*"

Her mother turns to Craig. "I've never liked it when she works for the police, even when she was working for LysisCo."

I'm right here, Mother.

Craig shakes his head like a teacher whose favourite student has turned in a C paper. "I'm afraid I have to agree with your parents on this one, Pandora. The police deal with some shady characters. The circles I'm in, I hear things. And not particularly savoury things either. Forgive me for saying this, but I think it's highly inadvisable for a woman like yourself—and especially from this family—to be carrying out scientific trials for the police."

Penny is livid. Who does Craig think he is? Just a few minutes ago she'd thought him amiable and charming. The pompous oaf! He needs to get his head out of his arse. Since when does making public policy entitle him to decide what she should do?

"You see? Even Craig agrees," her mother concludes, as if Craig's are the last words to be said on the matter. "It's far too dangerous. You'll have to phone them up immediately, Pandora. Tell them to get someone else."

"I'm sorry, Mum, I can't do that."

Her mother's eyes flash. She points her chopsticks—like a witch's wand—at Penny. "But surely, since we're shareholders, we get a say, don't we, Hing?"

Dad's expression is stony. "As Pandora's *parents*, we get a say."

Penny throws down her napkin and pushes back her chair, a pang of disappointment at leaving the rest of the *fun see chow wan yee*. It can't be helped. In the short space of one evening, her family has managed to negate two centuries of women's suffrage. Someone has to make a stand. "I'm sorry, I've just remembered something I have to do."

"But you haven't finished your dinner," her mother wails.

"It's really quite urgent."

Urgent that she get out of here.

"Pandora!" Her father stands now, the sound of his chair grating on the schist.

Bum. If her father is prepared to step away from his favourite dish, then it's serious. Penny stops, waiting for his rebuke.

"Since you're going to insist on being imprudent, then I will insist that Matiu go with you at all times." He speaks in a near whisper.

"But..."

"Pandora."

There's no point in arguing. Penny wishes she'd never agreed to the loan. She should've known it would come with strings attached. Who's she kidding? Her parents don't need the threat of calling in their loan to manipulate her. Suddenly, she catches sight of Matiu chasing a slippery piece of *pak choi* around his bowl with his chopsticks. The look on his face. He's smirking! Knowing that by this point she must be as pink and sizzling as a shrimp on a hotplate, Penny glares at her brother.

He did this.

Exasperated, she turns on her heel and, grabbing her satchel, makes a stormy exit. It's not until she's out on the street that she realises she's stuck. Without Matiu she's got no way of getting back to the lab.

CHAPTER 6

- Matiu -

As the door slams, Matiu stands and spreads his hands in a placating manner.

"I'll go talk to her," he says, putting down his napkin. "It's been a big day. You know our Pandora, doesn't cope very well under pressure."

"Yes, well," Mum says, tapping her wine glass with one manicured nail, "that's why I don't think she should be getting herself mixed up in this police business. You go talk some sense into her, darling. She listens to you."

"That's right," Dad agrees, his voice relaxed but the tight set of his shoulders speaking volumes. He turns to Craig. "So, this new biofuel prospect in the Waikato, who's behind it?"

Dismissed, Matiu nods to their dinner guest and heads for the door. Pandora isn't in the hallway, so he presumes she's taken the lift to the ground floor. He calls the elevator and descends to the parking garage.

Cerberus isn't tied up where they left him near the car—*No, of course you can't bring a dog up here,* Bituin had said on the phone, *your mother will have a fit*—so Matiu scoops up the blanket, tips out the water from the bowl and tucks these, along with the dog's biscuits, into the back seat. Penny might be a temperamental little princess sometimes, but she's not silly enough to go walking the streets of Auckland after dark without some sort of protection. He guns the engine and swings up the ramp, headlights sweeping the footpath and dark shop windows. Tapping and swiping the screen of the onboard GPS, he quickly locates her phone and pinpoints her location, one block over.

She's walking, shoulders hunched, Cerberus straining at the leash, in the direction of the lab, which is just silly. It'll take her an hour to walk that far, if she makes it at all. Lot of nutters between here and there. He winds down the passenger window and pulls in to the curb.

"Hey lady, wanna ride?"

"Sod off," she growls.

"Just hop in. I'll take you to the lab."

Penny stops, wiping one hand across her eyes. "Shouldn't you be hauling me back in front of our parents for another interrogation?"

Matiu snorts. "Hell no. I needed an excuse for us to get out of there. You storming out was as good as any."

She glares at him through the open window, her eyebrow raised suspiciously. "You wound me up just to get out of dinner? What are you up to?"

Matiu spreads his hands in mock innocence. "We've got a case to investigate, sister. Crime never sleeps and all that."

"Those cutesy puppy-dog eyes don't work on me, remember?" But nevertheless, she opens the back door so that Cerberus can clamber in and settle on his blanket, then slides into the passenger seat. "You can talk and drive, right?"

Matiu checks his mirrors and pulls onto the street. "You're cute when you're angry. Craig's gonna love that when you're hitched."

"Shut up about Craig and tell me about the dogs. And what, specifically, do you think you're going to find on Fletcher's laptop?"

"Porn, probably," he says, "but hopefully not dog porn. That'd just be gross."

"I'm so glad we can agree on *something*," Penny deadpans.

"I've got an idea about the dogs. But I need to know who Fletcher was in contact with before he disappeared."

"Care to share?"

"Not yet. Mum and Dad aren't even happy with you being involved with the police. They sure as hell wouldn't want you getting mixed up with the people *I* know."

"You see?" Penny throws her hands up in frustration. "This is the thing I just don't get. I'm the responsible one. I'm the one with an education and a career and some life skills, but they treat you like their golden boy. You, who went to *prison* for possession and aggravated assault. You, who, freaking well *talks to himself* when you think no one's listening. How in the hell are you the model child, and I'm the one they constantly think they need to *fix*?"

Matiu nods a little. "What can I say? I'm the prodigal son. Fell in with the wrong crowd is all. Cleaned myself up, paid my dues. You, you'll always be their little girl. More than I was ever their little boy. They look out for you, that's all. Leave me to look out for myself."

Penny's mouth opens, but she closes it again without speaking. Matiu keeps his eyes on the road, letting the words sink in. She knows as well as he does that they were never equals, growing up. Pandora's mother had had an obligation to *whangai* the young Matiu, bringing him into their home and raising him as their own when it became apparent her sister couldn't care for him. And Matiu had taken after his biological mother in that regard, a black sheep of sorts, for reasons he could never explain to his adoptive parents lest they medicate him into a waking stupor. How do you tell your distracted, craven father and your hand-wringing, guilt-ridden mother that you have an imaginary friend who actually talks to you, *all the freaking time*? And that with the sort of shit he tells you, about yourself, about other people, it's no real surprise Matiu used to lose his wicket and lay into the other kids far more often than was reasonable, even for a kid of his age. Or that when he was old enough to make the right contacts, he delved into whatever substances he could lay his hands on in the vain hope of making the voice at his shoulder just *shut the hell up* for a while.

Not that anything ever worked, until he'd started driving. Spending nine months in a cell with Makere had nearly driven Matiu absolutely bat-shit crazy. It was there, behind bars, that he'd learned to deal with Makere as best he could, and where he made his resolution to stay clean and out of trouble when he got out, just so he'd have a chance to work as a driver. Because when he was driving, for whatever reason, Makere couldn't taunt him. He had the family connection to land a driving job, but even Daddy Yee with his lucrative government transport contracts wouldn't let a drugged-out thug behind the wheel of his cars. So Matiu got out of prison, stayed clean and held down his job, and Makere was pushed a little further from his mind. Eventually, he just might push him all the way out. But Makere was a tenacious bastard.

"You know that's not true," Pandora says quietly. Dank streetlights flare and decay through the windshield, painting her face in waves of burnt umber, jaundice, and shadow.

Matiu shrugs, swinging onto a side street. "Don't see them making any effort to marry *me* off."

He flinches as she hits him in the shoulder. "Think yourself lucky. I mean, Craig Tong. Seriously? Here, daughter dearest, please marry this delightful Investment Fund. What a creep."

He spares her a glance. "Yeah, but with all your science and shit, you could probably slip him something and make it look like a natural death, right? I mean, once all the legal stuff is done, and you're his sole benefactor and all that?"

Penny stares at him, horrified. After a moment, she finds her voice. "You can't be serious? Please tell me you're not serious."

Matiu turns back to the road. "Hey, I'm just saying." The bewildered shock in her eyes is priceless. He holds his composure for a suitably dramatic moment, then chokes back a snort of laughter. "Chill out, sister. You're too uptight."

The car slides down the alley. The lab is dark.

"Looks like Beaker went home."

"Good," Matiu says, parking the car and pulling on the handbrake. "I reckon we might find out some things he doesn't need to know."

- Pandora -

A soft shaft of orange neon spills onto the benches from across the road. It's a pity Matiu took Cerberus to do his business, Penny muses, because she could be entering the Kingdom of the Dead, and it would be comforting to have the slobbery rambunctiousness of a dog loping along at heel. But the poor dog has been shut up for days: he needs a run and a pee, Penny isn't having him exercise either of those functions in her lab, so Matiu has taken him off for a quick tour of the park. Instead, she contents herself with the welcoming hum of the refrigerator and the cheery hello of her shoes in the gloom. She turns on the lights, fumbling to manage both the computer and the satchel, and blinks a second as the luminosity changes from 1 to 1000 lux, the recommended level for work tables in research environments. Popping the gear on those well-lit work tables, she goes to her coat hook, switches Beaker's lab coat to the correct hook—*honestly, Beaker*—then takes down her own.

"Where shall we start?" she says to no one in particular as she buttons her coat. The refrigerator replies with a change in vibration.

"So, you reckon the clothes, then?" Penny answers. "I agree, it'd help if we could determine that the garments were Fletcher's. I think I'll run a DNA comparison of the saliva from the toothbrush with any DNA found on the clothes. That way we'll be able to safely assume they belong to him."

The refrigerator hesitates, then hums again.

"OK, OK, you're right. Or they could belong to whoever borrowed his toothbrush last." Penny screws up her face. "Eeew. Sharing a toothbrush. Yuck. I can't think of anything worse."

The refrigerator groans its agreement.

Oh my God. Penny snorts at her own silliness. What is she doing? All that furtive muttering under his breath and Matiu's got *her* talking to herself now? Although it's odd that he should be doing that again. Penny would've thought he'd have his childhood demons under control by now. God knows, he's had enough counselling over the years; he's practically moulded to the couch. But she definitely heard him mutter the name of his imaginary friend when they were in Fletcher's apartment.

Makere.

That's it. Penny hasn't heard that name in a long time. Matiu's childhood friend, invented to keep him company. There hadn't been a lot of playdates; the other kids had found him too strange—or worse. Doctors had suggested Asperger's since Matiu exhibited several symptoms typical of the disorder: struggling to look people in the eye, inappropriate responses in social situations, weird stimming behaviours like talking to himself, and pacing the room as if he were a lion taking a wide arc, sizing up the herd.

Oh, and occasionally bashing the shit out of other kids.

Yes, it's fair to say he didn't always see eye-to-eye with people. Even now, Matiu has this Aspie off-the-wall way of looking at things. That's the beauty of the condition. Its sufferers—or those gifted with the condition, depending how you look at it—perceive things without all the usual constraints and conventions that normal, neurotypical people apply to their thinking. It's as if they approach problems from a different dimension, examining and reorganising them into new, often startling, permutations, the way a poet arranges words to reveal the obvious in a fresh and surprising way, or how van Gogh saw moonlight as a dappled swirl of blues and golds. For a long time now, Penny has wondered if all the world's original thinkers have had an element of Asperger's or Autism in their make-up. The social scientists seem to think so. Einstein, Turing, Mendel, even Isaac Newton, all thought to have been Aspies. So perhaps Penny's appreciation of her brother stems not from their familial connection but from the fact that scientists and Aspies both have an innate need to examine things: Penny testing her hypotheses through method and rigour, and Matiu looking for answers in his own inscrutable way. Oh sure, there's all the normal sibling dynamic between them, the bickering and the teasing, but it's a smoke screen. A trick with mirrors. Because for all his weirdness, Matiu really gets her, and Penny has learned to read her brother better than anyone. She trusts his instincts. Although, to be fair, she doesn't always listen.

The refrigerator hums pointedly: 'He didn't like Cordell, did he?'

"Shut up!" *You're a refrigerator. You are not sentient. You don't get to offer an opinion.*

The whiteware shudders, but continues its quiet murmurings, obviously miffed. Penny ignores it and begins to remove the samples from her satchel, lining them up on the bench. Maybe she should pay more attention to Matiu's ramblings. Especially if Makere is back on the scene. What is it they say about misery and company? Matiu's imaginary friend has a tendency to turn up when Matiu is at his lowest. The last time, Matiu had ended up in a bit of trouble. Actually, that's understating it. Using 'a bit of trouble' to describe Matiu's past is like using a candle to light a canyon. Penny's parents had tried to protect her from it, but for a while there, Matiu had been a regular prince of the underworld.

Penny considers the samples. Since there are several of them, and not because anyone told her to (she glowers at the fridge), she decides to start with analysis of the hairs found on the clothing. Taking a pair of sterilised tweezers, Penny lifts the sampling tape and holds it to the light to study the single ash-blonde strand. Is that a hint of pink? Penny hopes the hair hasn't been chemically treated. These new Breadmaker™ sequencers are fantastic at providing discriminatory analyses with limited material. In fact, they're so sensitive that in 62% of cases the machine can deliver a profile from a single hair *without* the hair root, using just the hardened cornified nuclear material in the hair shaft. Amazing. But mass production always has a downside, and one thing these bench-top models can't do is sequence DNA which has been degraded by chemical treatment in the enhancement studios, they wreck your hair that much. Mum always said so: 'You've got beautiful hair, Pandora. Leave it alone. Don't ruin it.'

Penny rotates the sample. It looks like the follicle's intact, so that's something. Carefully placing the hair in a cuvette, Penny pops it in the centrifuge, then heads to the fridge for the reagents Beaker made up earlier: the DDT/proteinase incubation solution, the manufacturer's recommended lysis solvent, primer, and the polymerase. It takes her a few trips to bring them all across to the analyser, the fridge rattling each time she closes it.

Still miffed then.

Using a pipette to fill the relevant compartments in the machine, Penny turns her back on it, more interested in what's really bothering Matiu. Mum and Dad were overbearing this evening, but then they always are, so it can't be that. It must be something to do with the case. The scene in that storeroom was pretty gruesome. Could that be it? Matiu did seem upset, and sometimes the smallest thing can set him off. It's funny really, because all the textbooks say Aspies lack empathy. Which is so wrong because if anything Matiu feels more than a neurotypical person does. He feels so much, and so acutely, that for him it's like a physical pain. How researchers haven't worked this out has Penny flummoxed, since she's known it forever. She'd discovered it one weekend in her second-to-last year at primary school. Sent to find Matiu for lunch—he can't have been more than four and already he was doing one of his disappearing acts—she'd found his upturned tricycle in the downstairs lobby. Of course, an eight-year-old Penny had gone looking, slightly panicked that something might have happened to him. She'd found him in the cleaner's cupboard, near the lock-ups. Penny hated going down there. It was dark and spooky and full of spiders, but she'd pushed open the door and there he was, curled up on the concrete amongst the coils of grey vacuum hoses, his hands over his ears, his eyes screwed up, his body trembling, and his face streaming with snot and tears. He was crying, only he wasn't making any sound. Like he hadn't wanted anyone to know he was there. Penny wasn't sure he knew she was there, until she'd touched him on the shoulder.

"Matiu?"

He'd turned then, and flung himself at her, howling and screaming, *pleading* with Penny to please, please make Makere stop, to make them all stop because he didn't want to feel any more. It was hurting him. Hurting his head. Hurting! Penny's first thought was the boy in the back apartment. Had he been bullying Matiu again? Is that why her brother was hiding out here in the murk? But Matiu was clinging to her—this kid who didn't like people touching him—so it wasn't just that. He was hysterical. His fingers squeezing her arm, leaving little dents in her skin. Then she'd seen the graze on his knee, the tiny droplets of blood beading in the torn skin, and something, she's not sure what, had made her bend over and brush her lips over the graze. She'd kissed it better. Kissed the hurt away. Well, it was what you did when babies hurt themselves, wasn't it? She'd only meant it as distraction, because that scrape wasn't the real reason Matiu was upset, but it had worked because Matiu stopped crying, wiping the snot on his shoulder and giving a last sniff-in sniff.

"S'OK. Dey gone now."

Just like that. Weird. Penny had never mentioned the thing in the cupboard to their parents, but she'd understood that something in Matiu's head hurt him, and that Makere, Matiu's imaginary friend, wasn't always a friend. Penny had kept her little brother close after that, and like a duckling he'd taken to following her around. For a while, he'd been like her own little fandom. That is, until he hit his teens and discovered that you didn't need to *feel* anything to have a crowd of people flock to you: all you needed was a decent set of abs.

Switching off the centrifuge, Penny slides the cuvette into the Breadmaker™, closes the lid, and starts the machine. There. She checks her watch. It should incubate at 65°C for an hour, and when that's done the machine will vortex off the buffer, holding back the eluted DNA solution for the subsequent annealing cycles and the enzyme digestion phases, which it does automatically. And just like baking bread, the machine pings when it's done. Honestly, if science gets any easier she'll be out of a job.

- Matiu -

The ringtone buzzes in Matiu's ear.

"Yo, bro," floats the disembodied voice down the line.

"Hey," Matiu says. "How's it?"

"Thought you'd ended up inside again or something, been so long. Where you holed up?"

Matiu shrugs, though no one can see. Cerberus is lifting his leg to a power pole. Good dog. "Been working an' shit. Keeping out of trouble."

"Nah eh. But now you're calling me. That's trouble all by itself. What gives?"

"Scour, I gotta ask a favour."

"What sort of favour?"

"Got an old lappy I need to crack. If I patch you in, can you hit it?"

There's a pause, not much, but enough that Matiu notices it. "Hard core?"

"Dunno. It's a personal machine, old school. Like, 2020s old."

"What's in it for me?"

"Bro, don't make me blackmail you. Do it because we're family."

Scour sighs. "You're not gonna get me into any shit, are you?"

"I'll let you know once you crack it."

"Riiight. Make sure your connection's secure. I don't need this shit getting back to me."

"All good," Matiu nods. "I'll be ten minutes. Say, any idea what happened to old man Hanson? He still around, doing his thing?"

"Fuck man, why you wanna know about him? You said you were trying to stay out of the shit."

"Just curious."

"Well, he's not gaming in the same spot anymore. Had to move around a couple times, even had the pens raided once so he's gone to ground out in the rurals.

Someone'll know, but chances are as soon as you ask, he'll know you asked. And he'll want to know why."

"You let me worry about that. Catch you in a bit."

"Laters, bro."

Matiu swipes the call to end it and whistles to Cerberus, who's wandered off to investigate an overflowing rubbish bin. The dog trots over and lets him attach his lead. Pondering, Matiu heads back towards the lab through the humid night air.

Pushing through the heavy doors and locking them behind him, he hears Penny's voice in the back section of the laboratory. "Yo," he yells, "you talking to yourself again?"

Her reply is a small squeal of terror, accompanied by a tinkle of breaking glass.

"Oops," he says, coming around the bench to find her crouching on the floor. "Did I frighten you?"

"Oh, shut up," she growls. "You made me drop important evidence."

"That's all right," he says, "I'll let you clean that up. Where's the laptop?"

"Over there," she points, her face a thunderstorm in a teacup. "Now stay out of my way." Matiu sidles over to the desktop that serves Penny as an admin desk and boots up the laptop. "Sit," he tells Cerberus, who promptly lies down and starts to snore. Reaching under the desk, he finds a coiled up Ethernet cable, grimed in dust that Penny must never have seen, and clicks it into the machine's port. "Yip," he mutters to himself, "real old school." Hell, most machines don't even have USB anymore, much less Ethernet ports. The fan hums to life, and Matiu wonders how much precious battery life that anachronism will suck up. Once Scour cracks the OS security, Matiu doesn't expect to find passwords conveniently stored in a text file or pre-populated at secure web addresses, but he should be able to get the ball rolling, at least.

Swiping Penny's desktop, Matiu brings up a floating window and opens a browser to sign into his inbox. Grabbing the LAN properties and pasting them into an email, he taps out a message to Scour:

U R IN. Deets below.

Send.

"Watcha doing?"

Matiu all but falls out of his chair at Penny's voice over his shoulder, and Cerberus is suddenly on his feet and barking with excitement.

"Shit, you gave me a heart attack!"

"Oops," she says, glancing over the laptop's login screen, one hand drifting to the dog's neck to ruffle his fur and settle him down. "But seriously, what are you doing?"

"What do you think? I'm cracking his password so we can look at his emails."

"And why do you think he'd leave anything useful on a cruddy old machine like this? Looks like he dredged it up out of the twenties."

"Call it a hunch, whatever. We won't know until we try." The laptop flickers and goes dark, then the start-up window kicks in. "Magic."

Penny frowns, noticing the dusty blue cable snaking down the back of the desk. "Hang on, you weren't even using the keyboard. How did you crack the password?"

Matiu shrugs. "I've got a little help on the line."

"Someone's on our network, hacking his security? Is that even legal?"

"Yeah," Matiu says, deadpan. "This is legal hacking. Perfectly legit."

She lurches for the laptop, but Matiu grabs her wrists. "You can't do that! You can't make me a part of this, this, something…criminal! If they find out they'll track it straight to my lab and I'll be…"

"Pandora, relax." Matiu crosses her arms in front of her, pulling her close to him, their faces inches apart. "This guy's missing, right? Might be dead, but he might not be. Which means there's a chance we can find him alive."

Penny jerks against his grip, before sagging. "There are procedures…"

"And if they worked, the cops would've found him already, but they haven't. So we try something else."

"The cops don't have his laptop! We do! Illegally!"

"Yes, we do. And it's in better hands than it would be with those IT geeks the cops have working for them. You know they're on minimum wage, right?"

Penny fumes. "I don't know what you're doing Matiu, but if Fletcher has any sense, he'll have something a little more sophisticated to protect his online accounts than some backroom hacker you met in a pub in Waitakere will be able to crack. After those photos of Hayley Nevada with that pig got loose…"

"It's not his social profile or his bestiality selfies we want." Matiu smirks. "I reckon he uses this dumpy old machine for personal stuff that he doesn't want floating around where anyone could find it. OS is likely so old no one's bothering to write viruses for it anymore, so it's pretty damned safe—safer than any new machine." Cautiously, Matiu loosens his grip on Penny's wrists, her skin flushing red where his fingers were. "Let's just step in, have a look, see if we can find any clues. That's what detectives do, right?"

"We're not detectives. We're just handling the evidence. The *stolen* evidence."

Matiu fixes her with a glare. "Your precious detectives don't even know what they're looking for, much less where to start looking. If we find something helpful, we'll pass it straight along to the cops, right?"

"You're sure no one will know you were doing this from here?"

Matiu opens his mouth, closes it again. Nothing's certain when you start cracking the lid on the sort of shit he's delving into. But he smiles and says, "Sure." Turning back to the desktop, which is popping up shortcut icons at a painfully slow rate, while the ancient hard drive grinds and whirs under the brushed chrome casing, he slides the mouse towards the local email client. "OK, Mister Fletcher, who have you been talking to?"

Penny raises a finger to protest, but falls silent as she scans the list of senders that pops up as Matiu opens Fletcher's inbox. She chews on a nail, a nervous habit Matiu thought she had trained herself out of ages ago. "Who's that one from? Buchanan. Why do I know that name?"

He looks at the subject line. *Re: Re: Re: Treatment Options.* The message preview is garbled. "He's a doctor, maybe? Must be important, he's used some sort of plugin to encrypt the message internally. Paranoid, much?"

"Maybe he didn't want his nosey sister reading his emails," Penny muses. Something beeps on the other side of the lab. "Hold that thought," she says, and scurries away.

Matiu leans closer to the screen and continues to scroll through the inbox. Halfway down the page, he sees another name that just might prove his hunch right: Hanson's Canine Services. He hovers the mouse over the email link.

Clicks it open.

CHAPTER 7

- Pandora -

The explosion wakes her, sending her scrambling from the couch and dashing into the aisle where Beaker emerges like an astronaut from a cloud of green smoke.

Penny scrubs at her eyes. "Beak! What the hell?"

"It's OK. I'm OK." Beaker shoves his safety goggles up on top of his head, blinks a couple of times, then promptly pulls them back on as the murk engulfs them.

Penny's bench partner may be alive, but clearly things are *not* OK. The air in the lab is putrid. Sickly and sulphurous, it's the stench of the dead, their bodies washed up on the beach to bake and bloat and burst in the sun. Malodorous gases prick at Penny's eyes and make her throat burn. Her mind guns into overdrive. Some kind of chemical bomb? In her lab? Why would anyone want to bomb her lab? That can't be right. And yet the far end of the lab is billowing with noxious fumes. Who would do this? Could it be something to do with this new case? But who even knew she was working on it? Only Cordell...

"Beak—" she croaks.

"I know, I know. No flames, but these fumes could be toxic. We need to get into the corridor where it's safe." Taking his phone from his pocket Beaker bustles Penny towardsthe exit. "Come on. Let's get out of here. I'll get on to the chemical spill squad."

Mention of the Tox Team stops Penny in her tracks.

Over my dead body.

Whirling, she swats at the phone, batting it out of Beaker's hand and onto the bench. Beaker lets out a little cry of alarm as it skitters across the surface and spins to a stop.

"And get us a citation for contaminated premises? Beaker, what makes you think they'll treat us any different to a dirty meth lab? You call them, and we may as well shut up shop now."

While Beaker stands flat-footed and confused, Penny plunges her hand into a cardboard box of disposable respirator masks, yanking one over her head and face, tugging frantically at the elastic when it snags in her pony tail. "For Christ's sake, don't stand there, Beak, get the fume hoods on," she grunts through the mask.

"Riiight," Beaker says, his loyalty to Penny finally winning out over his need to adhere to standard spill procedure. He turns a full 360 degrees, trying to get his bearings, and for a second Penny wonders if he wasn't injured in the blast and is only just feeling the effects now.

"Fume hoods, Beaker," she says again, slower this time. "Turn them on—full tit—then get out."

"Fume hoods. Full tit." Penny imagines him colouring at the word *tit*, but the billows of smoke are forcing her to screw up her eyes, so there's no way of knowing.

"Right."

"Wait." Penny shoves the box along the bench at him. "Put a mask on first." They might be flimsy and cheap-looking, but these little filters are capable of protecting a wearer from sub-micron particles—99.8%—and biological contaminants—99.1%—as well as non-volatile liquid mists.

Except there was an explosion. Which means whatever they're huffing is definitely volatile. Shit. Penny's got to get some air in here before they both pass out.

Holding her breath, she doesn't waste time casting around for her safety googles, rushing instead to the window, throwing it open, then moving on to the next, going down the length of the lab towards the corridor like pencil traced from point to point along a number line. But even in her haste, Penny notes that there are no broken panes.

She's just flung open the last window when the lab ventilators crank into action, slowly gathering speed like a couple of old freight trains. Her eyes full of tears, Penny dashes out into the corridor.

Pulling the mask down around her neck, Penny bends over, her hands on her knees, and breathes in large desperate gulps of air that taste of polish with undertones of decades old linoleum.

"Penny? You OK?"

"Uh-huh." She stands upright, sucks in another breath. "You?"

"A bit dizzy and my ears are still ringing, but I'll live…"

Penny yawns, then slaps her hand over her mouth. "Whoops. That just slipped out."

But Beaker only shrugs. "No offence taken. You're in shock. Waking up to an explosion is just the kind of stimuli to set off a person's fight and flee mechanism.

Or maybe it was the CO_2 saturation. That'll cause yawns. I'm pretty sure you were holding your breath when you ran out of the lab."

You've gotta love an employee who provides scientific hypotheses as excuses for your rudeness, but this isn't the time. Penny places a hand on Beaker's shoulder. "Beak, what the hell just happened?"

Beaker slides down the wall until he's sitting on the marbled lino, his hands resting on knees not covered by his lab coat. Penny lets her hand fall away as she drops to the floor opposite him.

"I don't know," Beaker says. "When I got in this morning you were asleep on the couch. Matiu said you'd stayed up late to run some assays? You must've come in late because I didn't switch off the lights until close to nine." Sitting cross-legged, her back against the wall, Penny wipes her face with her hands. So Beaker *did* stay on. Penny hopes he didn't mention that to Matiu or she'll be down the price of Mum's Christmas present and a week's worth of ribbing from him. In fact, she'll be lucky if it's only a week. "Anyway, Matiu said not to wake you because you'd not long ago nodded off. He said I better keep the clinking to a minimum because if you woke up you'd be, you'd be..." he stammers, searching for the right word.

"Grumpy?"

Beaker's eyes drift left. "Um, yes. Something like that."

Just wait 'til she gets hold of Matiu.

"Anyway, your brother said he needed to take his dog out for a bit, run a couple of errands, and I was just to carry on..."

"How long ago did Matiu leave? Do you think someone could have slipped their foot in the door before it closed?"

"What for?"

"To give them time to roll the Molotov cocktail into the lab."

"Molotov cocktail?"

"Well, maybe it wasn't strictly a Molotov cocktail. I don't think it was petrol. Did it smell like petrol to you? It might have been some other flammable solvent. I thought it smelled like sulphur. Not carbon disulphide, thank God. Any contact with air and that stuff turns into a fireball..."

Beaker is completely dazed. Maybe Penny should get him checked out at the hospital after all. He might have a slight concussion.

She tries again. "Beaker, I'm talking about the explosion. The one that caused all the smoke? The reason we're sitting on the floor out here in the corridor?"

At that, Beaker raises his index finger in his own version of a Eureka moment. His face lights up in understanding. "And you thought someone was trying to sabotage the lab?"

"That's not what happened?"

"No."

"Then what?"

Beaker shakes his head like a disappointed school marm. "Really Penny, you should know better than to jump to conclusions. It was the *Breadmaker*. I'd set up one of the biological samples from the crime scene and then left it to run. I must have done something wrong. Maybe I accidentally substituted the wrong reagent. I don't know. I'll need to check. But something definitely happened. I'd left it—I was looking at the results from the assays you ran last night—when the machine started moaning and sighing. It was like something was alive in there trying to get the hell out. As soon as I heard it, I knew something was wrong. I was on my way to turn the machine off when the thing blew. I had to steady myself against the fridge. At least the lid was down: I think it contained the blast."

"I'm very glad it did. Otherwise, you could've been seriously hurt," Penny says, hoping to make up for her earlier yawning gaff. Inside though, her hopes are lower than a pimp's morals. She needs to be kind to Beaker right now. If the Breadmaker™ is irrevocably damaged then their chances of completing the DNA analyses and seeing out this case are a big fat zero. Penny's liability insurance won't run to replacing the machine. Not without a huge hike in premiums which she can't afford. She'll be out of business almost before she's started, and poor Beaker will be filling out forms at Work and Income. She pats him reassuringly on the knee. "We'll give it a few minutes for the gas to dissipate and then we'll sample the air using Teflon impingers, and titrate the samples through barium chloride-thorin substrates—just to eliminate any risk. It's what the Tox Team would do, right? Only we'll be quicker and there'll be no need to close the lab down. We'll check there's nothing too noxious lingering about, and after that we'll see what's what. You're right. It was premature of me to jump to conclusions. We can't make a call about the cause of the explosion until we have more information."

Beaker looks glum. "It was probably my fault."

"Beaker, honestly, I'm just glad we've established it wasn't a bomb. It wasn't anyone's fault. Mistakes happen. Anyway, the machine's new, so maybe something was off with the factory calibration before it was sent out. In that case, it should be under warranty. Let's just wait and see, shall we?"

Penny and Beaker are still in the corridor when Officer Clark and Matiu turn up, Cerberus bounding along the corridor behind Matiu.

Clark crinkles his nose. "What's that god-awful smell?"

"That? It's nothing." The dog thrusts his nose playfully into Penny's crotch as she pushes herself to her feet. "My colleague Beaker here thought he'd have his breakfast in the lab," she says, hoping she sounds nonchalant. She nudges Cerberus away with the flat of her hand, then stoops to scratch him behind his ear, teasing a grass seed out of his fur. "But he forgot to set the timer and managed to burn his toast and eggs." Smiling, she pushes the door open and gestures for Clark to enter. "It was a bit pongy so we came out, but we can go in now."

Beaker hurries around them. "I'll just get rid of that…toast," he says. He disappears into the back of the lab.

Remembering that Fletcher's computer is still out on the bench where Matiu had been dissecting it last night, Penny steps sideways, hoping to block it from Clark's view, but the officer doesn't appear to have noticed. In fact, Clark is staring past her at Cerberus.

"Dr Yee, I don't think your dog is too happy."

Penny turns to look. Cerberus is backing up towards Matiu, his hackles raised and his eyes rolling back, the whites showing stark and panicked. A low growl rumbles in his throat, his lips curling upwards over his canines, snarling softly as if his master had returned, plank in hand, to flay the skin off his bones.

And when Penny looks at Matiu, her brother's expression tells the same story.

- Matiu -

It washes over Matiu, a cold dread whisper, a rasping of sand across barren places, a swaying of his senses, broken blades of sound stabbing through him from somewhere beyond the veil. His coffee cup suddenly burns his palm, the fried rewa-bread with cheese he bought from the street vendor around the corner catching, clumping, choking in his throat.

"The fuck—?" he manages to gasp, as he reaches out to steady himself against the wall. It's the hand he'd been holding the coffee in, and the paper cup hits the floor with a hiss, rolling in long wet arcs towards the door. Matiu can't hear anything over the menacing chuckle beside his ear.

"Don't get weak on me now, bro. Not now. when things are starting to get interesting."

Makere is at his shoulder, darker somehow, larger than Matiu remembers, or maybe that's because Matiu is sliding down the wall. He fights to find his balance, goes down hard on one knee. The pain brings him focus, and then there are hands on him, under his arms, lifting him back to his feet.

"Matiu! Are you OK?"

Matiu pushes Penny away, perhaps more roughly than she deserves. Clark, on the other hand, is harder to brush off. The cop is giving him a hard look, the kind that cops bring out for Persons of Interest. Matiu's winning grin slams into place like an iron mask. "I'm all good, just spilt my coffee then slipped in it. They should put a warning on the cup, eh? Who'd've thought you could find a hot cup of coffee in this part of town, anyway?" He doesn't try to seal the deal with a laugh. That'd just sound wrong.

Penny chimes in, predictably, with her watery tinkle. It sounds wrong too, only Matiu doesn't know why. She's hiding something, and Matiu has to hope Clark isn't the sort of copper who can smell that from a distance.

Clark looks from Penny back to Matiu, then unhands him, straightening up his ruffled jacket. "You should get a mop, clean that up before someone gets hurt. Safety first."

Matiu bobs his head. Was a time he would've chafed at being talked to like that, but the last thing he needs right now is to wind up the five-oh. It's bad enough that he's got an illegally cracked laptop, which also happens to be evidence in a missing persons case, sitting on Penny's workbench, but for the cop to turn up at what looks and smells literally like a bombsite? With smoke pouring out the door? Matiu shakes his head. It's Penny's lab, not his. Her record is shiny clean, so they won't suspect her of anything. In fact, as Clark turns back to Penny and starts asking about the results of the crime scene analyses she's been working on, Matiu realises that it's merely his own guilty conscience working against him. The cops have simply come to collect what they're paying for, and given how pressed they are for leads and resources, maybe a smoking shambles that can deliver results is better than no lab results at all. Not the best look, for sure, but as long as Penny can string them along, they should be fine.

But the feeling of dread has eased and Makere, too, has vanished like a rat scuttling back into a sewer, after poking his teeth out just long enough to bite, to remind Matiu he's there, and that he isn't going away. Leaving Penny to deal with the inconvenience of the copper on the doorstep, he slips away to find the broom cupboard. Cerberus, still growling low in his throat, follows when Matiu slaps his hand to his thigh.

The smell gets worse as he moves through the lab, but he can hear fans blowing, so Beaker must be on it. As he clatters about in the broom cupboard, dragging out the mop and bucket, he ponders the feeling that washed over him as he stepped into the lab. The sudden, empty cold, like he was laid out beneath the glittering stars with nothing below him but frigid, shifting sand and there, in the back of his mind, the sound that had twisted his guts into sudden, unspeakable terror.

The baying of dogs at the moon. It was a raw and hungry sound, the more so for the desolate ages it echoed across to reach him.

CHAPTER 8

- Pandora -

When Clark had left to run their DNA results against police databases, Penny insisted that Matiu drive her back to her apartment for a late breakfast and a shower. Nothing could be achieved until the lab had been thoroughly decontaminated, and Beaker insisted on doing that—probably out of a misplaced sense of guilt, since he'd been the one who'd loaded the sample into the Breadmaker™. Well, Penny wasn't about to look a gift horse in the mouth, not when she hadn't had a change of clothes since being called out to the crime scene at the warehouse yesterday. Yesterday! She must smell totally rank with the filth of a day and a night of murder investigation on her. And now, with the stench of sulphur clinging to her hair and seeping into her pores, she could have crawled out of a sewer. Even Cerberus is giving her a wide berth, and let's face it, dogs will eat their own shit…

Dropping her satchel, she makes her way down the hall. For once, Matiu hadn't argued with her. He'd been rattled when he arrived back at the lab this morning. Rattled enough to collapse. Clark may have bought his 'oopsey-I-slipped-in-my-coffee' routine, but not Penny. She knows her baby brother better than that. And he can't tell her it was the fumes either. He'd only been in there a few minutes, and by that point the pea-green clouds had pretty much dissipated. A lingering waft or two is all, so it definitely wasn't that, individual variances in susceptibility notwithstanding. Perhaps it had something to do with the information he'd discovered on Fletcher's computer? He'd mentioned last night there was something on there that they should probably check out. But enigmatic as ever, he hadn't specified exactly *what* and Penny, up to her elbows in labwork, had been too engrossed to ask. Is that what he'd been doing this morning while she was asleep? Following up a lead on the case without her? Penny frowns. He better not have. Unfortunately, in the short drive to her apartment there hadn't been time enough to go into it, and once here Matiu hadn't hung around, mumbling about needing to check in with his probation officer. No matter. It'll keep. For the moment, she's going to stand under the shower and let the water wash over her until she feels human again.

In the ensuite she turns on the tap, giving the water time to run hot while she returns to the bedroom to search out some clean clothes. Naughty of her. Clean water is a finite resource. Still, she'll be quick. Bottom drawer for a pair of jeans. Second drawer for T-shirts. She shuts the drawer and opens another. Rummages about. Aha, here it is: a soft cup bra, because the blasted underwire on this one has been driving her crazy, digging into her all night. Laying the clean clothes out on the bed, she strips off, stuffing the dirty ones into the hamper, then steps into the shower. Tiny needles of hot water thwack at her shoulders and back. Standing still, she closes her eyes. Breathes deeply.

Oh God, that's good. Best thing by far all day. Although learning that the Breadmaker™ was intact had been a huge relief. It remains to be seen if the assays are still accurate, if the results are still dependable, but just looking at it, Penny had been encouraged. Standing in the corridor with Beaker, she'd been convinced her lab career was going out the window with the fumes. But amazingly, apart from being slightly blackened, the Breadmaker™ didn't appear to be seriously damaged. A few failed LEDs, but nothing much else. Lucky for her, the manufacturer had installed an automatic cut-out in case of operator error—they must have had an inkling about Beaker. Anyway, whatever it was that caused the blast had imploded inside the reinforced machine casing, forcing the lid open and spewing lovely green fumes throughout the lab, but happily containing any major damage. There was nothing left of the sample to analyse, but there wasn't much they could do about that. Overall, things could have been a lot worse.

Cupping her left hand, Penny pumps a shot of shampoo into her palm, then works the foam into her hair. The cleansing scent of tea-tree saturates the shower stall, infusing her with a sense of calm. Bucolic.

That's when the name pops back into her head: Buchanan. She and Matiu had seen it on Fletcher's computer. Penny remembers now where she'd seen that name before. It was on a death-by-suicide case she'd consulted on a couple of years ago with Noah…with *LysisCo*, Penny corrects herself. She massages her fingers into the scalp at the back of her neck. If she remembers rightly, on that occasion, the victim had been suffering from advanced pancreatic cancer, but wasn't responding to treatment. He'd become sufficiently demoralised to commit suicide. And his oncologist?

Buchanan.

Could Fletcher also be Buchanan's patient? If their victim has cancer and is struggling with depression, that might explain the motivation for his disappearance. But surely Rose Fletcher would have mentioned it? Or perhaps her brother hadn't told her? It wouldn't be the first time a brother kept something from his sister now, would it? Rose did say Fletcher had lost a lot of weight recently. Rapid weight loss could point to cancer. And if he did have advanced cancer, he might consider a quick death a blessing. Horrible disease. Centuries of research and still no easy cure. Rinsing the suds from her hair, Penny remembers downloading a few of Buchanan's papers. She'll have to look them up again, but she vaguely recalls that his treatment protocol at the time had been experimental, and not always successful, which was why his patient had chosen to take his own life. Of course, the Buchanan in Fletcher's records might be another Buchanan altogether. It's a common enough name. Or if it were the same one, Fletcher might have contacted him for another reason. Perhaps their correspondence was related to a Dish-It investigation. Well, one thing's for sure: she's not going to find out while standing in the shower. Ignoring the twinge of guilt she makes no attempt to move. She's steamed up the bathroom big time: she can hardly make out the mirror. Little rivulets snake their way down the tiles. She really should get out. Her daily water allocation will run out soon, and she still hasn't had anything to eat. Besides, Matiu will be all impatient, out there on the street waiting for her. Then she remembers how he kept her waiting yesterday. Turning his phone off. Ignoring her calls. His cheeky toot when he finally arrived forty minutes late.

Tilting her head to one side to allow the shower jets to work their magic on her neck, Penny figures, to hell with it, a few more minutes won't hurt.

- Matiu -

Matiu sets the teacups down with a soft ceramic clink, steam spooling away from the rims like *wairua* leaping off the edge of the world. The woman sitting in the worn armchair barely registers, looking past him through the window, through the years, nodding in that distant way that is so familiar to him. Moving like a cat, he eases himself into the chair beside her, lets the moment sit quiet between them for a bit. When she's ready she'll talk. There's not much point starting into anything before that. She knows he's there. Sometimes it just takes her a while to arrive at the same place, in the same time. Such a lot of distance to cover between here and wherever it is she goes.

Where she has to come back from.

Matiu settles back, sips his tea and waits, even though his nerves are as frayed as the edges of the throws on the old armchairs. A breeze stirs the bead curtain. Just outside the back door, Matiu can hear Cerberus, whimpering quietly. The heat, the haze of summer, sits heavy on the house. But for a short while, Matiu has no choice but to sit quietly, to feel the warm wind wafting through. It should bring him some peace—normally, it does—but not this time. The heat, the quiet are oppressive, weighing him down. There are things he should be doing, like checking in with the probation office, but none of it can happen until this conversation has taken place.

"Mārama, I brought you tea," he says, gesturing to the cup. It's as much of an ice-breaker as he's willing to risk. Pressing her into conversation can tip her over into one of her episodes, and he can't afford that, not today. Today, he'd appreciate it if she could be having one of her lucid periods.

Her nodding pauses and she looks past him, as if towards something far away growing steadily closer. Then she turns to him, and a phantom of a smile crosses her lips. "My boy," she says, and her fingers twist one against the other, tug at the wrap which shrouds her shoulders. "Always such a good boy."

"How have you been?" he asks. As ever, he struggles to start the conversation, never quite sure how close she'll be to this reality, how far lost in the other. Wonders, as he always does, if this is what he too has in store as the years wear him down.

"I stood on the beach," she says, her voice little more than a whisper. "The tide was coming in, and it just kept coming. Right up the beach, covering the sand, and the stones, and the flax and the dunes, and the water...the water was cold. Really cold. Too cold for swimming. So I just stood and watched from under the waves. The sand, Matiu, it swirled up and around me as the tide washed in and out, and it was hard to breathe, with all that sand and water in my mouth. *Aue.*"

Matiu nods, as she reaches down to pick up her teacup in hands that tremble. "Everyone's good," he says, moving right along. "Pandora's taken on some police work. If she can keep that up she might be able to stay afloat, with her lab and all."

"*Tino pai*," she says, smiling, and for a moment Matiu thinks he can see through the distance that falls away behind her eyes, see the Mārama he has known from time to time, on those rare occasions when the inexplicable sadness retreats, and she emerges to face the world with her bright and shining self. "You should bring your dog in to say hello."

Matiu shouldn't be surprised. Walls and doors seldom hide anything from Mārama if she chooses to see past them. Obedient to her every request, he goes out to the back porch, unties Cerberus and leads him inside. The dog sits beside the armchair, tail swishing slowly back and forth, floppy ears twitching. He looks from Matiu to Mārama and back, before settling on his front paws. "We're looking after him, Penny and me."

"Penny and *I*," Mārama corrects absently. "What's his name?"

"Cerberus."

"Of course. Quite a monster, by the looks." Cerberus' dark eyes stare up at her. She stretches a hand towards him. "*Kia ora, e kuri*," she says.

Matiu watches, transfixed, remembering what happened the first time he touched the dog. Partly, he hopes the negative energy that had been clinging to the dog is gone now, grounded out through him in Fletcher's apartment, but he also hopes that something remains, enough of a trace that Mārama will touch, sense something. She rubs the top of the dog's head, and he leans in to her. A frown crosses her face, though her eyes remain distant. Matiu can feel the silence as it falls across Mārama's shoulders, across the room. She sets the teacup down in its saucer with a small staccato of clinking china and places her other hand on the dog's head. She closes her eyes.

Matiu sits perfectly still, his mouth dry, half-expecting Makere to whisper suddenly in his ear, startling him silly. But his unseen companion says nothing, even though Matiu can feel his presence, there in the shadows behind his eyes, watching, anticipating. He won't show himself, Matiu knows. He can't hide from Mārama. He *fears* Mārama. But he's not too afraid to spy on them.

She looks up, and her eyes are clear, bright with sadness. "You know?" she asks Matiu.

He shrugs. "A little. Not enough."

Mārama releases the dog and sinks back into her chair, the shawl wrapping around her like a cloak to ward off bad spirits. She takes several long breaths, as if coming up from a deep place, hungry for air and light. "Every time I come back here," she says, looking past his shoulder to the sunshine that glares across the windowsill, "all I see is more darkness. It follows us, clings to us, like a sickness, like…wild dogs. Wraps around us and ties us to the world."

Matiu waits.

"It's the dark that keeps us, Matiu. The dark that owns us." Mārama lifts her teacup, blows across the tannin surface of the liquid, inhales the steam. Sips at it reverently. "He couldn't bear to see it die. You know that, right? He couldn't sacrifice his friend."

Matiu nods. However cryptic, he had felt a hint of it in the warehouse, when the walls had screamed. "But something had to die. Something that mattered."

This was the way of all sacrifices.

"This is not your fight, Matiu. The shadows grow long around you. You have no need to walk any deeper into them."

Matiu stares at his cup, trying to ignore the tiny ripples that flutter out and back, out and back, across the tea. He doesn't even like tea, only drinks it because Mārama does, and she doesn't have coffee in the house. Because it's something they share which *doesn't* terrify him. "Someone has to."

Mārama's eyes flick up, scouring him like sudden flame. "I thought you would've learned by now when to walk away."

Matiu resists the urge to stand and leave. She doesn't deserve that, not for caring about him. Not for wishing he could step out of the darkness, the danger, and put it behind him. Not when the darkness is such a part of him. "There was another dog. I'm pretty sure it came from Hanson. I thought he was out of the game, but it looks like he's back at his old tricks. Need to shut him down for good."

"If this was just about Hanson, I'd have no issue with it. Hanson's a soulless murderer, and I'd be as happy as you to see him fed to his own dogs. But it's more than that. I can see it, you can *feel* it. There's a tide coming up the beach, Matiu, a drowning flood. We should be running from it, as far and as fast as we can. Those who stand on the sand and watch it come, who try to hold it back...? They'll be the first to be dragged under. I can't bear to think that you'll be on the beach, digging your toes into the sand, when the tide comes in."

"And what about the others?" Matiu asks. "What about those who are on the beach but can't hear it coming?"

"They're not your concern."

"Some of them are."

"You're too good, child. You will put yourself through this; you'll be made to suffer, and no one will ever know. No one will care. The world doesn't care for the likes of us."

"Where can I find Hanson?"

The light seems to fall away from her, like a cloud drifting over the moon. "If you fall, Matiu..."

"I won't."

"Without you, I will be nothing."

"Where's Hanson?"

She tugs the shawl closer around her shoulders as if, despite the humidity and the sweat that crawls down Matiu's spine, the room has just grown cold. Her voice, when it emerges from her small, bent shell, is a hollow whisper. "Woodhill Forest. The old ranger station up Tarawera Road, west of Helensville. He keeps them tied up in the storage sheds at the bottom of the valley."

Matiu nods, committing the address to memory, and trying as best he can to forget the way the light—and the hope—slide from her face as she tells him, like the information isn't a tip-off so much as it's a eulogy. Like they might be the last words she will ever share with her son, before the tide comes in, and sweeps away the world they know.

CHAPTER 9

- Pandora -

Penny's still eating when Matiu returns. With her toast in one hand and her coffee in the other, she buzzes him up with her elbow. Draining her coffee, she pops the mug in the sink. Then, the last of her toast still in her hand, she opens the door. Cerberus bounds in, leaping playfully on Penny, his paws reaching nearly to her shoulders. It's just as well she'd finished her coffee.

Laughing, Penny holds her toast out of reach. "Hey, you big oaf. I'm finally clean and you have to go and jump on me with these dirty great mitts. Come on, off me now. Sit."

Obediently, the dog drops to its haunches, his dark eyes fixed on Penny's corner of toast. Penny waves the crust across her body. The dog's eyes follow the movement.

"Oh well, there's the truth of it. And here I was thinking you were pleased to see me. Go on then. It's all yours. No snatching now."

Penny opens her hand and Cerberus nibbles at the toast, picking it up in a movement delicate enough to pass at a duchess' high tea, then settles down under the coffee table to enjoy his treat.

Penny turns to find Matiu leaning on the door frame. "I thought you were going to wait downstairs," she says.

"And I thought you were going to be ready."

Penny looks up sharply at his tone. Something is off. This is getting to be a habit. He was off-kilter at the crime scene yesterday, and again later in Fletcher's apartment, then he catapulted his coffee all over the floor at the lab this morning, and now this? Matiu's not so much leaning on the door frame as propping himself up. It doesn't take a gas-liquid chromatograph to detect when he's masking something. His stationary phase may look solid enough, apart from those dark hollows under his eyes, but uneasiness is pouring off him in volatile waves. Like he's just seen the Ghost of Christmas Past.

"Yeah, sorry. I had some stuff to do," Penny says. She crosses the living room and skirts around the kitchen island.

Matiu steps into the room, part of Cerberus' lead dangling from his back pocket, the chain clinking softly. Glancing pointedly at Penny's satchel, still where she'd dumped it on her way in, Matiu takes a gander down the hall to where the last wisps of steam are leaking from the bathroom. He raises his eyebrows. "Yeah, so I see. Good shower was it?"

"Shuddup," Penny retorts. Pumping antibacterial soap into her palm, she rinses her hands and places them under the blower, cleaning off the dog slobber. And speaking of dog, Cerberus had been upset this morning, too. Was that the dog's natural empathy making him susceptible to the anxiety of his human companion? Could Cerberus be that attached to her brother after just a day in his company?

Penny turns her hands in the air blades. Normally, she'd do this to optimise drying, but she does it now to give her time to think.

Plenty of historical studies support empathy in canines. Although, it's probably too soon for the dog to exhibit that kind of rapport. More likely he was responding to an emotional contagion, the way one baby in the nursery cries and sets all the others off. With babies it's not empathy—those feelings don't typically kick in until a child is about two—just a kind of Mexican Wave effect. So when Matiu had been startled in the lab, he'd provided the stimulus, and Cerberus had simply responded in kind? Penny shakes her head, rejecting the theory. No, it wasn't just that. Matiu had been shaken, so if it had been a simple case of emotional contagion Cerberus should have had his ears folded back and his tail tucked under his belly. Instead, the dog had shown all the signs of an animal set to attack: standing tall on his toes, hackles raised, and his lips pulled back to expose his teeth. She steals a sideways look at the dog. Under the table, Cerberus is gnawing away at the crust, struggling to anchor the tiny morsel between his front paws. He seems OK now…

Penny removes her hands, the action automatically switching off the blower. "Look, Matiu, about this case, we really need to talk."

"Any coffee still in that pot?"

Looks like some solid phase micro-extraction is going to be required. "Come on, Matiu. You've been acting really weird ever since I took this case. What's going on?"

"Caffeine deficiency."

"Matiu."

"OK, good idea, Pandora," Matiu says, opening a cupboard and grabbing a mug. He slams the door shut. Penny gives a little jump. "Since you brought it up, let's talk about what's going on, shall we? Why don't you tell me what the hell happened in the lab this morning?" He pours his coffee—black—then swings around to face her. "And don't give me any smoke-and-mirrors bullshit about overcooked eggs."

"Oh, that," Penny says, suddenly on the back foot.

"Well?"

"It was nothing. At first, I thought someone had rolled a Molotov cocktail into the lab—"

"Because people do that regularly, do they?"

"No, of course not." Penny titters. "I thought it was Cordell, or maybe something to do with the case…"

"Cordell? You mean Noah? What would your ex have to do with it?"

"Nothing. Nothing at all. He's just…the first person who came to mind." Seeing Matiu's frown, Penny rushes on. "Look, it turns out there are some teething problems with the Breadmaker—it's a new machine and they're highly sensitive. I didn't want Clark to find out because I can't risk him thinking my company is flaky. He'll pass it up the line to Tanner. They'll show me the door. I've only just managed to get my foot in." Penny stops. Matiu, pensive, is off with the fairies somewhere.

"What?" Penny insists.

Matiu shakes his head. "Nothing."

"Tell me."

"What was in your Breadmaker?"

"I'm not sure. A sample from the crime scene. Beaker set it up, so I'd have to check with him."

Penny could swear she sees Matiu's body sag. He looks like an overloaded coat rail, only barely holding up under the weight.

"Matiu, if you know something—"

Matiu exhales through puffed cheeks. "It's probably nothing. Just a hunch." He tips his coffee in the sink and pulls the lead from his back pocket. At the sound of the chink, Cerberus clambers out from under the table, vaults Penny's satchel and hovers at Matiu's feet, his tail wagging. "We should go," Matiu says. He secures the lead. "C'mon, boy."

Stopping first to put the cups in the dishwasher and switch off the cafetière, Penny gathers up her satchel and hurries after them. Another fail. How does he do that? Twist her words around so she's the one being grilled. Penny wishes she had that skill. Matiu probably picked it up going through the court system, she thinks, as she closes the door.

Then again, who is she kidding? He only had to watch Mum and Dad.

Downstairs in the car, Matiu is on the air to despatch. "So you see, Carlie, I'm tied up all day, driving Pandora about for her police investigation. Yes, you could say Mum and Dad authorised it." Matiu's eyes meet Penny's and their discord from earlier drops away as understanding flashes between them.

Mum and Dad? Authorised? Ordered, more like.

They exchange knowing smiles, and Matiu returns to the conversation.

"And I'm turning off the GPS," he goes on. "Yes, all day. I know, it's against company regulations, but we can't have the details of our movements noted on civilian records." There's a pause. Matiu purses his lips and taps his fingers on the steering wheel. Penny imagines Carlie's rebuttal. No doubt along the lines of Mr and Mrs Yee expecting to be informed of their whereabouts at all times. Matiu inhales slowly. "But this is a murder investigation. Pandora has to follow up leads, interview witnesses, that sort of thing," he says, his voice deliberate. "Yes, Carlie, if that information got out, she could definitely be at risk. You'd do that? Because Pandora and I don't want to get you in trouble: they can be pretty scary." He laughs, overloud in the vehicle. "You're a doll. I knew you'd understand." He rings off, and starts the car.

Penny shakes her head theatrically. "All that crap you give me about Beaker," she teases.

"It got her off our back, didn't it?"

"For now. They'll find out, you know."

"It'll be fine."

"They'll be pissed."

Matiu pulls out into the street. "Yeah, well, that's OK, sis, because I plan on blaming you."

Penny snorts. He will, too. She'll have to make up some nonsense about police procedure. Or failing that, marry Craig Tong.

"Anyway, I thought this morning—what's left of it—we should make a visit to Fletcher's Dish-It offices. Staff there might be able to fill us in on his movements over the past few days, maybe give us some clues about his state of mind—"

Penny is interrupted when, between them, Matiu's tablet buzzes.

Penny picks up the device and reads off the caller's name. "Erica."

"Fuck." Matiu slaps his temple. "Fuck-fuck-fuck-fuck-fuck," he raps, marking each expletive with a fist-thump to his thigh.

"Who is she?"

"My probation officer."

Dan Rabarts & Lee Murray

"Ah. Given your reaction, I thought maybe you'd got her pregnant."

"Very funny."

"What do you want me to do?"

Matiu grimaces. "Just leave it."

More buzzing. "You sure? She's pretty insistent."

"Yeah, leave it. It'll just be about an appointment."

Appointment…appointment! That reminds her about the name they saw in Fletcher's online diary. She rejects the call and tells Matiu everything she remembers about Buchanan: his research, the case she'd worked with Cordell, even gives him a summary of the post mortem findings on the guy who committed suicide. Then she tells him her suspicions about Fletcher, and the evidence leading her to think he might have cancer—a likely motive if he did kill himself.

"We'll see what Scour turns up," Matiu says when she finally peters out. "I've got him checking out the names we found on Fletcher's computer."

"Maybe Fletcher's colleagues will be able to help with that, too," Penny says cheerily. The Buchanan discussion concluded, Penny takes a proper look out the window as Matiu slows the vehicle, and turns hard right at a wooden sheep run, weathered grey from years in the sun. Penny's heart sinks. This isn't the city green belt. On either side of the road, a couple of straggly beech trees, shying from the prevailing sou-westerly nod their assent.

"What the heck, Matiu. Where are we? This isn't the Dish-It office, this is the Back of Beyond."

"Well spotted, sis. I found something else on that computer that we should check out."

They continue on in silence. The road narrows as it dips into the valley.

CHAPTER 10

- Matiu -

The landscape spreads out around them, kilometre after rolling kilometre of overstretched farmland encircled by rusting fence lines of razor wire topped with solar-powered LED security lights. A few vehicles patrol the dead zones between plantations, biodiesel LEVs and electric ATVs. The buggies might be jokes compared to the Holden as it chews up the horizon, but the grim-faced security staff with their equally grim submachine-guns are nothing to laugh about. "No stun setting on those puppies," Matiu chuckles as one such security patrol does a U-turn to match their approach, then attempts to keep pace with them along the dirt track between the looming fence and the crumbling road.

Penny says nothing. She's shrinking a little further into herself with every curve of the road that stretches between Auckland and wherever the hell it is Matiu is taking them. She has her tablet out, maybe reviewing her lab findings, maybe just staring into the safe borders of her screen so she doesn't have to see the brutal lines of fences beyond the windshield.

"We're only ever five good meals away from revolution, you know that?" Matiu says. He's not trying to wind her up again, honestly. Not even trying to upset her. But he has a hard time hiding from truth, and it feels to him like this is a truth that *matters*, now more than ever. "If it all turns to custard at lunchtime today, there could be war in the streets by dinner-time tomorrow."

"Shush," Penny says, and Matiu can tell from the slight quaver in her voice that it's taking her a lot of effort to sound relaxed. Beneath the calm exterior she's taut, like a violin string wound too tight. Ready to snap. "People are too civilised for that."

"Yip," Matiu says, nodding. "That's why the government farms are guarded by armed patrols. It keeps the masses civilised."

"You're the one driving us out here. You still haven't told me where we're going."

"That must be pretty infuriating," Matiu agrees, and they drive on, leaving the suspicious stares of the hired guns behind. Ahead, as they crest a rise, sunlight glints on water.

"We're miles from anywhere," Penny finally says, her frustration bubbling to the surface.

"Not really. That's Kawau Parua Inlet up there, and we must be less than a mile from it, surely."

Penny holds up her tablet. A green and blue map is spread out in stiff, stilted blocks. "Miles. From. Anywhere. Not even enough signal to get a proper map up. How can this possibly have anything to do with my case? For crying out loud, Matiu, I've got work to do. You've had your little joke—and it's not even funny, just so you know—now explain yourself or turn this car around and take us back to Auckland. Right. Now."

Matiu sighs, theatrically deep, then slows the car to a stop. The wheels crunch in the gravel on the roadside. In the back seat, Cerberus raises his head, hopeful. Matiu nudges the central locking button on the door, and the locks pop open. "Feel free to try your luck hitch-hiking home, sister." It's cruel, he knows, but also a little bit hilarious, to watch the colour drain from her cheeks.

"Cut it out."

There's a real edge of fear in her voice, and Matiu deflates. For once he feels a thread of shame tighten around his chest. He locks the doors again. "In the old days, the spirits would travel north, across these lands, to reach Rēinga. It was their last journey, to the place where the sea swallows up the land forever, and there they'd throw themselves into the setting sun. To be free."

Penny's brow furrows. "We're going to throw ourselves into the sea? What the fuck, Matiu…?"

Matiu shakes his head, holding up a hand. "Not us. The point is, this is the ends of the earth, right? We're driving towards the end of the world. Every click further we get from Auckland, the further we are from what you like to think of as civilised, if that's what you want to use as your benchmark, for want of a better word."

"So…?"

"So if I was the sort of person who was in the business of…doing things that were a bit uncivilised, I'd want to be as far from the eyes of civilisation as possible, right?"

"I trust you're going to get to the point eventually."

"Not yet. Because if I told you, you wouldn't hesitate to get out of the car if I unlocked it again. You'd rather risk the road than where we're going."

Penny laughs a little laugh, a brittle sound of broken glass in a drainpipe, a sound that wants to be cheerful but which can only rattle with fear. "Now you're just trying to freak me out."

Matiu puts the car in gear and pulls out. "No, I want you to know that where we're going will be dangerous. You won't like what you see. It'll make you sick, it'll haunt you for years to come. But you need to see this."

"What? Why?"

Matiu doesn't take his eyes from the road ahead, but he knows she's looking at the door again, at the lock, at the road rushing by. Weighing her chances. "Because this is your fight as much as it is mine. You need to know what we're fighting for."

"I'm not fighting *anyone*. Enough with the cryptic bullshit. Are you back on the wacky backy?"

Matiu's jaw tightens. Proud as he is of the fact that it's been years now since he's touched the smoke, he can't really blame her for thinking he's gone off the rails. But she has to see, has to understand how serious it is. "You love dogs, right?"

Penny glares at him. Her lip is trembling.

"Fletcher bought a dog to sacrifice, instead of Cerberus. He bought it from a guy named Hanson, who keeps dogs in captivity and raises them to fight each other in pit battles for money."

Penny freezes in the act of tapping out a message, presumably to Dad.

"We're going to Hanson's farm."

"So we can...question him?"

"Yes," Matiu says, his face as grim as the men on the fences, as bleak as their machine-guns. "To question him."

He tries to ignore the way she stares at him, her face a mask of outrage and terror. If that's how she reacts to the idea of what lies in store, he hopes she really will be able to handle herself when they reach Hanson's. Because she has a job to do, and if she can't do it, then they really are driving to the end of the world, to throw themselves into the setting sun.

"Hang on," Penny says, the air suddenly even cooler in the car, "what did you mean? Sacrifice?"

"That's why we're going to question him, aren't we?"

"I don't like this."

"Neither do I, sister. But it has to be done."

- Pandora -

Penny doesn't need to look him up. Hanson. Fraud, theft, trafficking, inciting to violence, grievous bodily harm, manslaughter, murder. The guy's a regular peach.

Hey, Hanson, we were just in the neighbourhood, thought we'd pop in for a cuppa.

She gnaws at the skin inside her cheek. Matiu was right to lock the doors, because right now she is seriously freaked out. Clammy palms, a racing heart, and a sudden urge to pee: Penny recognises the standard physiological responses to fear reported in Walter Bradford Canon's hallmark paper published in 1932. In the back seat, affected by the emotional contagion, or perhaps by Penny's own fear pheromone, Cerberus whines softly.

"Matiu, come on. It's not funny anymore. Turn around."

"Like I said, you can get out if you like. Hitch back. I won't stop you."

"Dad will cut your nose off."

Matiu curls his lip. "Really, Pandora? Chop my nose off? That's the best you can do?"

It *was* pretty lame. Instead, she imagines sliding bamboo shoots under his finger nails where the nerve endings are exquisitely sensitive and ramming them in hard. But Penny needn't worry: if they ever come back from this, and their father sees the gas bill, he will add tortures Six through Ten to the list of Five Punishments.

Hugging her arms to her chest, she looks out the window, feeling almost wistful as they leave behind the last of the government farms with their Get-Lost gunmen, Fuck-You fences, and Bugger-Off barbed wire. From here it's just gravel road, scrub and loneliness all the way to the coast. Maybe tapping her foot will dissipate some tension. No. That's just winding her up even more.

"At least put the GPS on," she snaps. Even patchy reception would give the olds a general idea of their whereabouts.

"Nuh-uh."

Penny could clean out his innards with a chopstick, he is *that* infuriating. "Why not? Someone should know we're out here," she says, wishing she didn't sound so wheedling. "In case…"

She clamps her lips shut as Matiu slows the Holden to take the turn. On the gatepost, a dilapidated sign reads *Hanson's Canine Services*. Matiu stops the car.

They've passed the point of no return.

Penny slips her tablet down the side of the seat. Then, steeling herself, she throws open the door and steps into a dried pool of mud. Time to find out if they really *are* throwing themselves into the setting sun, as Matiu so eloquently put it.

Because, quite honestly, meeting with Hanson isn't the scariest thing her brother has suggested today.

CHAPTER 11

- Matiu -

Matiu sits for a minute, scanning the paddock, the fence line, the trees that mark the boundary of Hanson's property. It used to be Conservation land, back before budget cuts forced the Government to sell off large chunks of regenerating coastal forest just to keep their parliamentary lunch bill paid. He's been here before, of course, once or twice, back when he used to work the fringes of the Auckland pit-fighting rings, usually just watching the perimeter, keeping an eye out for the five-oh. Still, that was close enough. He'd still *heard* what was going on inside those walls. The screams of the crowd, of the dogs. Screams that drove through him like nails, but work was work. Sometimes things have to be done.

The farm was where Hanson brought new dogs, the ones that had to be broken, ready for fighting. Some had a killer instinct that could be honed for the ring; some had none, and needed to learn the fear and desperation of battling tooth and claw, fighting for their lives. Or at least, of putting on a good show for the punters.

Not that different, Matiu thinks, than the outcasts who found themselves fallen so far that they were working for a creature like Hanson. Either way, he has some idea of what he'll find on the other side of the hill. He picks out the pole with the small black camera, cunningly concealed beside the nikau palm near the gate. He leans forward for a better look. From memory, he should be parked far enough back from the gate that he won't be visible, but even so, something looks not quite right about the surveillance camera. Either the wind has knocked it, or the screws have come loose, but it's tilted almost straight down, so it won't be monitoring the whole fence line like it should. He remembers standing in the ranger station, years ago, watching the screen for anyone driving up to the gate. It had once been his job to guard this guy and his bloody little empire. Irony's a bitch.

Someone must know the camera's misaligned, and will probably be coming to fix it, and that could be a problem. But he'll take his good luck when he can get it. It doesn't come along often, after all. And there's always the chance not everything is well and good over that rise, under those trees.

He climbs from the car, throwing open the back door so Cerberus can leap out. The dog shakes itself as Matiu slides on his sunglasses, a black mask to hide behind. He reaches into the back seat and pulls out his jacket, black leather that falls halfway down his thigh, soft from years of use. The sun on the leather is scorching, but he'd rather be too hot than go anywhere without his jacket. Armour against the world. He slams the door shut, walks to the locked gate, hoists himself onto the post and jumps deftly to the dirt road beyond. Penny hurries to keep up, clambering over the fence with all the grace of a lab technician, or lack thereof. Cerberus shames them both by clearing the gate in a single bound, and then proceeds to raise his leg to the fence-post and baptise it.

"You don't think the locked gate might mean he's not in the mood for visitors?" Penny asks.

Matiu points to a service road on the left that snakes down the hill into the cover of old-growth pines, towards the coast. "You head that way. Try not to be seen."

"What? You can't expect me to go off on my own? Are you nuts?"

"If I turn up with someone Hanson doesn't know, he'll be suspicious. While I've got him talking, you sneak around the other side. Get a look in through a window, record everything on your phone. We're going to need evidence."

"We're not actors in some thriller show, you know. This guy is dangerous. What if he has guards?"

Matiu shrugs in exaggerated exasperation. "I *said* try not to be seen. Given what he's into, if I show up at his door he'll assume I've brought something I'd like to sell him." Matiu clips Cerberus' leash to his collar. "Would *you* rather be the bait?"

"This is crazy."

"No," Matiu says, shaking his head only slightly at how dense his sister can sometimes be, for such a clever girl. He sets off towards the old ranger station beyond the rise and the stand of twisted pōhutukawa. "This is what lies beneath our veneer of civilisation. This is the first circle of hell."

"Thanks," Penny mutters as he leads the dog up the road. "That's really reassuring."

He keeps walking. Part of him wants to turn and run, get in the car and keep driving, not even back to Auckland but further, down to the lake, maybe to East Cape, or the Wairarapa. Plenty of places a guy could lose himself out that way. Somewhere he can hole up, hide from the world, hide from what's coming. But he's not that guy. He can't run and hide. Because what's coming won't leave him alone. What's coming is coming to find him.

"What's your plan, *e toa*?"

Matiu flinches at the suddenness of the voice at his shoulder, but chokes back a cry of surprise. Damn it all if he's going to let Makere see that just under his leather-and-sunshades exterior there's a frightened boy, the same boy who had more than once cowered in a crying heap in the basement, terrified of the voices in his head, of the things he saw that nobody else did. "Like I'm going to share with you." His fists clench and flex. He doesn't appreciate the mocking tone Makere has taken with him of late, nor of his choice to call him *e toa*—warrior. Matiu doesn't want to be a warrior. He doesn't want this to be his war. But it has to be, or else it'll be everyone's.

"You're just going to march on up to old Hanson's place, him with all his boys around, and probably a few you won't be able to see, more than one of them packing, and do what? Tell him you want to sell him a Golden Lab as a fighting dog? Penny's right, you're nuts."

"Cerberus isn't a fighting dog. That doesn't mean Hanson won't see him as useful or valuable."

Matiu can almost hear Makere's face split into a cruel grin. "Oh, pitbait? You *are* a vicious bastard. I won't tell Penny what you've got planned, I promise. You can live with that guilt all by yourself."

Matiu glances back. Of Makere, of course, there's no sign, just a shadow on the back of his eyes, a chill on his spine. More surprisingly though, he can't see Penny. He'd half-expected her to still be standing there in the rutted mud, wringing her hands together and shifting her weight from one foot to the other in a paroxysm of indecision. He's pretty sure she won't have gone back to the car. She's too deep in this thing now, just like he is. She has to know what's going on, too. She's determined like that; it's the scientist in her. "You just believe what you like, bro. Always have, always will," he says, into the salty air, to Makere, gone but always listening. To himself.

He tops the rise, and the dilapidated station reveals itself, hunkered like a withered old man under the looming pōhutukawa. Not much more than a cabin, really, with a double garage at one end, its roller doors rusting quietly in the steady sea breeze. Only four rooms inside; an office, a bunkroom, bathroom and a kitchenette, a pantry for dry stores. On the outside of the building there's a little storeroom where the DoC rangers used to keep the possum-baits and the rat-poison. Stinks in there, and if the wind's blowing from the right direction you can smell it inside the house. For a guy like Hanson to hole up in a dive like this, things must've got pretty hot with the five-oh back in the city. Nothing like the luxury he's used to.

Now in full view of the house, Matiu tries to mentally scope out the floor-plan, guess where the old man will be sitting, how many thugs with shotguns will be standing by the windows, watching him come. There's no one on the porch. He doesn't see the curtains twitch. He tries to walk with a calm certainty, the sort of walk that says he's meant to be there, nothing furtive in his step, no cause for concern here. Cerberus strains at the leash, and Matiu ignores the fact that the dog is not pulling forward, but off to the side, as if trying to get away.

"I know, boy. I can feel it too."

The closer they get, the more Matiu can taste the wrongness of the place. It's not just the neglect and decay that hang in the air, the soft rotting of old timber and the acidic tang of salting rust. It's a bitter reek of despair, and something more, something deeper, older. He's almost at the porch step now, and he knows that when he reaches out and grabs the rail, he'll learn a whole lot more—more than he wants to. So he keeps his hands close, one in his jacket pocket, where a cold, comfortable weight rests against his fingers, and the other wrapped around the leash, tight to his stomach so that Cerberus can't strain too far. Even so, as he climbs the steps, a coldness seeps up his legs, through the soles of his shoes. A heaviness, like grave-dirt sucking at his feet.

He reaches the porch, and the two steps that bring him to the door are the longest he's ever taken, like stepping out across a vast void and arriving somewhere alien, haunted. Letting the jack-knife fall from his fingers back into the bottom of his pocket, he reaches for the door handle. The sea breeze moans through the branches of the pōhutukawa, the cries of lost souls fleeing to Rēinga. His hand freezes before he grabs the handle, suddenly aware his brash advance may be a little *too* bold. Familiar face or not, he's still not expected. Still might not be welcome. The door will surely be locked and barred, after all. Hanson's a long way from home, but he'll be no less careful. Paranoid, some would call it.

He raps his knuckles on the door. The sound echoes hollowly, but no voices, no footsteps, no gunshots rouse to greet him. He waits. Trying his best to look nonchalant, he glances at the sky.

Grey clouds swarm and coil on the horizon. Matiu frowns. He could've sworn it was clear, blue, stifling hot before he stepped onto the porch. He distinctly remembers sweating in his leather jacket under the sun, yet now a rivulet of cold creeps down his back. He fights the urge to tug his jacket across his chest. Refuses to feel the sudden chill pooling around him.

He knocks again. This time, when no one answers, he reaches out, wraps a hand around the door handle. It's cold as death in his grip. He turns it. With a soft crack, like the sound of the thin ice in the centre of a pond surrendering to some brave and foolish child's weight on a frosty winter morning, the door swings in.

- Pandora -

Penny picks her way down the track, half-crouched and half-running, making for the cover of the pines. The path is deeply pugged and although the real heat of summer is still more than a month away, the clay ruts are baked hard, making it tricky to negotiate without breaking an ankle. It doesn't help that she's wearing these summer sandals. Strappy and heeled, they're not the best choice for gallivanting about the countryside pretending she's an FBI field agent. Penny zig-zags from one side of the track to the other, side-stepping another pile of dried dung and praying she doesn't run smack into one of Hanson's men.

She glances back up the hill at her brother. Closing in on the top of the rise, Matiu is channelling his inner James Dean, wearing his sunnies and his old faithful black leather jacket. He's heading out to play with the gangsters, so he puts on his leathers? Does he think if he dresses himself like a thug and swaggers up the front path, the nasty lowlifes in there will recognise him as one of their own? This isn't a bloody costume party to go traipsing up to the front door without an invitation! Penny shivers. Matiu better know what he's doing.

Suddenly, the theme from *Star Wars* blares.

Da duh, da da da da duh...

Her phone.

Now she gets reception?

Quickly, Penny digs it out of her pocket. "Hello?" she whispers.

"Pandora." Her heart sinks. "Mum, this isn't a very good time…"

"When is ever a good time with you? You left in such a hurry last night, before the meal was over. We didn't raise you to behave like that in front of guests."

"Craig Tong, you mean," Penny hisses.

"You won't take that tone after I tell you the good news."

"Good news?"

"Wonderful news, actually. Craig says he might be able to get you a government job in science policy. Isn't that great? Of course, he can't promise anything, but you'd be out of the lab—"

The track curves like a natural skateboard bowl, and in the dip, Penny spies the roof of the house. Ignoring her mother on the phone, she ducks down. There could be sentries. Penny needs to get out of the open. She puts on a little spurt to cover the distance to the pines and has only just made it to the craggy grey canopy of the trees when she kicks up a stone. Chattering loudly, it skitters down the hill and into the natural bowl in the landscape, exacerbating the noise. Penny freezes, her pulse galloping, her heart about to explode. Is this how the last flightless takahē felt in the seconds before the dog killed it? She waits, not breathing, for a shout from one of Hanson's men. But the sound of the stone Dopplers away, and Penny relaxes. She waits a moment longer, then hazards a quick look back through the tree trunks. Matiu and Cerberus have vanished beyond the rise. She needs to get a wriggle on. Matiu will be knocking on the front door before she's had a chance to scope out the back.

She puts the phone back to her ear. Her mother is still talking. "Just imagine the doors a job like that could open…"

Speaking of doors, why *is* Matiu the one waltzing up to the front door? Why is he the frontperson? It should be Penny standing there on the porch. She's the consultant for the police: it's *her* job to collect evidence relevant to the case. Except Hanson would've told her to piss off back to town and get a warrant, and in the time it would take her to get Clark out here with one, Hanson would have the place wiped cleaner than the inside of an autoclave. That's why she's the one skirting round the back. There isn't time for a warrant, not if there's any hope of finding Fletcher alive, and Matiu knows that.

"Mum, sorry. I have to go. I'll call you back."

"Pandora, really, is Matiu there—?"

Penny turns her phone off and puts it back in her pocket. A niggle sticks under her ribs. Maybe collecting evidence on the quiet isn't the only reason she's picking her way through these radiata. Maybe Matiu's plan isn't so hot after all, and Penny's little detour is meant to keep her out of harm's way.

Shit.

It takes only minutes for Penny to reach the far side of the pines and the rear of the farmlet. Huffing from the exertion, she hunkers behind a rusted sheet of corrugated iron. Heading in from the coast, the breeze is a welcome relief. Penny takes a moment to catch her breath and study the outbuildings.

Closest to her, and on an angle, is a line of pens sufficient to house perhaps thirty dogs, but with the kennels blocking her view she can't tell how many of the cages are occupied. A chorus of barks tells her they aren't empty: the dogs are picking up her scent and warning her off. Penny watches for a corresponding sign of alarm from the house, but there's no movement, no short-tempered handler bellowing at them to shut up.

Clearly, Hanson's people are used to a bit of a ruckus.

Between the pens and the house is a low-roofed shed, probably for storage, and beyond the shed is the back wall of the house, its length broken by a long, high window. A farm bike has been abandoned near the back door. No other vehicles to be seen, but there must be something about. Penny's pretty certain Hanson doesn't get around on a farm bike, and they must have some way of moving the dogs.

Keeping an eye on the road, Penny runs across the space to the pens. Rounding the corner, the stench of neglect hits her full in the face. At a glance, there must be a couple of dozen dogs, the near pens housing big aggressive breeds, stocky barrel-chested animals with thick necks and muscled shoulders: Rottweilers, American Pitbulls, Pinschers. Good family pets if they've been well-treated. But these dogs have not. They've been abused: whipped and kicked and starved to a frenzy, all the better to tear each other's throats out. These dogs are good at that. They know how to sink their teeth into the soft fur at the base of the neck and grind and rip until the throat is laid bare and tendons and muscles shredded. They've tasted blood. Penny knows they have, because these dogs are still alive. The survivors. To them, everyone is a threat, including her. Slowly, Penny takes a step back from the pens, putting some space between her and the pack. But a grim-faced Chow Chow emits a low snarl, setting the others off.

The noise! Matiu said to be quiet.

Panicked, Penny drops to a crouch and swings her eyes back to the house. But again, there's no response to the dogs' barking.

"Shh," Penny murmurs, in an attempt to soothe the dogs. She drops her eyes to show them she's not interested in confrontation, and inches her way along the front of the pens. "It's OK. I don't want to hurt anyone."

When it's clear she's not about to kick them, nor is she going to feed them, the dogs start to settle. By the time she reaches the end of the line, the noise has largely died away. But at the end, in a cage low to the ground, a little Staffie leans forward and pushes his ruined muzzle through the wire. Stooping for a better look, Penny's breath catches in her throat. Desperately thin, the poor creature's in a pitiful condition. It looks at Penny with soulful, solemn eyes. This is no killer. It's been used as a punching bag, a ragdoll for the others to toss between their teeth. Old lacerations show through the animal's coat, its short hair growing at odd angles where the scars have puckered. Its nose is torn, and one of its ears is missing a chunk, leaving behind a ragged hanging tuft, like yellowed kapok pulled out of an old pillow. Pus leaks from the corners of its eyes.

How can people be so cruel?

Penny can't bear it. To hell with the risk, she's going to free this one. She *has* to. She yanks at the cage door. It won't open. She tugs again. That's weird. From this side, it should just click open. Frowning, she checks the mechanism. Her shoulders slump. Electronic locking. Hanson obviously isn't planning on letting any of his staff make off in the night with his cash cows. So much for honour among thieves.

Well, even if she could open the cage, this one isn't going anywhere. There's no mistaking the inflammation in the dog's hind leg. The limb is swollen and puffy. An infected nip left untreated, most likely. If neglected much longer, septicaemia will take hold and the dog will die. Penny can't help thinking that for this little fellow, it might be the kindest outcome. Fighting tears, she places the back of her hand against the wires, introducing herself.

"Hey there, Staffy," she breathes. The dog lets out a whine, the sound pitiful and defeated. "I know it hurts, sweetheart."

Staffy opens his mouth, and a little pink tongue licks at her skin, its touch comforting, like the weft of an old bath towel.

Penny squeezes her fingers through the gap in the wire and tickles the dog under his chin. She thinks of Cerberus: exuberant, bounding Cerberus with his bear paws and goopy dog slobber. There's a dog who's been well-treated. Darius Fletcher had adored his dog. So why would such a man be involved with Hanson? It doesn't add up.

On cue, Penny recognises a bark which can only be Cerberus' coming from the other side of the house.

Please don't do anything stupid, Matiu. If Hanson can do this to a dog...

Penny pulls her fingers out of the cage and whispers to Staffy, "Back soon."

- Matiu -

Tikau is staring right at Matiu. He's sitting on a chair in the main room, the kitchenette, his hand resting lightly on a shotgun which lies on the table beside him. It's a Benelli M4, US military semi-automatic. Nothing but the best for Hanson's boys, right? A shit-eating grin covers Tikau's face, like he's having some fine joke at Matiu's expense, but if he's laughing, it's all on the inside. He's also wearing sunshades, so Matiu can't tell if the mirth on his face is mirrored in his eyes. He dares a glance at the surveillance monitor on the wall. Nothing. Not even the paddock, just a slab of digital blue. Could be the sky, if the sky hadn't turned grey. If the camera hadn't been pointing straight down.

"Tikau, bro," Matiu says, relieved that at least here's someone he knows, and who knows him. Tikau won't blow his head off and ask his corpse questions later. Hopefully. "Where's Hanson at?"

Tikau says nothing, doesn't even nod.

"Yeah yeah, you're fucking hilarious. Killing me. What's going on?"

He tries to step through the door, but something holds him back. Cerberus is still on the top step, pulling against him, but the dog could be a thousand miles away. Looks like he's sitting in a spot of sunlight shining only on him, not on the steps, not on the house. The longer Matiu looks at the dog, the more he feels he's falling further from him, the space between them unchanged but their worlds torn apart atom by atom. Cerberus presses with all his strength against the step, muscles straining and tongue lolling as his collar bites deeper into his neck.

"Damn it dog, get in here." Matiu jerks the leash, with more force than he intends, and Cerberus slides across the warped timber towards him. The sunlight falling on the dog's golden hide drains away, leaving shades of grubby yellow, old dirt, rotting corn. Tikau doesn't even flinch. Just sits there, grinning. "Tikau bro, what the fuck…?"

Matiu crosses the distance to his drinking buddy of years gone by. They'd shared many a night on the turps, back in the day, after a spot of petty theft and thuggery. Shared more than one spliff, more than one girl. Dragging Cerberus with him, Matiu puts a hand on Tikau's shoulder and gives him a friendly shove.

Tikau topples to the floor, his sunshades spilling from his dead eyes even as his cold fingers drag the shotgun off the table.

"Shit!" Matiu staggers, falling to one knee as his balance goes out from under him. The blast of the shotgun as it hits the floor is enough to deafen him in the small building. Glass shatters, and there's a screech of splintering timber as Matiu rolls, instinctively covering his head and hoping like hell none of his anatomy has been blown off.

His ears are ringing, but he can still hear Cerberus howling, the sound growing more distant. "Shit," he says again. In his sudden panic, he's let go of the leash. But hell, the game's just changed. Now he's inside, he can smell blood, the stale, overripe tang of death several days old. He's lying on the floor with a grinning corpse. That wasn't in the plan. He's staring at the back of Tikau's head, at the gaping hole where his skull should've been. It's not a gunshot wound, but more like something has taken a bite, right through the bone, into the brain…

There's a hot, sharp pressure against the back of Matiu's throat. He chokes back the need to vomit. Something Penny told him, about disturbing the scene of a crime. He doubts vomit spatter on a murder victim's body will go over well with Tanner and the boys. Or with Penny, for that matter.

"You can stop swearing. He can't hear you." Something creaks in the shadows beyond the doorframe that leads into the cabin's back room, the room that Matiu remembers as the bunk room. Metal, maybe, and squeaking rubber? Hard to tell. He takes a deep shuddering breath, gets to his knees, and turns towards the voice. "Hanson," he says, before he can see the man. "What the hell is going on?" His voice is trembling almost as much as his hands. But where there's one gun, there's bound to be another.

"Your dog seems to be running away," the voice that is Hanson says from the other room. Either the curtains are drawn or the windows have been boarded up, because it's almost pitch black in there. Even without his sunglasses, Matiu can't see Hanson, despite the light spilling in from the front room.

Matiu shrugs. "He won't run far. He's a good dog."

A rasping noise, like an emphysemic's laughter, all hacking cough and wet flesh. "They all run, Matiu, even good dogs. You were a good dog once, but you ran too, didn't you?"

The creaking sound again, and Matiu recognises it this time. Wheels, plastic, on the wooden floor. A thump, and the groan of the tyres. Edging forward, against every rational impulse surging through his body, Matiu tries to get a look in the room. Why the hell is it so dark in there? He can make out shapes, something vaguely human, and something else, indistinct, shifting, serpentine. Shadows, he tells himself, playing tricks on his eyes, His ears are still ringing from the shotgun blast, and dimly he's aware that Penny will be in a panic, probably running towards the cabin but shit-scared of being seen. His other senses are probably off-kilter from the gunshot too. "I didn't run, remember? I got locked up. Spent some of the best months of my life inside for doing your dirty work."

"Free board, free meals, free education. Where's the gratitude?" That laugh again, a rattling, hissing sound. "Bygones, right? It's good to see you, Matiu. I've missed you."

Matiu creeps forward another couple of paces, hunting for the light switch. He can hear a dog barking, the sound coming across a great distance. Like an echo from another age. "What happened to Tikau?"

"Laughed himself to death. It happens. Why are you here?"

Any warmth Matiu might have imagined in Hanson's voice is evaporating. "I've always been straight with you, Hanson. You be straight with me for once, right?"

"Little dog runs away, comes home with big teeth, eh boy? You calling the shots now, are you?"

Creaking of wheels again. *Is he coming closer? Or backing away?*

"Just doing a job. Looking for someone."

"And you thought you'd find 'em here? I got a couple spares lying around the place. Take your pick." Hacking, shredded laughter.

"I think he came here for a dog."

Silence falls, sudden and heavy, like all the sound in the place is tumbling into a void. The moment stretches out, achingly quiet, like the long dead spaces between the stars. "He's not someone you want to find, son. Let it go. You'll thank me later."

"Can't do that." Matiu takes another small step towards the room, straining against the unnatural gloom to see something, *anything*, through that black doorway. In the back of his mind, he knows he's stalling, trying to give Penny time to get somewhere she can see in from outside and record what's going on. But he needs to get a light on in that room. And at the same time, he doesn't think he wants to see. Because there beyond the doorframe, in that sucking darkness, all is not well. "I've got people depending on me. This guy might be dead, but he might still be alive." Like Hanson cares if some rich fucker lives or dies. Take his money, that's all that matters to a guy like Hanson. In his mind's eye, Matiu sees Tikau, those dead eyes, that hole in the back of his head where something has chewed away his skull. Thinks of all the dogs this wheezing prick has sent to slaughter. Life doesn't mean shit to Hanson.

The old man cackles. "Not much chance of that, son. Not with what he was into. Not much chance for any of us, really. Not anymore."

The wheels creak again, and this time he's coming out of the shadow for certain. Shoes, trousers advance into the light spilling from the kitchen. Matiu had been expecting a wheelchair, though Hanson was never an invalid when he knew him. No, there are the little plastic wheels of a cheap office chair, rolling forward, but if he's not using his feet to shuffle himself, then how the hell is he moving? In the darkness, something wet hisses across the floor.

Matiu steps backwards, losing his hard-won ground in a flush of inexplicable terror. For a moment he thinks he glimpses another figure moving in the deepest shadows at the back of the room, then his attention snaps back to Hanson, the chair advancing, revealing thighs, hands intertwined in his lap, all crinkled skin and liver spots, blackened nails rubbing against each other in a slow rhythm of clutch and scrape, clutch and scrape. Dimly, Matiu is aware that Hanson's not using his hands to move the chair, either. He'd thought he might've had a walking stick of some kind, or a crutch, and was using that to propel himself. But the chair just keeps creeping up, inexorably. Vague shapes continue to bend and twist in the dark behind Hanson, and the sound of something slick and liquid drowns out the baying of the dogs, of someone shouting. Penny, probably. Matiu's stomach lurches, his legs suddenly burning with the urge to run, to help his sister with whatever pile of shit she's managed to drop herself in, but he's paralysed. He can't look away from the horror that is Hanson, inching forward from the darkness. He can hardly breathe, yet he manages to summon words from his dry throat.

"The dog was a sacrifice. Why? What was he sacrificing to?"

Hanson edges from the dark, light falling across his face, a craggy mass of wrinkles, age, and old sorrow, his eyes sunken black holes. "Told you son, you don't want to know."

Something moves in the darkness, whipping towards Matiu with a liquid hiss. Years on the street, dodging swinging fists and jabbing knives, lend him the speed to hurl himself backwards like an acrobat. The mass, whatever it is—Matiu is moving too fast to see—sluices through the air where he'd just been standing. Not a stick, not a fist. Something large, fluid, a vague shape in his periphery as he hits the floor on hands and knees, slides, collides with the table. It's a long time since he's been in a fight, a twinge shooting up his back as his muscles contort.

The shotgun brushes against his knuckles, and he grabs it. Longer time since he held a gun. Its weight is reassuring, and terrifying, as he propels himself to his feet again, spinning and bracing the M4 towards the darkened doorway.

The paralysis that had claimed his legs now spreads to his arms, to his hands, to his trigger finger. *To his mind.* For a moment, his grip on sanity teeters, as he looks at the thing rising from the shadows, swelling to fill the room. It's not a man, but something alien, something terrifying, something that defies reason, and all Matiu can do is stare in horror as it draws ever closer.

CHAPTER 12

- Pandora -

The way the storage shed is positioned—and the slope of its roof—if Penny could get up on the roof and lie flat, she should be able to look through the long window and inside the house. That way, she'll be able to keep an eye on Matiu and take some photos on her phone, all without being seen. She scans the darkened windows. Still, no sentries that she can see. They're probably watching the front: the road's over in that direction, and Matiu had approached from there. Now, how is she going to get on the roof? That rusty old forty gallon drum? It's tetanus-in-waiting, but she could climb on top of it and jump across.

Having established a plan, Penny dashes across the gap, keeping the shed between herself and the house. But up close, Penny can see the drum is too far from the shed—only a metre or so—but still too far for her to leap to the roof.

She's going to have to move it.

She tips the rim towards her to test its weight. Liquid sloshes in the bottom, but at least the drum isn't full. She might just manage. Penny tilts the bulky container, then, as if it were her dance partner, twists it nearer to the shed wall. Blimmin' heck. Her dance partner could do to lose a few kilos. One more turn. There. She lets the drum rock backwards to the ground. The liquid inside sloshes violently. As soon as the drum is stable, she clambers up, her sandals clunking on its metal sides. Penny doesn't bother to peer round the side of the shed to check if anyone is coming. No one had paid any attention earlier, and the quicker she's up on the roof and out of sight the better. But even standing on the drum, it's going to be a bit of a stretch. Ignoring its schmear of creamy bird poop, Penny grabs the lip of the roof and, arms straining and legs scrambling, hauls herself over on her stomach. She lies there a moment panting, flicking her eyes across to the pens. On his feet in his cage, Staffy is watching her, his little tail wagging. Penny could swear the dog is cheering. She throws him a grim smile.

We're not out of the woods yet, boy.

Penny inhales, preparing herself for the climb, and battles a wave of nausea. Phew, that's ripe. Just as well she's lying down or the stink coming from the shed might've made her keel over. Still, it's too rank to be dog food, unless Hanson and his men slaughter their own. She remembers the cow pat on the track on the way down here. That might explain it. Or the shed might conceal an offal pit, a tip for dead or dying animals, the ones Hanson no longer has any use for. After seeing the state of the dogs, Penny wouldn't put it past him. Staffy's wounds still haunting her, she suppresses a surge of rage.

Time to get some evidence.

Taking her phone out of her pocket, Penny turns it on and, holding it in one hand, crawls up the roof until she's lying flat on the ocean side with only her head popping over the ridge. Made up of odd boards and chip, the sheeting is slippery, so it's a bit of a job not to slide back and over the side. Penny digs her knees in. She peeps over ridge.

Where are you, Matiu?

The sun is directly overhead, so the windows of the house appear dark. Penny strains her eyes, sure she can detect movement inside, grey and shadowy, like smoke. Hang on, is that Hanson? Penny raises the phone to take a photo.

Da duh, da da da da duh...

Penny jumps with fright and the phone slips from her hand. She lunges to save it, catching it and juggling it in her fingertips but, in doing so, she slithers down the roof. Desperately, she scrabbles for purchase, digging her heels into the sheeting, bruising her elbows and knees as she tries to slow her descent.

Shit.

She turns her body mid-slide and extends her fingers, using her nails to cling on. She grits her teeth. The phone moans as it's dragged across the sheeting. Mercifully, she stops sliding. Once again she lies, not moving, while she waits for her 4,5-β-trihydroxy-N-methylphenethylamine spike to reduce. That was too close. She gives Staffy a reassuring wave, turns the ring tone to mute, then checks the screen: Beaker.

Can't talk now, sorry Beak. Collecting evidence.

Pushing her heel down hard, Penny twists to climb back to the ridge. But the roof creaks, then collapses, the timbers exploding beneath her. The noise is brief and deafening, like a cannon blast, or a gun shot. Penny shrieks, her free hand grappling at the air, splinters and debris raining about her, as she descends. Outside, the dogs howl.

"Oaaf," grunts the man whose body cushions Penny's fall, the pair of them prone on the shed's dirt floor.

"Sorry, sorry."

Why's she apologising? These guys run an illegal dog fighting outfit, for heaven's sake. But Penny opens her eyes to a blank stare from a bloated blue face. The tongue lolls forward and a maggot wriggles from the eye socket. Penny has fallen into the arms of a dead man. She screams again. Instinctive and visceral, it incites the dogs, setting them off again.

"Oh my God, oh my God!"

But he grunted. She definitely heard him groan. Did she kill him in the fall?

Immediately, Penny's adrenalin levels hike. Her heart hurtles along, a train *à grande vitesse*. She's killed him.

She scrabbles to her feet, her head spinning, and leaps away from the body.

Don't vomit, don't vomit. You'll contaminate the scene. Contaminate the scene? It could contaminate her!

Trying not to think of cholera, entero-viruses, hepatitis, and the raft of parasitic diseases she might have just exposed herself to, Penny takes some deliberate breaths, her chest heaving, and wills the peristalsis of her stomach down.

Calmer now, reasoning kicks back into play. He's dead, but she didn't kill him. She'd noted the smell before, when she was up on the roof, and maggots don't infect healthy tissue, *Musca domestica* larvae preferring to feed on decaying organic matter. Since it takes around 24 hours for the eggs to hatch and the larvae to emerge, the man has to have been dead a day. Maybe less, given the temperatures, which are even hotter in the confines of this shed. The grunt was caused by pent-up gases, released when she collapsed on the cadaver. Penny didn't kill him. He was already dead.

Alive, he would've been around thirty, Polynesian, dark hair and of solid build. His eyes might have been brown. Possibly grey. He might've been nice-looking once. Somebody's brother, maybe a husband. But the tarnished yellow fingernails point to poor nutrition, and the hollowed cheeks and open skin lesions suggest he'd been a meth user. And being dumped unceremoniously in a back shed like this implies he didn't die peacefully of natural causes, either. Penny feels a pang of sadness. It's not only dogs who suffer here.

In any case, it's not Fletcher. That would've been too convenient.

She'd told Matiu this was a bad idea. She should probably get out of here. Someone might have heard her shout when the roof caved in. Someone *must* have heard that ruckus. She doesn't want to be caught here if Hanson's lot come looking. Hurriedly, she casts about for her phone, dropped in the fall...

It's fallen not far away, its screen still illuminated. Penny brushes away the debris with her elbow, and uncovers a plastic bag of dried blood. Her stomach lurches. But still...blood samples already bagged up and ready for the lab?

The inside of her t-shirt serving as a rudimentary glove, Penny picks it up.

Oh please don't let them be fingernails.

She lifts the bag up to the shards of light filtering in from the hole in the roof. Microchips? There are nineteen of them, gristle and bristly dog hair still attached to each. Penny examines one of the chips through the clear plastic. The bloodied morsel has been ripped out of a dog's flesh and then damaged—stabbed like a Horcrux.

So the authorities can't trace them.

Hanson's lot must have been collecting the chips until they had a chance to dispose of them—buried in a pit at the back of the farm, or maybe chucked in the ocean. It doesn't really matter how. Once the chips had been rendered ineffective, there was little chance of the authorities ever tracking the dogs out here. But her discovery means there's hope for Staffy and his companions because these dogs were once registered, which means they've got owners somewhere. Still using her t-shirt as a barrier, Penny stuffs the gruesome bag in the front pocket of her jeans. Illegal evidence, but the dead body should negate that.

Yeah, show me the judge who can ignore that, Tanner.

There's a scraping at the base of the door.

Penny freezes. Shit. Someone's heard her. Frantic, she looks for somewhere to hide. There's nowhere. This stinky little shed is too tiny. There isn't enough space to hide a child. For a second, she contemplates crawling under the body, concealing herself beneath the putrefying carcass, but the man's maggot-ridden gaze makes her stomach lurch. She can't bring herself to do it. It's too late, anyway.

The door rattles, bowing inwards, as if someone has put their shoulder to it. Penny squares herself up, prepared to confront whoever might be out there. The door remains firmly shut. Why aren't they coming in? Maybe they can't? Someone injured? Creeping forward, Penny puts her ear to the wooden slats. From the other side, she hears scrabbling, a scuff. There's a faint clink of metal. A padlock opening? Her heart hammering, Penny presses her thumb to the latch and, keeping the door closed, pushes down slowly. She tries the door and finds some give. It's not locked. She listens again. More scratching. Whoever it is can't open the door.

"Matiu?" she whispers. "Is that you?"

The scratching intensifies. Cautiously, Penny cracks the door open, just a sliver, to allow her to see…

Cerberus bounds in, his lead clinking behind him.

"Cerberus? What are you doing here? Where's Matiu?" One hand twisted in the fur of Cerberus' neck to stop him from dashing off somewhere else, Penny pops her head out of the shed and scans the yard. She sucks in mouthfuls of fresh air. No sign of Matiu. What's happened to him? Puzzled, she steps back into the shed and closes the door. She needs to take photos and look for Matiu, but first she has to secure Cerberus.

But the dog slips from her grip, the smell of death and decay sending him into a frenzy. He paws at the body, nudging at it forcefully, desperate to sample this glorious thing.

"Come away, Cerberus," Penny hisses.

The dog moves, but only to change position from one side of the body to the other. He steps on the man's stomach in his haste to explore, releasing more gas, which excites him even more. It's as if his favourite squeaky toy has been shoved down the man's trousers and Cerberus is determined to retrieve it. He tears at the man's shirt with his teeth, yanking away the fabric, and burrowing at the waistband of his pants.

"Cerberus!" Penny whispers, horrified. Seizing the dog's lead, she hauls him back towards her. He'll be getting dog slobber all over the body. She may as well give herself up now, hand herself in to Tanner and confess to everything, since between the pair of them they'll have obliterated any evidence of the real killer. Cerberus strains against the lead.

"Come on boy, that's enough. Come away. You're going to choke yourself."

The dog yelps, dragging himself forward, and the chain slides out of Penny's hand. Cerberus flies at the body, jamming his back paws under the body to stop his slide. His muzzle over the corpse, he snaps at the dead man's waistband and reveals a tuft of wool.

A pouch? Penny is about to yank Cerberus back but something in the way the dog teases at the fabric gives her pause. He's too patient. Penny watches as, with quiet determination, Cerberus gnaws gently at the wool. Finally, he pulls the prize from the body, holding it, triumphant, in his jaws. It's a beanie, which had been tucked into the waistband of the dead man's pants. Penny is baffled why Cerberus would go to so much effort when a wallet slips out of the bundle.

"So, *that's* what all the fuss was about?"

Penny ignores the beanie. In any case, Cerberus doesn't look keen to give it up. Instead, she stoops and, in an almost futile gesture at this point, uses the bottom of her t-shirt to pluck the wallet out of the dirt. It's stretched to all hell by now anyway, the fabric sagging pitifully at the hem.

Penny gives the dog a quick scratch behind his ear. "Good boy. Not a bad bit of detective work. Let's see who he was then, shall we?"

Holding the wallet awkwardly with one hand, she shakes it gently, using gravity to flip it open. Her mouth agape, Penny stares at the ID card tucked in the front panel. Penny recognises the wavy hair, square jaw and dazzling blue eyes. No wonder Cerberus was so insistent. Whoever the dead man at her feet is, this isn't his wallet. The wallet is Fletcher's.

Suddenly, the blast of a gun shakes the air, rattling Penny to her bones.

She whirls, dropping the wallet.

Matiu...

- Matiu -

Writhing tentacles turn lazy arcs across the ceiling and slide over the floor. In that fractured moment as Matiu gapes in utter shock at Hanson, he understands it's not Hanson anymore. The glutinous, twisting masses are a part of the old man, six, at least, maybe eight, emerging from his back. Three are lifting him off the chair, his own legs hanging limp and useless beneath him. The others—how many, he doesn't dare count—roil and snap, warping the air above them, a sick shade of purple like bruised clouds, heavy with thunder. Hanson's black eyes glitter in his sallow face, his mouth sagging open, wide, wider, revealing an infinite pit within. A hell of blindness for Matiu to fall into, a black hole where his nightmares might be swallowed and spat out. "There's no point running away, doggy," Hanson says, in a voice that cascades across aeons, splinters reality. "All bad dogs get their whippin'." Black-clawed hands and questing tentacles stretch for Matiu.

The gun booms, deafening him again, the recoil tossing him back towards the door. There's a screech, a howl of pain that can't be human, and he glimpses a tentacle falling, spraying dark ichor. Then he's running. He doesn't remember pulling the trigger, just knows he must have, because if he hadn't, the thing would have taken him, dragging him into that soul-sucking blackness.

A blast of hot wind hits him as he barrels through the door, so strong it might be trying to drive him back into the darkness and the creature's waiting maw. Stormclouds boil overhead and he's running, yet the distance between door and porch grows ever wider. Matiu chokes back a scream. He's had nightmares like this, running but standing still, screaming but suffocating, unable to escape the terrors at his back.

He dares a glance back, refusing to believe he's still in the cursed doorway, still trying to break free from the hell he's stepped into.

The creature is advancing. Behind it, emerging from the shadows, the third figure, the one Matiu glimpsed, but hadn't rationalised. The one he recognises, even though he's never seen his face. The scream tears from his throat, rage and betrayal and defiance, and then he's falling. The stairs rush up to greet him and he slams into the ground, the wind knocked from his lungs. Stunned but not broken, Matiu scrambles to his rump, wrangling the shotgun around to face the doorway as he struggles to his feet, fighting to suck down a breath.

A tentacle pushes through the door, slow, probing, as if it, too, is fighting the hot, driving wind. Matiu pulls the trigger, once, twice, the acrid burn of gas propellant stinging his throat as the M4 cycles fresh ammunition into the breach and discards the smoking shells onto the dirt. Pain blossoms in his shoulder with the recoil and the second shot goes wide, sparks bursting from the side of the cabin. Black cables fall from the sky in a haze of wood dust. Satisfied with the horrific shriek that comes from the creature and the burst of white liquid that douses the porch, Matiu turns and runs, still heaving for breath. Somewhere, he can hear Penny calling his name, and he heads towards her voice. He wants to be relieved that she's alive, and that he's out of the cabin, but his mind is numb. He'd rather not feel anything anymore. Not after what he saw.

The creature that has spawned in Hanson's place is horror enough, but it's what was stepping from the shadows behind the monster that has shaken him the most. Because it was a little piece of him.

Makere.

CHAPTER 13

- Pandora -

Penny doesn't wait. She drops the wallet, flings open the door and sprints into the open. Where did that shot come from? Inside the house? Should she take the back door? Penny hesitates. If Matiu's been hit, if he's down, she can't help him if she runs into the house and headlong into the shooter. She'll get herself killed, and she can't help Matiu if she's dead, too.

If Matiu's been hit, and it's on account of her, Mum and Dad will kill her themselves.

"Matiu!" she yells, indecision paralysing her.

In the pens, the dogs are going ape-shit, yowling and yapping. Some of the bigger dogs hurl themselves at the wires, fevered with excitement, their jaws dripping saliva. Trained to sense desperation, to take advantage of an opponent's *weakness*, they want a piece of whatever's going on out here. Penny catches Staffy eyeing her, his ears twitching.

"Matiu!" she screams again.

"Penny!"

Penny almost dies of relief. He's not dead. Penny can barely hear him, but he's outside somewhere. The front of the house?

Cerberus' canine instincts serve him better, and he streaks off ahead in a blur of gold. A minute later, Penny rounds the side of the house only to discover Cerberus on his way back and Matiu dashing towardsher, gripping a shotgun, the sides of his leather jacket flapping. He waves her back.

"Penny, back the other way!" he shouts. At least he's moving freely. There's no sign of any blood. No wound. That's good. The gunshot she heard must have been a warning note: Hanson playing the heavy. Penny slows, her panic subsiding now she's seen Matiu's OK.

"No, we need to confront this Hanson guy. He's involved somehow, Matiu. There's evidence: a body in the back shed—"

Matiu's face is tight. "Tell me later, sis. Right now, we need to get out of here." Cerberus obviously supports that idea because he races past them both, heading back around the corner.

"But Matiu—"

Grabbing her elbow, Matiu yanks her around roughly, pulling her face to his. He raises the shotgun in his right hand, his fist clenched white against the black barrel.

"Penny. Do you see this gun?" he says evenly, dark eyes blazing.

"Yes, I was wondering what you—"

Matiu shakes her. "I got it from the guy back there. The guy who's trying to kill me. Who is coming this way."

Oh shit.

Penny surrenders as he pulls her bodily by her elbow, hustling her along the way a harassed parent ushers a misbehaving toddler from the supermarket. Ordinarily, Penny would balk. She's not a sack of potatoes to be manhandled by Matiu. But a glance over her shoulder shows her someone *is* coming. Someone large. Dark. Hanson? Whoever it is, he's moving slowly. Lurching. Did Matiu injure him? The shadowy form passes behind the spreading pōhutukawa, its massive central girder and weighty boughs blocking her view. Penny shakes her head, not trusting her eyes. Perhaps she bumped her head in the fall, because that arm looks strangely sinuous like...*a tentacle*. Immediately, she dismisses the idea. A branch, or a trick of the light, surely. The man must be carrying a gun, his arm curled around its length...

Matiu drags her around the corner.

Penny snaps to. "There's a farm bike by the back door," she says, shaking herself free. "I didn't check yet to see if the keys..."

But already Matiu is running towardsthe bike. In true James Dean fashion he throws a leg over it and revs the engine, as Penny hurries to join him.

"Wait, Matiu. Where's Cerberus?" Penny looks around wildly.

"Damn it. Cerberus!" Matiu roars, revving the bike and sending up a cloud of exhaust. Cerberus lopes out of the shed, the beanie held in his mouth, and Penny realises it must be Fletcher's too. The dog whirls and takes off past the pens.

The wallet. She left it by the body. Penny starts for the shed but, on the bike, Matiu surges forward, cutting her off. Leaning out, he grabs her arm again, his grip bruising.

"Matiu, the evidence—" she gasps.

"Leave it. We'll call Clark. Let him find it."

"By the time he gets here, Hanson will have destroyed it."

"I'd rather it be the evidence than us. Come on."

"No."

"Penny, please, get on the bike."

"I can't." Flatfooted, Penny wrings her hands. She stares across the yard at Staffy. The little dog lifts his ruined muzzle, his nose twitching as he searches for Penny's scent on the air.

He's not the only one twitching. A muscle jumps under Matiu's eye. He turns to check the corner of the house. "Penny, someone is coming who intends to kills us," he says. It's almost a plea. "When he rounds that corner, believe me, we don't want to be here."

"The dogs, Matiu. We can't leave them here."

Matiu's eyes widen. "You're right. Excellent idea. We'll let them out."

"But the cages won't open. I tried. They're on some kind of central locking."

Matiu throws something at her. Instinctively, unintentionally, Penny catches it. She opens her hands: it's the company card for the Holden.

"You go. Follow Cerberus. Run for the car. I'll free the dogs."

"But what about…?"

"If I'm not there in five minutes, you forget your stupid hang-ups and you drive, you hear me? You get the hell out of here."

"Matiu—"

"For fuck's sake, Penny, just go!"

Penny runs then, as best she can in her stupid summer sandals, dashing by the pens, her heart breaking as she passes the little Staffordshire, and runs after Cerberus. She's only covered half the ground to the corrugated iron sheeting when she hears a shot before the latches clunk open in unison. Matiu's done it. He's opened the cages and freed the dogs. Penny risks a quick look back to see the pack charge *en masse* around the back of the house. She prays Matiu is nowhere near that pack of wolves: they'll shred him to tatters in seconds. She turns, intending to follow Cerberus into the pines. But the Chow Chow steps out from behind the grey metal sheeting. Alone, the animal has come wide and cut her off. It curls its upper lip, emitting a snarl from low in its throat. Penny falters as the animal bares its teeth, its coat bristling with anger.

Quickly, Penny drops her eyes, and takes a slow step back. If she appears submissive perhaps the dog will back down.

It doesn't work. This dog has menace and threat ingrained in its psyche. Fighting is all it knows. It crouches, preparing to leap. Penny lifts her arms to protect her head and neck.

Suddenly, Staffy dashes in—was he following her, wanting her to rescue him?—and nips hard at the Chow Chow's paws. The Chow Chow tosses its head and snarls, its pushed-in face mean and hostile, but it stands its ground. Staffy ducks in again, worrying at his opponent's haunches, his nips demanding attention. The Chow Chow snaps and twists, its jaws clamping down hard, and comes away with fur in its mouth. Her hands over her mouth, Penny gasps as Staffy dives away, but, persistent, he comes back, this time leaping on the Chow Chow's back and biting down hard. The Chow Chow yowls in pain and anger. It shakes its torso, brutally tossing the smaller dog, who's whiplashed from side to side. Penny, paralysed, can only watch on in horror. At last, the Chow Chow disengages itself, hurling the smaller dog off. With a yelp, Staffy rolls away. But he's achieved his purpose. The enraged Chow Chow has forgotten all about Penny. It rounds on Staffy, and the little fighter, knowing his business, tears off, his gait an excruciating one-two-three-limp, as he leads the Chow Chow back towards the pack.

Penny knows the Chow Chow will catch the little Staffordshire eventually.

Tears streaming, she turns and stumbles through the pines.

CHAPTER 14

- Matiu -

Matiu vaults onto the low roof of the pens, shotgun counterbalancing the tricky manoeuvre, and crouches low, running lightly along the creaking tin roof towards the house. The living mass of dogs swarm around the side of the building, a wave of claw and tooth and slavering drool, all barking and jostling against each other in the frenzy of sudden freedom and the wild rush of hunger. He comes around the peak of the storage sheds, gaining a view of the open space in front of the house.

The thing that Hanson has become is halfway across the dirt road now, ichor dripping from ragged wounds, one tentacle dragging limp behind it. Matiu, his stomach dropping at the sight, kneels, bracing the shotgun and sighting down the barrel. He was right to keep Penny away. Her sane and rational mind wouldn't cope with this.

The dogs, however, have no such fear. They know only hunger and rage. They know the face, the smell, of the one who beats them. Matiu can't look away from the sudden snarling mass that piles on Hanson, all slaver and fury. Man and tentacles alike go down under the tide of tooth and claw, the shrieks of pain as much human as they are otherworldly.

Matiu's finger hovers over the trigger, considering putting a round through Hanson to end his misery. Then he relaxes his grip. He tells himself this is because he can't hit Hanson without taking out at least a couple of the dogs at the same time, and not even fighting dogs should go out that way. Not because this is the exact bloody fate the old bastard deserves.

A tentacle lifts above the savaging pack, slams down, skittering canines aside, but they gain their feet and rush back in—most of them, anyway. The tentacle flails, and then is torn free. On every side, the dogs are hauling dripping body parts away from the carnage at the centre. Tentacles, mainly, their soft flesh easily ripped apart by jaws built for tearing muscle and bone, but is that a hand? The dirt underneath the growling mass of bodies is rapidly turning a putrid mix of red and glistening white, scattered with torn sinew and blood-stained fabric.

Swallowing bile, Matiu slowly rises, lowering the shotgun. Hanson won't be walking away from this. A movement catches his eye and he glances up, at the doorway which stands open. The sun is shining bright from the clear blue sky on the dilapidated porch, throwing the interior into bleak shadow, but Matiu can see someone there. A black shape, legs and torso and arms, shoulders bent, face hidden beneath the overhang, but he knows who it is. How, he doesn't know, except that something has happened here. Something that Fletcher is a part of, something that can't be undone now it's started. The veil between the worlds, sometimes thinner than others, has been torn. Things can slip through, step between this place and the next, if they know how. If they can connect.

That can't be a good thing.

Matiu scampers back along the rooftop, drops to the ground and hops back on the dirt bike. Stowing the shotgun in the utility bag behind him with the shovel and the axe, he twists the throttle and speeds away in a cloud of dust. He can't leave this place behind fast enough, but even as he rides, with the roar of the engine in his ears and the thunder of his heart in his throat, he knows what has happened here will follow him.

All the way down.

CHAPTER 15

- Pandora -

A hand on the dash and the other clutching the edge of her seat, Penny tries to stop her shaking while the Holden takes the corner, Matiu barely slowing as he speeds them away from the horrors of the farm, back towards town.

The wait in the car had been an eternity. It was like getting a call from the doctor's office, one of those ominous messages asking you to please come in and discuss your latest test results, and the agonising wait to find out whether or not you've contracted something terminal. Her fist buried in Cerberus' fur and biting her cheek, Penny had watched the horizon, wondering who would appear: Hanson or her brother. But when the bike had finally come into view, she'd recognised Matiu's black jacket as he careered up the valley, gunning the engine—he slid in just metres from the gate, throwing up a cloud of grit and dust. Placing one hand on the post, he vaulted the barrier, his face as grim as a pallbearer's. Quickly, Penny had scrambled across the centre console to the passenger side, shooing Cerberus into the back, while Matiu stowed the gun out of sight along the door sill.

Since then, he's said nothing, his silence scarier than the dead man, scarier than an enraged dog…

When they've passed by the government farms—the ubiquitous cameras turning to trace the Holden's route and the nervous security men glaring at them through narrowed eyes—Matiu pulls left at a derelict sheep run and follows the farm track away from the road. It's weedy and pitted from disuse so Matiu creeps along it, his speed positively funereal. With a jolt, Penny realises he doesn't want anyone to see the dust. They're hiding. Why? Is Hanson still after them? Penny spins in her seat, almost choking on the seatbelt as she strains to look.

But they dip below the hill-line and soon after the track peters out, its original purpose long since obscured by scrub and weed. Right now, it's a bolt-hole. Matiu reverses the car into a thicket so they're facing the track before cutting the engine.

Then, the gun resting across his knees (and alarmingly pointing her way), he puts his head back and closes his eyes.

"You're kidding me. You're going to go to sleep now?" Penny is aghast. After what just happened back there? "Where's Hanson, then? What happened to him? He looked injured. Did you shoot him? Oh my God, Matiu, did you shoot him? But the dogs, the dogs are on the loose. We have to let people know what's going on out there. There was a body in that shed, Matiu. A dead body, just dumped there, and he'd been dead a few days, with Fletcher's wallet down his pants! I *told* you I didn't like this. We need to call Clark, get him to get his people out here…"

"And you need to shut the hell up and calm down," Matiu snaps, his mood as black as his jacket. The door slams. Matiu, his head down, storms up the track, still clasping the gun. He doesn't go far before he pulls up.

Just far enough to get away from her.

Penny winces. She's behaving like a shrew. She looks at her feet and inhales deeply, trying to get a grip on her fear.

"Stay there," she says to Cerberus as she unfastens her seatbelt. With Fletcher's beanie tucked under his chin, the dog seems perfectly content to lie on the back seat. Penny gets out of the vehicle and approaches her brother. He has his back to her.

"Matiu. Sorry, I shouldn't have gone off my head like that." When he doesn't move, Penny does the moving, coming around to face him, forcing him to meet her eye. "Matiu, come on. I said I was sorry."

His nod is so tiny it's almost nonexistent. He rests the gun on the ground, its muzzle buried in the weeds, and runs his free hand through his hair. He seems tired, grey, as if he's the one with a terminal disease. After a time, he says: "So your victim in the shed, how did he die?"

"He was a meth user."

"He died from an overdose?"

"No, I didn't see…he'd been dead for a day or so."

"What was the cause of death?" Penny falls quiet. "You did examine the body?" He keeps his voice even, but Penny can tell he's livid because that muscle below his eye is twitching again, setting the dark swirls of the *kiri tuhi* trembling.

"I didn't have my satchel, did I? And besides, Cerberus charged in and started grubbing around with the remains."

"Can you at least tell me if the death was suspect?"

"That whole place was suspect, Matiu. All those poor dogs, some of them injured, it was inhuman."

Matiu sighs. "You don't have a clue, do you?"

"No," Penny whispers, hanging her head. Yanking the gun out of the weed, Matiu stalks back to the Holden.

"I was flustered, OK?" Penny hurries after him. "I fell through the roof onto a dead guy."

"It's your *job*, Penny. Scientific consultant to the police, if I recall. I guess Tanner should've screened you better: made sure you didn't fall apart at the first glimpse of a corpse." He stops, faces her.

"He was crawling with maggots, and I didn't have my gloves!"

"Well, heaven help us if you get your precious fingers dirty."

Penny puts her hands on her hips. "That's just not fair, Matiu. I don't know why you're making such a song and dance about the cause of death anyway. I'll find out later. Clark and Tanner will secure the scene, track down the dogs and get Hanson into custody, and then they'll call me in to take samples. Maybe even send in the *coroner*. Determining the cause of death is *his* job."

Matiu pulls open the driver's door. "You're so sure they'll call you back?" he growls over the roof of the vehicle.

"They have to, because the cases are connected. As soon as they discover the wallet, they'll realise that."

"And you'll explain how you've already contaminated all the evidence. Not exactly pristine procedure."

"I'll tell them the dogs were loose, so I climbed on the shed to avoid being mauled, fell in and found the body. It's plausible. The wallet's clean. I was careful about that..."

"A web of lies, Pandora..."

"Well, I wouldn't have to, if you hadn't waltzed up to Hanson's front door like a Girl Guide selling cookies. I don't know why you're getting all high and mighty, anyway. You're the one who removed a gun from the scene, if I recall rightly."

"No choice. Hanson threatened me."

"So, you confiscated his gun," she retorts accusingly, "and turned it on him."

"I doubt he'd have it registered..."

"Hang on, did you shoot him?"

"No." Matiu's eyes waver. He seems to have found something highly interesting to observe in the thicket behind her. Penny covers her mouth with her hand. "I didn't shoot Hanson," Matiu insists.

"Matiu, you better be damned sure, because if that man was shot, even just clipped, the police are going to be looking for that gun."

"It's OK, sis, they won't find anything." He climbs into his seat and starts the Holden, closing the subject. Penny rushes to get in.

"So, here's what we'll do," Matiu says, as he pulls out of the thicket and onto the track. "You call Tanner and his boys, get them out to the farm…"

"I could tell them you took the gun in self-defence…"

"No!"

"Because of the dogs…"

"Penny, don't mention the gun."

"We have to."

Matiu shrugs. "Fine, your call. Go ahead. But you'll have to explain it to Mum and Dad."

"What are you—"

"Send me a care package, will you?"

Suddenly cold, the air is squeezed out of her, like she's a boob stuck between two plates of an old mammogram machine. They'll have to hide the gun. She's going to have to lie. Ex-cons on probation aren't allowed within cooee of a firearm.

- Matiu -

Sunlight bleeds down the tenements and high-rises that march gaunt and unyielding across the Auckland skyline. Matiu stares through the windscreen as the canyons of glass and concrete, flaring on one side, dark on the other, swell upon the horizon like gravestones in the setting sun's harsh rays. Imagines those towers, one by one, bursting into flame, the smoke blotting out the sky. He can almost *see* it, can almost hear the dull roar of a city burning, the high thin cries of people dying. A tide sweeping in.

"Shouldn't we have ditched it by now? The gun."

Matiu chews the inside of his cheek. Too many thoughts are battering at his skull, trying to find a way out. Damn, what the hell is happening? What's Fletcher started, and why the fuck could he see, *see* Makere standing in that house? Fuck's sake, he'd almost convinced himself that the voice in his head was just a broken part of his own psyche, voicing thoughts he didn't want to admit to. But he'd been there in the back room behind Hanson, and later, standing in the doorway, watching the dogs tear the old man to shreds.

Makere had *been there.*

His *imaginary* friend, standing tall in a house haunted by a madman with tentacles growing from his spine. Matiu mightn't have seen his face, but he knows his longtime companion by his presence. By the way he feels so much like himself, yet so different. A distorted reflection.

Part of him doesn't want to stop driving, because soon as he does, Makere will be at his shoulder to taunt him. Or he won't. And Matiu's not sure which would be worse.

"Matiu? The gun?"

He takes a long breath, sliding his sunnies onto the top of his head as the Holden dips into the lengthening shadows. "I know a place. We can swing by."

"I'd ask if you're OK, but I know the answer. Try to relax, little brother. We've got all we need to let the police take over from here. We'll be able to forget about all of this pretty soon."

Matiu can't help it; he lets slip a bark of laughter. He contemplates some witty, acerbic response, but knows there's no point. Penny will only believe this shit when she sees it. Anyway, her phone is buzzing, and she answers it.

"Hey, Beaker…Yeah, we're just coming…um…heading back now…Hey… Hey, slow down. Big breath. Right, start again."

She listens, and Matiu tunes it out. All he can see are those legs, standing in the shadows. The light pouring like blood, like fire down the city walls.

"OK," Penny's saying, her words filtering through the haze of Matiu's dark contemplations. "See you shortly." She swipes the call away, bites her lip. "Clark's been trying to reach us. Something about the crime scene. And Beaker has something he wants to show me, so we'd best head back to the lab first."

"Before we ditch the gun?"

"Beak seems to think it's pretty important."

Matiu's stomach twists. Last thing he needs is to turn up at the lab, GSR on his hands, shotgun in the back seat, and have the cops turn the car out on account of he and Penny having been suspiciously absent all day. "Five minutes. That's all you get."

Penny lets out a long, hard breath. "Fine."

Matiu turns the wheel, the city's crown blazing overhead as the sun falls drowning into the sea.

CHAPTER 16

- Pandora -

Beaker is as pleased to see Penny as she is to be back. Wearing a relieved expression and a freshly laundered lab coat, he hurries to meet them, holding the door open as the threesome pile in, looking dishevelled and no doubt smelling like an offal pit.

Poor Beaker. He's done such a sterling job of decontaminating the lab—the sulphurous stench of this morning's misadventure now overlaid with the clean fragrance of Cleanase—and here she is, traipsing in with Cerberus in tow, the both of them having just cavorted with a dead body in the initial stages of putrefaction. Not to mention the mud, cow pats, and guano-encrusted shed roofs. And there's no telling what Matiu might have stepped in after setting the dogs free.

Erring on the safe side, Beaker has drenched the place in product. Phosphate-free and nontoxic, the radioactive decontaminant is powerful stuff, removing both DNA and DNAase and, since it's residue-free, it won't degrade any subsequent samples they decide to test either. Naturally, products like Cleanase don't come cheap. Penny imagines the bill for today's little mishap, wondering if she'll ever be able to step into the lab without calculating how much it costs to run. She sighs.

"I'm really sorry, Penny. Honestly," Beaker says, obviously misinterpreting her reaction. "I wouldn't have bothered you if I didn't think it were important. I tried calling earlier, but your device was switched off…"

"Yes, I know, sorry about that. Matiu and I were following up on a lead, and I…um…was having a bit of a breakthrough when you called me." Over at the sink, Matiu is attempting to fill a large watch-glass with water for the dog. He glances at Penny from under his lashes and smirks.

Well, at least one of us is feeling brighter.

"That's OK," Beaker replies. He rubs his hand forward through the blades of pīngao sedge sprouting from his head. "I guessed it must have been something like that."

"So, what'd Clark want?" Penny says, striding to a cupboard for a plastic container. She hands it to her brother. "Here, use this."

The watch-glass was never going to work. Too shallow. Cerberus would have to be a fruit bat to get a drink out of that.

"He said Tanner's given instructions to take the tape down at your warehouse scene this evening," Beaker says, "so if you're inclined to do any more sampling, you'll need to get…um…yourself…back there pronto." Beaker favours her with one of his spectacular blushes, allowing Penny to guess what might actually have been said.

"They're shutting up shop after only a day?" Penny replies. "Geez, that's quick. Those other seventeen cases the department is working on must really be chewing through police resources."

"Nineteen," Matiu mutters, the words barely audible over Cerberus' slurping.

Beaker goes on. "He rang again later, wanted you to call him. And I wanted to show you—"

"Right. I'll do that now, then," Penny agrees, swiping at her tablet and bringing up the police officer. "Officer Clark? It's Penny Yee."

"Oh, yes, you should probably do that…"

Beaker's response is drowned out by Clark's voice: "Where have you been?"

"Sorry. I—"

"Never mind about that. All hell has broken loose where I am, so I've got to be quick. Firstly, those DNA results you wanted me to check? The ones for the dog?"

"Yes?"

"I've checked them against the city's Dog Control database, made some matches with the police logs, and discovered the dog's owner reported the animal missing a week ago, on the twenty-fifth. Dog Control hadn't picked it up, so I had an intern check up on a couple of canine dealers known to the police…"

He knows. Penny's heart sinks. Her first solo case and already she's botched it. "Officer Clark…"

"Hang on, I'm getting there. Anyway, it was weird—but I was trying to get hold of one dealer: a character named Hanson—when we got a call from one of the government farms out by the coast backing on to Hanson's property. The staff there were complaining about a pack of marauding dogs on their border, threatening the stock. Now, I'm not a man who believes in coincidences, Dr Yee."

"No, of course not…" Penny's stomach twists.

"What?" Matiu whispers, his eyes boring into hers. Penny shakes her head.

"So I got a car out to the site…" Penny wants to throw up. "And turns out I was right to be suspicious: there are three bodies out here."

She spins.

"Three bodies," she mouths, holding up three fingers as if to double-check the maths. Three? Was Hanson one of those? Who was the other?

Matiu turns to face the windows.

"We think there was some kind of internal gang dispute going on," Clark explains, "and one of the players let the dogs out, a decision that backfired. Anyway, I wanted to let you know that there's definitely a connection to your man Fletcher. We found the guy's wallet out here with one of the bodies, along with a bag of microchips. Bloody horrible things, torn out of the dogs, most likely so they couldn't be traced."

Penny's stomach flips. She'd forgotten about the chips. She pats her pocket with her free hand. Empty. She must have dropped the bag when she heard the shot and ran from the shed. Maybe it was just as well she did. Could she have left any prints on it? Possibly. She'd been in a hurry.

"You still there?" Clark asks.

"Yes, yes. Sorry. It's just, I'm just taking it all in. Three deaths."

"You're telling me. You should see the mess. It isn't exactly a garden party. Two bodies with the backs of their heads blown out, and another one reduced to blood and pulp. Been policing a long while, and this is the first time I've seen anything to rival it…Look, I'll get someone to run the wallet out to the sister tomorrow, confirm she recognises it, but the ID inside says it's Fletcher's. And with a bit of luck — actually we'd need a lot of luck—but the microchip for the butchered dog just might be in this baggie and the information salvageable."

"Right."

"Since the cases look like they're connected, we'll need you out here tomorrow morning, first thing, to do your sampling. I'll forward you the directions. You'll need to drive right down to the house. Whatever you do, don't park at the gate: for the moment that pack of dogs is still on the loose and they'll tear you apart as soon as look at you. If you see them, stay in the car."

"Right," Penny says again, resisting the urge to ask if there'd been a little Staffie with a limp somewhere in that pack. "I'll do that."

"Did your assistant tell you that we're pulling out of the warehouse?"

"Yes, thank you, he did."

"Sorry, couldn't be helped. Patisepa Taylor got her lawyers in, demanding that the police compensate her for the disruption to her business. Seems Fletcher made prior arrangements for her to show the site to a representative from the museum. Extra storage, or something, and Taylor doesn't want to miss the opportunity. Anyway, Tanner says the department isn't paying, so we have to wrap it up. You've got until end of the day today. Shoot, gotta go. The coroner's here. See you tomorrow."

"We better head straight off," Penny announces when she gets off the phone. Matiu calls Cerberus to him. They've made it halfway to the door when Penny sees Beaker's shoulders slump, deflated.

"Was there something you wanted me to look at?"

"It can wait."

"No, that's all right, Beak. We can spare a few minutes." Penny ignores Matiu's pointed glower.

"It's the Breadmaker."

"I thought it was OK?"

Please let it be OK.

"Yes, I think the machine is fine. That is, I ran a couple of calibration tests and it seems to be functioning normally, running through the correct cycles and with reproducible outputs. But I found a manual read-out in the machine when I was decontaminating the apparatus after the…" He glances uncertainly at Matiu. "After the egg incident this morning. The paper was jammed in the feed and I had to prise it out. I didn't want to lose it if there was a chance we could salvage the results, you know, in case the machine had completed its cycle before the implosion. As it was, the paper was close to disintegrating."

"Let's take a look, then."

Beaker scurries away to his workstation, returning seconds later to hand Penny a crisp white sheet. She looks at him, her eyebrows raised.

"Oh," Beaker says, as understanding dawns. "It's a copy. By the time I got the original out, it was barely legible. I enhanced it."

Penny considers the graph. Looks again. Carrying the paper to the lightbox, she clips it up and peers at the sequence of nucleotides listed underneath the multicoloured peaks. Those bases! A threose sugar backbone. TNA? But TNA is only formed under strict laboratory conditions, which the bloodbath at the warehouse was not. Finding TNA in the sample would mean it was made up of a different kind of genetic material altogether. *Some other form of life.* Penny shakes her head in disbelief.

"That's not possible," she breathes. It can't be. It has to be an aberration caused by the implosion.

"What's not possible?" Matiu says, his head snapping up.

"I agree, it has to be a glitch," Beaker replies.

"Absolutely," Penny says.

"Caused by the implosion."

Penny nods. "I should probably calibrate the machine again. Not that I distrust you…"

"No, no, you should," Beaker says hurriedly. "It's what I'd do."

Matiu peers at the results on the lightbox. "How do you read this goobledy-gook?" he asks, tilting his head to the right as if he were a tourist at the Leaning Tower of Pisa, before the demise of the iconic building in the late 2020s. "What does it say?"

"Nothing," Beaker mumbles.

"It's a mistake," asserts Penny. She puts a hand on Beaker's arm. "I'll calibrate it again later. In the meantime, you head off, Beak. You've done enough, and heaven knows I can't afford to pay you overtime."

Beaker blushes violently. "I wouldn't ask for overtime. You know that."

Behind her assistant, Matiu rolls his eyes and clasps his hands to his chest. Seriously, if she could reach him, Penny would hit him.

- Matiu -

Winking at Beaker, Matiu snatches down the printout and makes for the door, Cerberus at his heels. Actually, he thinks, Cerberus seems to be following Penny to the car, not him, but Matiu doesn't let that irk him. Dog's probably sensitive to the bad juju he's been feeling, and wants to keep his distance. He runs his eyes over the scanned, enhanced printout from the Breadmaker™. Mostly letters and numbers, but here and there, a few incongruous characters. Like that stupid Wingdings font, but not quite the same. He's seen printers spit out crap like this when they've been fed corrupted data, or the drivers have been compromised, or the machine it's hooked up to has had a virus go through it. Something definitely went wrong with the Breadmaker™ during that sample process, and Matiu might be inclined to think it was just a software glitch—if not a malware attack—except that doesn't quite fit with the symbols scattered through the alphanumerics on the page.

Putting on his practised, relaxed grin, Matiu slides into the driver's seat, dropping the sheet into Penny's lap. "That's fucked up." He starts the engine and pulls out of the alley.

"The machine glitched. We can't trust anything it generated."

"Correction," Matiu stabs a finger at the sheet as he brakes for a red light. "You can't trust anything it's generated *since* that result."

"What do you mean?"

"Whatever was put into that machine—something from the crime scene—the hardware didn't know how to deal with it. Screwed with its logic boards or something."

"It's DNA, Matiu. Nucleotides and base pairs. You can't put anything organic into the Breadmaker that it can't recognise. There *had* to be something volatile in the sample, some inflammable contaminant."

Matiu pulls into the intersection, checking his mirrors as he goes. "Mister Clean let a dirty sample get into the machine? Whatever."

"It might've happened. He's been working long hours."

"Yes, and all for *you*." He resists the urge to make kissy faces at her. "He wouldn't slip up, not like that. Never has before, has he?"

"Well, no, but there's always a first time." Penny lifts the report, slips on her glasses, and tries to examine it more closely.

"There's another possibility, but you don't want to hear it."

She scours him with a glance. "I'm sure I don't. Just drive the car, and leave the science to the scientists, all right?"

Matiu runs a hand over his forehead, suddenly hot. She's right, of course, as far as she knows. She hadn't seen Hanson, not like Matiu had seen him. Still, he can't keep a lid on what's bubbling towards a boil in his gut. "That's only DNA as we know it. Right?"

Penny is silent for a moment. Matiu isn't sure if she's trying to decide just how crazy he's become, or if what he said has put a serious chill through her. "Science is backed up by evidence, and there are decades of research that confirm what we know about DNA."

"OK, OK, don't get your tits in a tangle," Matiu says, raising one hand in surrender. "But if it was a contaminant, why did the machine still put out a complete result, and not just shut down mid-operation? You know, just worth asking."

Penny doesn't answer. Honestly, Matiu isn't sure he wants her to.

CHAPTER 17

- Pandora -

Tanner didn't muck around: the police vehicle is already gone and the sun just beginning to wink behind the buildings when Matiu pulls the Holden into the ground-floor car park in the warehouse.

"Looks like Clark's boys have already cleared out," Matiu says.

Penny grits her teeth. "Damn it. I hope the cleaners haven't been in yet."

Well, Penny isn't mucking around either. Leaving Matiu to lock up and deal with Cerberus, she scuttles across the parking lot, skirting a large grate in the concrete, and up the stairs, her heels clattering and her satchel banging against her hip.

She flings open the splintered door. Flicks the switch. Yellow light bounces off the shiny black walls. The room is quiet. It smells of fresh paint, faded now, but still noticeable. Plastic DO NOT CROSS tape still sags from the cones surrounding the blackened tarn of blood. A couple of fat blowflies buzz contently at the edge of the pool. For a fly, that's got to be the definition of nirvana. If the insects have their way, there'll be no need for cleaners. The only thing that looks different from yesterday are the three floorboards partially removed from the north end of the room—where Clark's men have checked for a body stowed in the crawl space.

Penny breathes out. The site is as it was, still uncontaminated—well, relatively uncontaminated. Apart from the flies. And Matiu—puddling his big fat foot in it yesterday.

Speak of the devil.

Matiu appears on the sill of the door.

No Cerberus. Good. He's already had his muzzle in one cadaver today.

Matiu is hesitating at the door, probably expecting Penny to bite his head off for cluttering up her crime scene.

"No cleaners, then?" he ventures.

"No, thank goodness."

He enters the room, each step slow and cautious, as if he expects the bogeyman to pop out and frighten him half to death. She must have really put the wind up him when he touched the bowl yesterday.

"Try not to step in anything," Penny warns anyway.

His shoulders tense, Matiu arches an eyebrow. "Says the girl who had a lie-down on a dead body earlier," he quips under his breath.

Ignoring him, Penny circles the site, examining it for any clues she might have missed the first time. Stepping gingerly over the missing floorboards, she crouches to peer into the pool of congealed blood.

Dog blood.

There was that bag of microchips at Hanson's. Could that be the reason for all this? Was someone removing a dog's identity chip here? Was that what the bowl was for? Penny stands up, edging around the bloodied mess. But if that was the case, why risk doing it here, where there was a chance of the dog ring being detected? Something doesn't quite balance in this equation. Surely it would've been prudent to keep those activities away from the city, to keep them out at the farm?

She looks at the ceiling. Blast. She forgot to ask Clark to have the vents checked. He might have done it anyway, but in case he didn't, she should probably look herself. Only, she's going to need some way of getting up there, a ladder or something large to stand on. She steps out onto the landing. Matiu follows her.

"So what do you think, now you're back here?" he asks.

"About what?"

"About what I said in the car?"

Penny sighs. "Matiu, you said a lot of things in the car. Can you be a little less cryptic?" Ah there, in the stairwell on the landing between flights: an old wooden pallet. Perfect. "Here, help me with this, will you?"

Obliging, Matiu lifts the pallet onto his shoulder, stabilising it with one hand. Penny heads back up the stairs to the crime scene, beckoning him to follow.

When they're back in the storeroom, he says, "Remember I said this case had all the trappings of a sacrifice. Look at the evidence: you've got your locked room with the blackened walls, discovered just days after Halloween. Then there's Hanson and the dog connection. Even that little bowl. And no sign of any bodies. Then, today, at the lab, your Breadmaker readout—"

Turning on him, Penny cuts him off. "Don't be ridiculous, Matiu. This is the 40s for heaven's sake. People don't believe that kind of superstitious mumbo-jumbo nowadays." She points at a spot against the wall.

Matiu sets down the pallet. "You'd be surprised what people believe. Our mothers' people used to make sacrifices to the war god Tū, for example: usually *amonga tapu*, people from neighbouring *hapū,* but sometimes a dog was offered."

Waving away a fly, Penny says, "I'm not denying that sacrifices happened in the past, but all that is ancient history. We've moved on. *People* have moved on."

Matiu shakes his head. "I'm not so sure. People can resort to crazy things if they think they're dying. Maybe Fletcher was one of those."

Penny has to concede it's a possibility—people do seek solace in strange ways—but even if he were about to die, would Fletcher really murder a dog? His business persona may be fairly sordid, but he really doesn't seem the type, given how well Cerberus has been cared for. Even his attention to his sister—the regular supper meetings—suggests the man had *some* compassion. Anyway, at this point it's all supposition. Until they speak to his doctor, they're not even certain Fletcher had cancer.

She snaps on a pair of gloves. "I need to check the vents. Can you hold the pallet steady a sec?" Using the structure like a ladder, and with one hand on the wall, Penny climbs the rungs.

"You're wasting your time," Matiu says from behind her. "There's nothing up there."

"How do you know that? Did Clark already look?"

"No. But I know there's nothing there," Matiu says, his voice rising, "because that's not where bodies go in a sacrifice."

Penny wobbles, nearly toppling off the pallet. She holds her breath, steadying herself against the wall. That was close. She could've fallen head first into the hole in the floor.

"Matiu, can you leave off with your stupid theories for five minutes?" she admonishes. "I'm trying to conduct a scientific examination here. And hold the damned pallet steady, will you?"

Carefully, she pushes up the vents. Peeks in. Even in the low light it's easy to see that the dust here is undisturbed. It doesn't look like any bodies went out this way. "Hand me my phone will you? It's in my satchel." She waggles a hand behind her. Matiu rummages in the bag at her hip, and slips the tablet into her palm. She takes a few photos and passes the phone back.

"Sampling tape."

Matiu repeats the procedure, this time putting the tape in her hand.

Penny takes a few samples of the dust inside the vent. "You know, it smells of almond up here," she says when she's finished. "What do you think?"

"Let me have a whiff."

Penny gets down and switches places with Matiu. Holding up the vent cover with one hand, Matiu pokes his head through the gap.

"Yeah, you're right. It does smell kind of fruity. Like Rose Fletcher's baking."

"Almond slice," Penny says, puzzled.

"Was it? That'll be it then. Almond."

Matiu drops the vent cover, the clang startling her and making her jump.

Bloody hell, Matiu. Getting the wind up her with his talk of sacrifices.

They're on their way out when Matiu points out the real estate agent, Patisepa Taylor, in the car park.

"The vultures are circling."

"Yeah. We haven't even found the body and already they're carving up the remains," Penny says. But with her eyes on the agent, Penny isn't looking where she's going and her heel gets wedged between the bars of the grate.

These bloody summer sandals. Honestly.

She slips her foot out of the sandal, then bends to pull the heel of her sandal out of the grill. A thought strikes her. *Why is this grate here…?*

Quickly, while the real estate agent is here. Penny turns and hop-slides towardsPatisepa Taylor, putting her shoe back on as she goes.

"Penny, where are you off to?" Matiu calls after her, exasperated.

"Got to have a word with the real estate agent," Penny replies, her voice as jerky as her gait. "Ms Taylor?" The woman turns, her silky mane billowing. Penny slows her limp. "I'm Penny Yee. We met yesterday."

The agent casts her eyes disdainfully at Penny's sandal, still hanging half off. "The girl with the police. Yes. I remember," she says curtly. Her face, already stiff from enhancements, hardens some more. She folds her arms across a formidable chest. "I hope you aren't here to beg for an extension. I already told your Chief Inspector that I won't tolerate any further delays."

"Oh no, Ms Taylor. I'm not here to get in your way. In fact, we're all done. Although you might want to avoid the actual crime scene—"

The real estate agent's head snaps up. "I knew it!"

Penny rushes on, "No no, you're good to go. It's just…the blood. It's still there. The cleaners haven't been through yet. It's not exactly…pleasant. So you might not want to take your client through there."

"Oh, I see. Well, thank you for letting me know, Miss Yee." The woman turns, the interview terminated, at least as far as she's concerned.

"Ms Taylor, I wondered if you would mind if I asked you a couple of additional questions?"

"Why? I already told everything to the officer yesterday. I really don't have time for this. I'm waiting on a client." She purses her lips. She could do with a bit more polyfiller on her top lip.

Matiu joins them, strolling over, turning on his best smarmy-charmy smile for the agent. "Just routine questioning, Ms Taylor, for the files, you understand. Dr Yee would really appreciate your help..."

The real estate agent flutters her false eyelashes at Matiu. "Of course, officer."

Impersonating a cop. Again. Matiu doesn't correct her.

Taylor turns to Penny. "OK, fine. Ask your questions. But hurry it up, will you? My client will be here any second."

"What can you tell me about the history of the premises?"

"I don't see why this is important..."

Matiu throws her a grave the-future-of-the-world-is-in-the-balance look. "Please, Ms Taylor. Your expert local knowledge could be key here."

"Oh. In that case. Well, let's see. From memory there was a school on the site once. About a century ago. Can't remember the name of it. It'll be in the file."

"What about later?" Penny prompts.

"More recently it's been a shared office complex. Modular. With the car parking underneath on the ground floor."

"Yes, yes." Penny says, impatient. "What about before that?"

Patisepa Taylor runs a manicured fingernail along her jawline. "Some time or another, the building was used as a fruit processing plant. For apples, I believe."

"Can you remember the name of the company?"

"Fresh-Ap? Not sure. I really don't see how this will help locate my client, but like I say, it'll be on the file. I'll ask my secretary to send it to you if you like."

"Brilliant. Thank you, Ms Taylor." Penny holds out her tablet to sync their contact numbers. Taylor does the same. As the two devices touch, Penny resolves to delete the connection as soon as she has the file, to avoid the likely deluge of real estate newsletters.

"There's my buyer," Taylor says, interrupting Penny's train of thought. Penny looks up. A silver car has pulled into the far end of the car park. "I'm really going to have to go now." With glossy talons, Taylor slips Matiu her card. "Anytime I can help you with my expert local knowledge, just give me a call," she says huskily, before tottering away on her six-inch heels.

Penny wants to snort. Instead, she heads back to the grate and, taking out a standard Geiger pencil, slides it into the cavity under the grill. The pencil clicks away cheerfully. Penny withdraws it, checks the tiny readout.

Interesting.

She's putting the device back in her pocket when Matiu grabs her by the arm. "Penny, that woman with the real estate agent. Does she look familiar to you?" he says, frowning.

Penny squints against the last of the sun. The woman who has stepped out of the silver car is blonde and leggy. Penny shrugs. "Not really. A game show host? Or maybe you dated her once. She looks your type."

But Cerberus clearly recognises her. Barking furiously, the dog has scrambled to the front seat of the car, and, his paws on wheel, he blasts on the horn.

CHAPTER 18

- Matiu -

Matiu whips the door open and hauls the dog out. Its claws scratch horribly across the leather upholstery, one foreleg catching in the steering wheel. Then man and dog are tumbling out, Matiu struggling under the dog's weight, putting him off balance long enough for Cerberus to make a dash for it. But Matiu is faster, snagging the leash as it snakes away from him, the dog scrabbling up short as he encounters Matiu's mass, holding him back. Still, Cerberus strains at the leash, his collar digging into his neck. Matiu tugs on the lead, easing the big dog back towards him inch by inch.

"Fuck me," he gasps, rattled by just how fast and powerful the Lab had proven to be once he's got his steam up. "Com'ere, boy. Heel!" Vocal commands are barely worth a damn to a dog that's got its hackles up, even less when every word is punctuated by a jerk on the lead choking off a fraction more air, but repeating them helps Matiu maintain the illusion of control. For Penny, at least, not to mention the real estate agent and her client. He resists the urge to crouch by the dog and rub his head, which he can tell is what Penny wants to do, despite how Cerberus' gums are in full view, lips pulled back from the jaws, slobber hanging in ropy loops from his muzzle. A low growl rumbles in the dog's throat.

"Wow," Penny breathes, looking from the dog across to Taylor and her client. "I guess he's happy to see someone."

"You really don't know dogs, do you?" Matiu says. He tries to drag Cerberus closer to him, but the dog has dug its weight firmly into the tar seal, his every muscle tensed to run, to strike. "They're like people. Scratch the surface of the tame animal, and there's always something feral lurking just beneath."

Penny takes another look at Cerberus. "Oh," she says, and then, in a smaller voice, "Oh."

"The real question is, who the hell is that, and why does Cerberus want to run over there and give her a big ol' loving hug?"

Penny looks back at the silver car, where Taylor and the stranger are now casting awkward and not entirely friendly glances their way, before they turn and move into the building, pulling the door closed behind them. Firmly.

"I'm not sure," she says, "but come to think of it, she does look familiar. I can't think why, though. Where have I seen her?"

"I think we need to get to Buchanan's."

"It's late. Won't the clinic be closed?"

"And that will stop us from having a look around how, exactly?" Matiu turns to drag Cerberus into the back of the car. The object of his ire no longer in the vicinity, the dog is somewhat more cooperative, though Matiu can feel his racing heart, the unspent tension in his muscles. He's a spring, coiled to breaking point. Moments ago, he was the most placid dog Matiu had ever known, and he's known a few. In an instant, Cerberus had morphed into a veritable hellhound. Matiu wonders if he'll be in the right place next time to hold back the wolf lurking vicious behind the eyes of every dog.

"You're not suggesting that we…what? That we break in? This is a police investigation, Matiu."

"Is it? Are you sure? Because the police don't seem all that interested in what's going on here."

Penny puts her hands on her hips. "I'm sorry, have you not noticed the barrage of phone calls I've been getting? The pressure to tie this thing up? How much more of a police investigation could it be?"

Slamming the back door, Matiu puts his hands on the roof, fixing his sister with that stare he knows can strip the copper off a penny. "You said it yourself. They want to tie this up. They want a nice, tidy explanation, someone to blame, if they can, and a rubber stamp so they can close the case and move on. They don't *care* what happened to Fletcher. They don't give a shit about the dogs, or Tikau, *anyone* so long as they can dump the case and not lose their jobs or any sleep over it. And they're not going to get a tidy answer, not if they're looking for the truth."

Penny stares at him. To her credit, she refuses to crumble. There's a spine in there somewhere after all. "We're not on a ghost hunt. We're looking for a missing person, or possibly that person's killer. There are clues, evidence, all of which will lead us to a sane and rational explanation. We're not living in your fantasy world anymore. We never were. Please, just grow the fuck up."

They stand there, the space between them more electric, more desolate than Matiu has ever known it. For a moment, he pauses to question. Did he really see Hanson the way he thought he did? Or was it just the fear playing tricks on him? Maybe Penny's right, he's just bat-shit crazy, and he's never come to terms with it, never tried to fix himself: that's the real problem. Maybe she doesn't deserve for it to be hers as well. Maybe his mother's legacy need not be his own, if he chooses otherwise.

But if that's the case, then what's happened to Makere? The presence that has been with him since childhood, the voice that has questioned his every move, sown him with self-doubt, that will never just shut the fuck up and leave him the hell alone, is gone. And if what had happened at Hanson's was just some escalation of his own mental instability, then shouldn't Makere, being the most basic expression of that, be worse now, and not vanished completely?

No. Because Makere had been in Hanson's house, in that place that was not a place, where the sky had twisted grey and bleeding and he could hear the screams that rang silent and hollow between the stars. That was a place a guy like Makere— whatever he was—could call home. It was a world that Matiu—whatever *he* was— could step into, and out of. It was a place that dear, sweet Penny couldn't believe in, couldn't *dare* to believe in, because if she did it might truly drive her mad. And it took a very special sort of person to live with being slightly, truly mad.

Matiu nods. "Sure. Whatever. Get in the car, we'll go do a drive-by. Can't hurt to have a look, can it?"

Penny gives him a suspicious glare. "You don't give up on an argument that easily. What are you thinking?"

Matiu shrugs. "Just that the cops still haven't found our missing rich boy, and if we get to him first, we might get the reward money. Right?"

He slides into the car.

"Wait, what? There's reward money?" Penny asks, flustered, as she opens her door and clambers in.

Matiu drives out slowly, pausing long enough to wave his phone past the parked car's number plate. "Course there is. There must be. There's always reward money," he says, keeping a perfectly straight face. "You clearly need to spend more time talking to the women in these people's lives."

Penny pulls out her tablet and begins searching, even as she's putting her seatbelt on. "I can't find anything here about a reward."

Matiu shrugs as he pulls onto the road. "Don't disbelieve everything you can't find on the internet. Just because no one's ever said it doesn't mean it isn't true."

Penny pauses in her scrolling. "You're... Oh for goodness' sake. I almost believed you." She swipes several windows into oblivion and opens a new one. "The clinic's on Devon Lane, across the bridge."

"Punch the deets down to the GeePee," Matiu says, and passes her his phone. "Then see what you can find out about this." On his screen, a shot of the silver car's number-plate. "I'm allowed to do that, right? It's in public view, and all."

Penny grimaces. "Yes, you're allowed. But I can't see how our dog getting upset about someone's perfume could possibly be related to a police investigation."

Matiu clicks his tongue. "Didn't take you long to claim him, did it? Let's not forget that Cerberus here is the missing person's dog. And he probably recognised that woman's smell from somewhere and doesn't like her."

Penny's eyes narrow. "Hang on..." Her fingers flicker across the screen, and in a moment she has an image displayed. She holds it up for Matiu to glance at. "That's Fletcher, receiving the Bruniel Award in 2042 for Outstanding Reality Television Achievement. And that woman behind him..."

"...was the woman we just saw," Matiu finishes for her.

"I bet you, if we were to get a strand of her hair and compare it to the strands we found in the apartment, it would be a match. Her name is Sandi Kerr, according to this article. The link is tenuous, but it's there."

"So, his lover, then, who dear sister Rosie didn't like very much. And who was taking him away from beloved Cerberus for more than her fair share. Dog starts to learn that when she comes around, he gets bumped off to the sister. And now she's interested in purchasing one of his properties, even before his body's shown up in the river."

"In the river?" Penny frowns.

Matiu waves her off. "To coin a phrase. But I think there's something important we're overlooking."

"What's that?"

"We may not have recognised her, but Cerberus did, and you can guarantee that she recognised Cerberus, and that our friend Patisepa is going to tell her all about how we're working for the police to solve the case."

Penny stiffens, the colour draining from her face. "So, if she knows we're onto something, she might come after us next?"

Matiu shrugs. "Do we know anything? Really? You said it yourself, there's fuck-all evidence. The cops are stumped."

"I did *not* say 'fuck-all'."

"Moot point. Am I right? Do we have anything to pin this crime on Sandi Kerr?"

"Well, we have motive."

"I don't know if that stretches to motive. We know that she's seen an opportunity to buy a building before the commercial buyers swoop in. Sort of like insider trading. She would've known this if she was Fletcher's lover, easy."

"So nothing more than circumstantial?"

Matiu shakes his head. Neither of them looks back at the dog. "Cerberus hates her for a reason. I think I know why."

"Is this one of your *feelings*?"

"Maybe," Matiu says. "There might be something in that first report Beaker produced to back it up. We'll take a look when we stop. Also, we need to know why Fletcher had to drop Cerberus off every time he went out with Kerr. Do you think she was allergic to dogs?"

Penny nods slowly. "That might explain it."

They drive in silence for a minute. In his periphery, Matiu sees Penny wringing her hands together. "You all right?" he asks. "You're making me nervy, you know that?"

"Who is Tikau?"

Matiu's gut twists. "What do you mean?"

"You said before, that the cops don't care about the dogs or Fletcher, or Tikau? Who the hell is Tikau?"

Matiu grits his teeth. How'd he let that slip? "Tikau's a guy I used to know. We used to do jobs together."

"You mean you used to work with him?"

"Yes, Penny. That's exactly what I mean." Matiu stifles a sigh. Sweet, innocent Penny.

"And what does he have to do with this case?"

He takes a slow breath. "Because he's dead. His body was in Hanson's house."

"What…?" Penny twists in her seat, her mouth falling open. "You knew about that other body? How could you not tell me this? For crying out loud, Matiu!"

"Well, we've been kinda busy, and besides, he wasn't just *a body*. He was Tikau."

Penny throws her hands in the air. "I thought we were working on this together. I don't suppose you'd care to tell me how he died?"

Matiu swings the car into a tight corner, forcing Penny to grab the door handle. His blood seethes beneath his skin, remembering what he saw at the farm. Tikau's grinning face, the shredded mess that was the back of his skull. "I'm no crime scene investigator, but…"

"Yes?" She's hanging on his every word now. Normally, Matiu likes having her folding under his weight like this, but for once, he'd rather she wasn't. For once, her attention is almost more than he can bear.

"If I was to guess, I'd say it looked like he'd blown the back of his head out with a shotgun, only I know he didn't."

Penny stares, horrified. "And how, exactly, do you *know* that he didn't?"

"Because there would've been blood around his face, and the back of his mouth would've been gone, but it wasn't."

"So, the back of his head was gone?"

Matiu nods. "The same way Clark described your John in the shed. Looks a bit like both of them might've taken a shotgun blast to the side of the head, but not *quite* like that, if you know what I mean."

"I don't like the way you're speculating without the bodies to actually examine, Matiu. You could be jumping to all the wrong conclusions, misremembering what you saw, forgetting details." Penny's voice quavers though, like she just doesn't want him to go on, because she's afraid of what he might say. Because maybe she's seen it herself, and then it won't be an anomaly, or a coincidence. Then it'll be a pattern, and there's nothing that science likes more than patterns.

"It looked like something bit the back of his skull off. Something with a great big mouth that opened wide, clamped down, and tore out half of his head."

"Pull over."

Matiu swerves to the side of the road, hitting the brakes in time for Penny to scramble out and throw up on the footpath. Listening to the engine idle, Matiu drums his fingers on the wheel, waiting patiently for her to be done. It's not like he can help her chuck her guts up. After a minute or more of retching, Penny pulls herself back into the passenger seat, her feet still on the footpath, and she fumbles for her water bottle, swills, rinses, spits. Repeats.

"I'm sure," Matiu says at last to Penny's back, "that my storytelling talents aren't that good. You saw it too, didn't you? You've been holding that in for a while now."

Penny doesn't answer. Instead, she gets to her feet, opens the back door and grabs her satchel with the rest of her reports tucked inside. She eases herself into the passenger seat, as if she's sore from head to toe, and pulls the door closed with all the quiet aplomb she can manage.

"What did you want to see in the report?"

Matiu nods to himself. Tougher than she looks, his Penny. He puts the car in gear and pulls back onto the road. "Beaker reported that the blood was mostly canine, right? A Staffie cross?"

"Correct."

"That's a fighting dog. I'm not saying they all are, but it fits with what we've seen, right? There's a good chance that the dog whose blood was at the storeroom scene came from Hanson's farm."

"We haven't been able to prove that yet."

"We might be able to if we could get your friends at the cop shop to run Fletcher's and Kerr's number-plates through the government farms' security footage. They would've had to drive past them to get to Hanson's, like we did."

Penny flinches. "We can't do that."

"I know," Matiu agrees. "As soon as you ask for that, they'll see we were there too. Maybe best to assume that that's going to happen anyway and start planning your cover story."

"You're not helping."

"OK, OK. Can we just make a connection here—call it a hunch—that Kerr went to Hanson and bought a Staffie from him, for Fletcher, because Fletcher is a decent guy really and doesn't want to get messed up in that stuff."

"But we found Fletcher's beanie and his wallet at the scene."

"So he was there, but let's run a quick character profile. Fletcher is a frontman, all smiles and sound bites and PR. Kerr is a shadow dealer, his backup. Presumably she's running things in the background, right? Quietly, since even Rosie thinks they've broken up, that Fletcher's given her the heave-ho. But she's there, pulling strings. She gets things done. She's the one who goes into the house with Hanson, who goes and chooses the dog, who does the deal. Fletcher sits on the porch, walks around looking at the trees, all fascinated by being out in the rurals for once. Making small talk with the farmhand, who quietly swipes his wallet from his back pocket and his beanie from his jacket. Meanwhile he's wondering what the hell that smell is, not realising it's fresh air."

"You're conjecturing again."

"No, I'm profiling. It's psychology."

"You can't psych profile people you've never met."

"Yeah, I can. Aren't you listening to me? Sheesh, and you call yourself a scientist. Anyway, one day, not long ago, Fletcher gets home, picks up Cerberus from Rosie and heads upstairs. Man and dog go into the apartment, and what does the dog see? This woman, who he already dislikes, sitting in his house with another dog. In dog terms, you can't do much worse than that. That's a territorial invasion. All hell breaks loose. So, Cerberus now hates this woman for bringing another dog

138

into the house, and whatever Fletcher had planned to do with the dog, he can't do it there, not now. He needs somewhere else, somewhere private. Somewhere no one will interrupt him. An empty warehouse, perhaps?"

Matiu lets this sink in, his mind racing to put the rest of the pieces together. The pylons of the harbour bridge whip past them with a soft swooshing sound.

Penny is shaking her head. "But, why? What's the dog for?"

"I've told you, it's a sacrifice."

"Will you get off that idea already?"

"I'm telling you, sister. I felt it in that room, in Fletcher's apartment. There had to be a sacrifice. And Fletcher didn't have the balls to let it be Cerberus."

Penny holds up her hands. "Just stop, all right. You're so completely off the rails that I can't even bear to think about it anymore. None of the evidence supports what you're saying."

"Actually, all the proof is there, you just don't want to see it."

"There are holes in your theory I could drive a truck through."

"You can't drive a truck. You can't even drive a car."

"Shut up. Slow down, this is the turn-off to Devon Shore."

Matiu brakes and changes lanes. Absorbed in his musings, he'd stopped paying attention to the GPS. "Let's see what we find out at Buchanan's."

"Probably that the clinic is closed for the night?"

Matiu waves his hand. "A mere technicality."

"Fine. But you're buying dinner."

Matiu lifts an eyebrow. "You're feeling up to eating already? Wow, my little sister is growing up."

"Shut up," Penny says again. "And I'm your big sister. Don't you forget it."

"OK, little big sister." Matiu pulls onto the foreshore avenue. "Anything you say."

CHAPTER 19

- Pandora -

Stuck to the inside of the glass and facing the street, the disclaimer states that no sharps or drugs are kept on the premises. The doors are shut. They've arrived too late and the clinic is closed, the faint glow of white security lighting evident in the upstairs windows. Stepping closer, Penny makes a tepee of her hands, pressing them to the glass on one side of the disclaimer for a better look inside. With a bit of luck an employee may still be in there, working late. But only the deserted corridor is visible.

Damn.

Penny was hoping it would be the centre's late night, and the doctor still there. After Matiu's latest revelations, she was looking forward to the reassurance of a clinic, where everything is clean, and sharp, and ordered. Medical records, lab results, appointment dates. Psychology reports. Pharmaceutical samples. Squeaky linoleum floors. *Anything* to obliterate Matiu's crazy-arsed theories of sacrifices and scooped-out skulls.

Of creatures with tentacles.

Penny sighs. She's just tired. Working on assays half the night, she's hardly slept. She got maybe two hours sleep, three at most, and that's likely to be affecting her cognitive processing. It's the only sensible explanation.

Tentacles. Honestly.

She made them up. Those tentacles are simply the delusions of a tired brain. It's well-documented that lack of sleep leads to impaired reasoning. Besides, brains gobble around twenty percent of resting metabolic rate, and all she's had to eat today is a piece of toast, hours ago, before…Involuntarily, she wipes her mouth, wishing she had a breath mint to take away the lingering taste of vomit.

"Come on, Cerberus, boy," Penny says. "Nothing to see here tonight." Gathering up the slack in the leash, she turns back to the car and is halfway across the road when Matiu calls her back.

"Pandora, wait!"

She turns. Matiu is standing by the open door, his grin as wide as a stadium turnstile, and waving her in as if she has block tickets to the corporate box.

What the hell?

She glances up and down the street, then hurries forward.

"What did you do?" she hisses. "Pick the lock? Matiu, we can't just go around breaking and entering people's premises. I'm Scientific Consultant to the police. I have a responsibility to abide by the rules."

Matiu gives her a look that is all spring lambs and clover. "It was open."

"It was not!"

He holds up his hands. "It swung open when I pushed it. I swear."

"Well, too bad if it did." She folds her arms, the end of the leash tucked under her wrist, and taps her foot angrily. "We are *not* going in there."

"Penny, we're here. The door is open. We should take a look. What if Fletcher is still alive? Come on."

"It's trespass."

"It's a man's life."

Penny hesitates. Light from the clinic spills into the doorway, casting their shadows in the darkened street. Matiu cocks an eyebrow and mimes ushering her through the door. She bites the inside of her cheek. This is so confusing. If they go in and uncover some important evidence, how will they explain their presence here, unaccompanied and after hours, and without a warrant? She doesn't rate her chances of getting another police contract too highly after that. And Matiu's on probation. A citation for trespass could send him straight back to jail. But then she thinks of Rose Fletcher with her white hands, her violet sprigged crockery, and her tins full of almond slice. Poor Rose Fletcher who's waiting anxiously at home, wondering what's happened to her brother Darius, her only remaining relative. If Penny and Matiu don't go in, they could miss vital clues which might lead them to Fletcher...

In the end, Cerberus makes the decision for her, dashing inside and yanking her along with him. Matiu closes the door after them.

"Weird that there was no alarm," Penny says, shortening the lead again and reining the Golden Lab back.

"Yeah, weird that," Matiu replies. He crosses the wait-room to the windows and drops the Roman blinds before switching on the lights.

"I guess whoever locked up must have forgotten to arm it."

"Hmm," Matiu murmurs. He holds out a hand. "Any surgical gloves in your handbag?"

"Good idea." Penny slips her a hand into her satchel, passes him a pair and puts some on herself. "They're size XS."

Matiu takes the gloves anyway, grimacing as he snaps them on, his skin squeezed white beneath the latex. Then he slips behind the reception desk, where he starts pulling out drawers and rifling through the contents.

Da duh, da da da da duh...

Matiu looks up.

Penny checks at the screen and mimes the word 'Mum'. He smirks.

"Hello Mum? This isn't a very good time."

"You said that last time."

"I know, but it really isn—"

"You were going to phone me back."

"I haven't had time. I'm still at work."

"But that's just the point. Craig phoned. It turns out there is a vacancy in science policy. Isn't that marvellous? It'll be entry level, of course, but according to Craig the job has good prospects and you wouldn't have to work the ridiculous hours you're working now."

"That's great, Mum, but—"

"Craig's going to find out exactly what they're looking for..."

Spying the old-fashioned bell on the reception counter, Penny dings it. "Sorry, Mum. That was the Breadmaker completing its cycle. I have to take my assays down." She dings the bell again for good measure. "Better run. Bye... Don't say anything," she says as she pockets the phone.

Matiu smiles. "Never said a word."

"Hey, look at this." On the reception counter beside the bell is a flexible display magazine. Penny waves it at Matiu. "Here's our man here. Buchanan." She angles the magazine so they can both look at the cover image. A Caucasian in his mid-fifties, Buchanan has short salt and pepper hair, a thin nose, and fashionably neat stubble. His pale blue shirt is open at the neck in a look that is carefully casual.

Penny reads the headline aloud: "'Buchanan's Baby Bots: Auckland Physician's Revolutionary Cancer Treatment.' Feature article of a high-end medical journal. Very fancy. Buchanan must be raking it in." Laying the magazine flat on the counter, she transfers Cerberus' lead to her other hand, looping it over her wrist while the dog sniffs at a spot on the carpet.

"Not necessarily," Matiu says, returning to his search. "Not everyone who features on a magazine cover is there because they've made it. Could be Buchanan needs the publicity? That sort of promo doesn't come cheap."

"You're always the cynic, you know that?" Penny says, swiping one-handed across the screen. "Why is it so hard to believe that sometimes people do things that are worthy of recognition?" She stops at the feature article, her eyes skimming the text.

"I thought you said one of his patients committed suicide."

"Hmm?"

"Buchanan's patient. You said you worked a suicide case for Cordell."

Penny hears the name Cordell. She stops reading.

"What?"

"Buchanan vs Suicide Victim."

"Oh, that. It was a couple of years ago. Buchanan's treatment was still in development." She presses her index finger to the page. "Look, it says here that the procedure is undergoing trials." She quotes from the article: "'Buchanan's state-of-the-art protocol is a highly sophisticated form of chemotherapy involving cancer-specific nanobots. Currently in development, the activated preprogrammed nanobots are introduced into a patient where they attach to and 'digest' cancer cells, leaving the healthy cells intact. Particularly effective in certain localised cancers, Buchanan has recently expanded his trials to include investigation of the treatment for systemic cancers, such as leukaemia...' It goes on, although you were right: the article is mostly advertorial."

"So maybe his treatment isn't the silver bullet he makes out?"

"Whatever the disease, no treatment is 100 percent effective. There are always individual variations. And cancer is a hugely complex disease. Anyway, Buchanan was cleared of any blame in that case. The forensic data all pointed to suicide, and it was pretty clear that the guy in question was massively depressed."

Cerberus starts to whine.

"Shh, boy," Penny soothes. She knows how the dog feels. She wouldn't mind a quick comfort stop herself. Well, he's going to have to wait a few more minutes.

"What about Fletcher? Was he the type to take his own life?"

"I don't know," Penny says wistfully, stooping to scratch under Cerberus' chin. "His sister didn't seem to think so. A lot of people would say he had plenty to live for. But faced with their own mortality, does anyone know how they'd react?"

Matiu slides the last drawer shut, and blows hard through puffed cheeks. "Nothing in here."

"Of course not," Penny says, closing down the magazine and replacing it on the stack. "You're not going to find Fletcher's records by fossicking through a few file cabinets. Buchanan's patient files will have been uploaded to the Med-Cloud. We'd need the doctor's log-in and password to access those."

"But there'll be hardcopy records somewhere, right? I thought medical centres were required to keep them in case of a server failure."

"Technically yes, but it's possible they'll be stored offsite."

"What about Buchanan's research files?"

Penny looks up. "The article says trial participants get personalised treatment plans."

Matiu nods. "Let's find his office."

- Matiu -

The smoke hits him as soon as he pushes through the door. It boils forth like a dragon unleashed, swirling along the floor and ceiling as fresh air rushes into the back rooms. Matiu ducks, his eyes stinging, the acrid fumes burning his throat. "Penny! Get out! Call 111!"

Pulling his shirt up to cover his mouth and nose, Matiu moves down the corridor.

"Matiu, you can't go down there!"

He turns back, shouts through his shirt. "Why haven't the smoke alarms gone off? Someone must've disarmed them, which means they're trying to destroy something. I'll only be a minute." Then he turns back to the roiling wall of smoke and heads into the warren of offices and examination rooms at the back of the building, leaving Penny gaping, stepping backwards to escape the smoke. He doesn't wait to see if she does as she's told. Glancing through one door after another, Matiu sees no one, and nothing that might be useful. A couple of consult rooms, a medical supplies storeroom, a bathroom, a small theatre with a bed and overhead lighting and arrays of surgical instruments laid out as if ready to be used. Matiu frowns at that small detail, then pushes open the doors at the end of the corridor, into what appears to be a long, narrow laboratory. Stainless steel benches fill the middle of the room, obscuring the far side. Immediately, the heat hits him, flames licking up the far wall, crawling along the ceiling. Not unexpectedly, the fire is raging around a server cage, a blown-out monitor jutting from the flames on a twisted extension arm. Along the walls, glass jars are bursting in the heat, and plastic containers are melting, adding their toxic reek to the swarming smoke. Matiu strips the overly tight gloves from hands and crushes them into his pocket, his throat suddenly burning and his eyes watering. Through the haze, he can see a printer on the workbench, and a stack of papers in the output tray. Their edges are curling up in the heat, and in a second they'll be sucked into the vortex, but they might be just what he's looking for.

Matiu advances, low to the floor, his lungs screaming. As he rounds one of the stainless benches that line the middle of the room, he scrapes to a stop. "For fuck's sake," he coughs to himself. "Not again."

The body is sprawled on the floor behind the bench, one hand reaching for the server cabinet, the other jammed firmly in the pocket of their lab coat. Matiu snakes forward, coughing as the fumes scorch his throat, knowing he has only seconds before the smoke overwhelms him. He reaches the body and rolls it over.

Matiu nearly gags. He'd only glanced at the magazine Penny had shown him, but it could very easily be Buchanan, if not for what's happened to his face. The printer and its precious cargo abandoned, Matiu wrestles the comatose form onto his shoulders, ignoring the sticky pool of blood he's forced to lift him out of, braces himself for the hoist, and stands.

Immediately, he gasps a lungful of scorching smoke and stumbles, crashing into the bench and staggering to keep his feet. Grunting with the effort, his head spinning, Matiu pushes forward, the bench skittering away from him as he makes a break for the swinging doors. His legs are turning to rubber underneath him, and suddenly he's falling, the walls rushing up, and there's a moment of blinding pain against his skull.

CHAPTER 20

- Pandora -

With Cerberus in tow, Penny dashes out of the building into the street. She turns back to look at the façade. From the front, the medical centre appears the same, only the upstairs windows are illuminated. But inside, Penny has seen the fire, licking its lips, ready to make a meal out of everything.

Including Matiu if he doesn't hurry up.

Penny pulls out her phone, strips off her gloves, and punches the number for emergency services. The hollow voice of an automated operator begins her standard spiel. Penny wants to scream with frustration. It's an emergency, for God's sake. But she follows the woman's instructions to the letter: pushing 3 for fire, giving her current address, and providing informed consent for the emergency services to use her GPS location. Hoping that in a back room somewhere a real person is monitoring tonight's emergency calls, Penny hangs up. Stuffs the used gloves in her satchel.

Now there's nothing to do but wait.

And wait.

A couple of late-night walkers stop to see what's going on while Penny and Cerberus pace back and forth in front of the building. The Labrador is beside himself. The smell of fire has him in a near frenzy. He tugs at the leash until it becomes a tourniquet around Penny's wrist. Penny is grateful for the pain. It gives her something else to think about. Still no sign of Matiu. How long has it been since she left him at the rear of the building? Penny has lost track of time. Could it be a minute? Two? How old is this building anyway? When was it built? Just a hundred years ago, firefighters had around seventeen minutes to evacuate a structure before a fire took hold. These days, it can take less than three. Three minutes! Penny bites her thumb nail.

More bystanders gather.

Come on, Matiu. Get your arse out of there.

Upstairs, a window pops, raining glass on the street. Penny pulls Cerberus away from the shards, and, crouching, plunges her hands into the fur at the Lab's neck, the gesture as much to ground herself as to soothe the dog. Above them, a tell-tale orange glow flickers in the empty window frame.

"Matiu, come on."

Fuck!

He's taking too long. Frantic, Penny pulls off her satchel, rummaging inside for a safety mask and goggles. They'll have to do.

"Here, take my dog, will you?" she yells, pushing Cerberus' lead and her satchel at a bystander. She stoops to give Cerberus a reassuring pat. "Wait here, boy."

The man's eyes widen. "What, no! You can't go in there. Didn't you see that window? That place is on fire. You want to get yourself killed?"

But Penny waves him off. "My brother's in there," she says.

"Oh shit." The man takes a step backwards, his face pale. "You hear that?" he says to his companion. "There's someone in there."

"Tell the fire service!" Penny shouts over her shoulder as she runs across the road. Then she takes a couple of deep breaths and enters the building.

For the moment, the reception rooms remain untouched, Buchanan's face smiling from the magazine on the counter. Penny isn't fooled. The fire will be lurking behind doors, behind walls, gathering force, ready to ambush her. She slides the goggles over her eyes, and the mask down over her nose. Neither will save her. They're not designed to protect a wearer from clouds of toxic gas, but that's OK. All she needs is enough time to find Matiu and get him the hell out.

She drops to her hands and knees and crawls forward, the heat increasing as she moves into the building's interior. Turning her head, she scans the room to her left. A table and chairs. A water dispenser. A corner sofa. Staff room, by the looks of it. No Matiu. Penny crawls on. The room on the right is an examination room, the counter covered in boxes of medical equipment—cotton balls and tongue depressors—the centre floor-space taken up by a gurney which is half-obscured by a privacy curtain. When the fire reaches here, that curtain will go up in seconds. Not to mention the cotton balls. Penny hurries forward, keeping low, slithering on her elbows like a reptile. She chances a quick look up. Overhead black smoke billows. Flames lick at the ceiling. Deep orange flames, like candied peel.

Shit, that's bad. When carbon particles combust, they emit light, their colour indicating the temperature of the flame. She forgets what temperature deep orange

147

represents exactly. Somewhere around 2000°C. Fucking hot anyway. The floor above her is probably already ablaze. It could come down at any second.

Damn it, Matiu. Where the hell are you?

Finally, she sees him, a hump on the floor in front of her, his black leather jacket almost camouflaging him in the swirling smoke. He's exactly where she left him, on the sill of the office. Only, when she'd left, he'd been vertical. And alone. There's another form beyond him. In white. Someone else. Buchanan? Penny hasn't got time to check. Like a couple of chess pawns, both men have been bowled sideways, overcome by smoke. Penny's feeling pretty woozy herself. There isn't much time. She gets to her feet, and keeping her head as low as she can, grabs her brother by his armpits and slides him along the polished lino into the corridor.

Jesus, Matiu.

Still alive, at least. But she can't stop there. Abandoning Matiu, and coughing on fumes, she runs back into the office, into the flames, yanking the second man clear by the shoulders of his lab coat. Then she slams the door, trapping the fire in the office, and hopefully buying precious seconds. Except, even with those seconds, it's futile. There's no way Penny can pull both men out of the building. On his own, Matiu is nearly twice her weight. Who knows what the other man might weigh? She simply isn't strong enough, and there isn't time to come back a second time.

"Sorry," she murmurs, her lips barely moving as she grabs Matiu by the hands and tugs him towards the front, her sandals slipping on the lino. Maybe the fire service will arrive in time to save the other man. Matiu is her baby brother.

Her muscles screaming, she pulls Matiu past the examination room, her head spinning from the smoke.

Wait. The gurney!

Immediately, she dismisses the idea. There's no time. But she dives into the room anyway, crawling along the floor and almost crying with relief when she reaches it. The gurney has a hydraulic mechanism. Battery powered. She palpates for the switch. The apparatus whirs. Penny pulls her hands out of the way as the stretcher lowers until it is only a hand high. More luck. It's a bariatric stretcher—wider than normal. Quickly, Penny pushes it into the hall alongside her brother, accidentally running over Matiu's hand in her haste.

Sorry.

Now, the ceiling ripples with flame. It's an ocean of ripples. Dripping fiery sparks. Penny rolls Matiu bodily onto the gurney. The other man?

She can't. There's no time.

But her body has a mind of its own. She finds herself standing up and running crouched in the direction of the office and the second man. Fighting nausea, she slides him along the lino until he lies lengthwise beside the gurney. Her lungs are on fire now, her eyes watering, her muscles shrieking from an overdose of lactic acid.

Just a few seconds more. Is. All. I. Need.

Penny claws at the man, trying to lift him onto the trolley. He's too heavy. Even at floor level, she can't roll him on top of Matiu from this side.

Think, Penny, think!

Her head spinning, she moves to the other side of the gurney and, leaning over, she slips the gurney's safety strap through his belt-loop. Then, pulling on the strap, she hauls him up by his jeans, turning him towards her, her sandals wedged under the trolley. She grunts with effort. Her legs burn. Lungs burn. Eyes burn. Everything burns. Finally, she gets him on the gurney, his body slumped over Matiu's. Penny feels her legs crumple. She miscalculated. Took too long. Breathed in too much smoke. She slides to the floor.

Suddenly, there's a face in hers. Pushing at her mask.

Cerberus. Thank God.

With a surge of adrenalin, Penny gropes for the dog's collar and finds his lead. She loops it over the front crossbar of the gurney and snaps the catch closed. Then, she slaps him on the flank. Hard.

Go.

The words don't come. She has no saliva. Penny crawls then, dragging herself out of the building as the ceiling falls around her.

CHAPTER 21

- Matiu -

Matiu coughs, the world rushing back in a choking haze as fresh air floods his lungs. He's moving, bouncing and jostling somehow. In the distance, sirens echo around the walls, the streets. He's outside. Cracking his eyes open, he sees the footpath clattering by underneath him, flickers of red dancing across his periphery. There's a weight on his shoulders, and he tries to shift it by flexing his arms, but they're pinned underneath him. The weight moves, slides, and he pushes against it.

It's a body. There's a body on his back. He swallows a sudden urge to vomit, and rolls over. With an awkward sliding tangle of limbs, Matiu, lying on what appears to be a gurney, twists over, and the body which was on his back slips. The man's face is a mask of blood, his eyes gone, leaving only bloody holes raked with scratches staring into nothing.

The gurney slows and stops. Matiu pushes himself away, sending the dead man—he has to be dead, right?—sliding to the street, and then collapses to the footpath himself. Cerberus barks. Coughing, Matiu scratches the dog behind the ear and drags himself over to look at the body, presumably Buchanan, sprawled on the road. His lungs still burn and every movement is an effort, but he has to see. One of the doctor's hands is coated with drying blood, the other jammed into his pocket, his lab coat smeared with red. Gingerly, and quite sure he doesn't even want to know what the man has put into his pocket, Matiu reaches out and extracts the bloody limb from where it's hidden. His breath catches at the sight of a surgical scalpel, gripped death-like in the man's fingers. Something clings to the blade, white, viscous. In a moment of pure, horrific clarity, Matiu can see that shape of the blade where it has scored the flesh of the man's face, the lines where the steel has slashed his skin, cut out his eyes. His gorge rises. Something else tumbles from the pocket, yet Matiu can see nothing but the bloody blade gleaming in the firelight. His gaze fixes on the blood that covers Buchanan's fingers, and he knows, without knowing how, that Buchanan did this to himself. What did he see, that he felt the urge to take out his own eyes?

150

Cerberus barks again, pulling him back to the moment. It's a data sliver that fell from Buchanan's pocket. Quickly swiping the sliver and pocketing it, Matiu backs away from the body.

Cerberus is still barking, and Matiu looks around. The clinic is an inferno, with people gathering on the street as the sirens draw closer. Then someone is hauling him to his feet, a stranger, but he's pointing back at the building. "Hey, pal! Your lady friend, she went in after you!"

Penny!

Matiu stands and staggers towards the fire as sirens swell around him and the walls swim with strobing red lights. She's collapsed on the footpath just outside the building, overcome by smoke. He skids to his knees, the heat of the fire searing him. He hooks her under the armpit and hauls her to her feet. She's light, so dreadfully light, like she's made of air and smoke and dreams, nightmares. Then he's stumbling away from the fire, her feet dragging, his lungs burning. Shapes appear in the smoke around him, faceless silver ghosts. In what feels like painful slow motion, Matiu carries Penny away from the burning building.

Maybe it's a gas line, or a tank of medical oxygen, Matiu doesn't know. But the explosion that rips through the night and sends a great demon of flame billowing into the sky pounds through his spine, knocking the strength from his oxygen-starved legs. He goes down, loses his grip on Penny, and the road leaps up to slap him across the face. Swimming seconds of blurred darkness, confusion. Then there are more silver-garbed soldiers all around, and the air is full of wet mist and arcing jets of water, and someone is asking him questions he can't answer, and he just wants to collapse and throw up and sleep forever.

What happened to Penny? He was holding her, just here, a second ago, where is she? Where's his sister? He might be asking that out loud, he's not sure. He can hear the words, but he has no idea if they're coming from him, or merely echoing inside his skull. There's a mask on his face, a blanket of some kind around his shoulders, and someone's shining a light in his eyes.

Again with the questions.

"Mate, is there anyone else inside?"

He shakes his head. "Don't…know," he croaks. "Just us, the doctor, I think."

Then he's being wheeled somewhere, away from the noise, the heat, the lights that roar across his vision like so many swarming taniwha with their eyes torn out by their own claws, like blind raging tentacles, hungering for sight and air from a darker place. He closes his eyes and wishes he could sink into that place, tear out his eyes and never return.

- Pandora -

Yellow light oscillates. Sirens scream. Penny lies on her back on the pavement, looking at the sky. She blinks. No orange flames licking upwards. No billows of grey smoke. The air is cool. She's outside. She inhales deeply, filling her lungs. Auckland's atmospheric pollution quotient may be heinous, but as far as she's concerned the city's air has never tasted sweeter. She stifles a sob.

They made it.

Testing her limbs, she shifts to a sitting position, a surge of nausea threatening to overwhelm her. She sees stars.

Jeepers. She's tempted to lie straight back down again. Everywhere hurts. She struggles to breathe.

"Here, let me help you get off the road," someone—a paramedic?—says, giving her an arm. He helps her to a nearby bollard.

"Wait here," the man says when she's propped up like a dolly. "I need to get you an oxygen mask." He lopes away into the flash of lights.

Her safety goggles are long gone, but Penny pulls the mask down around her neck. It dangles from the elastic, the white filter now black with soot and ash. Licking her lips— wishing now that she'd asked the paramedic to find her some water—she surveys the damage. The medical centre has fallen in on itself, the explosion that gutted the interior causing its steel girders to twist and collapse inwards. Shredded blinds flutter at the shattered windows, and steam sizzles as water hits the fire-licked beams. Silver-clad fire service personnel, like ancient astronauts, move—in slow motion, it seems to Penny—to deal with the fire still cackling and spitting, while here and there uniformed police calm the bystanders.

She's lost track of Matiu, but just minutes ago he'd been upright beside her, dragging her away from the building, before the place went up, the blastwave sending them barrelling forward, and Penny landing on her fanny in the middle of the road. He'll be around somewhere. Maybe giving the paramedics a talking to. She should probably check.

But then she sees the mangled gurney. Flung farther along the street in the blast, it's lying on its side. Underneath it, Cerberus is struggling to free himself, his front paws scrabbling, his haunches pinned beneath the stretcher.

"Cerberus," she calls, unable to manage much more than a whisper. "Hang on. I'm coming." Using the bollard to support her weight, Penny gets up, waits a few seconds for the dizziness to subside, and stumbles over to the dog. Still unsteady, she sits down on her bottom on the asphalt and unclips the lead from Cerberus' collar. Then she lifts the side of the trolley, creating a space for the dog to escape. Entangled in the straps, Cerberus kicks his hind legs a couple of times, then clambers out from under it, immediately hurling himself at Penny, pushing her backwards and licking her face.

Flat out on the ground again, Penny lifts her chin, dropping her head onto the road to avoid his doggy kiss.

"Hey! Yes, I'm OK," she says, her voice gravelly. "We're fine. Good boy. Down now. Good boy, Cerberus."

Penny lies there and indulges the dog a moment, playfully rubbing his back and flopping his ears. God knows he deserves it. He may have evaded the bystander she'd left him with, but he saved Matiu's life, hauling that gurney out of the building. Suddenly, she remembers the other man. Was it Buchanan? Did he survive? Penny had been too preoccupied getting them out. Whoever the man was, he'd been unconscious. Hardly surprising since he'd been exposed to the smoke for longer than either Penny or Matiu. Although, now her lungs have had a chance to recover, she should get up off the road and go and find out.

"Cerberus, that's enough. Hop off me now." She pushes gently at the dog, who steps to one side. "Good boy," she says again.

Turning and kneeling, she unravels Cerberus' lead from the gurney. He's managed to get it completely twisted up. She's just refastened it to his collar when she glimpses the silver sedan roll out of the service lane behind what's left of the medical centre. The driver can't resist a quick rubberneck backwards at the devastation.

Sandi Kerr.

Arriving or leaving?

Penny narrows her eyes. She'd put her money on the woman just leaving now. It's too much of a coincidence that they should see her earlier at the warehouse and, now, here at Buchanan's surgery. Did she have something to do with starting the fire? She couldn't have got here before Penny and Matiu, but plenty of lowlifes in this city would be willing to send a building up in flames for the right money. Perhaps she's passing by to verify that what had been ordered had been done?

Evidence!

Penny needs to take a photo. Cerberus erupts in a fit of barking as Penny scrambles for her phone, remembering too late that she entrusted her satchel, including her tablet, to a passerby.

"Hey, you. Pandora. Science girl," a voice bellows. It's Tanner. The detective stalks towards her, oblivious to the building smouldering alongside, his hulking frame blocking her view of the retreating sedan. "What the fuck are you doing here?"

"Um...I was following up on a lead," Penny babbles. "We...that is...I discovered that Dr Buchanan was Fletcher's physician, and I thought I'd take the opportunity to interview him. Buchanan may have ordered blood work, which could corroborate the forensic evidence collected at the crime scene."

"Bit late in the day for an interview," Tanner says.

"You said you have seventeen cases, sir. And that you needed a quick solve. I decided to come straight here when I finished up at the warehouse. It was just on the off-chance really." Penny fiddles with Cerberus' lead. "Seeing as Officer Clark expects me to be collecting samples at the Hanson farm in the morning."

"Yes, the bodies do seem to be piling up on this one. I call you in to help with the backlog of bodies and next thing I know, there's a frickin' mountain of them." Like an old school detective, Tanner pulls out a notepad and tiny pencil, both dwarfed in his huge hands. He flips to an empty page. "So, you're saying the medical centre was still open when you arrived?"

"No, sir. It was closed, but the door was open," says Penny, feeling her face go hot at the lie.

Tanner cocks an eyebrow. "Open. Right. So you just waltzed on in?"

"Well, yes." She looks at her summer sandals; one of the buckles is nearly torn right off.

"You and your brother?"

"That's right."

"Matiu Yee, isn't it?" The detective shifts his weight to his back foot.

Penny looks up sharply. "Yes. Is there a problem?"

Tanner rubs his chin. "You forgot to mention that your brother has some history with the police. Bit of a naughty lad in his day."

Swallowing hard, Penny lifts her chin, meeting his gaze. "I didn't think it was relevant. Matiu did his time, Detective Tanner. He's not the same person he was then. He's moved on."

"Uh-huh. I'm sure he has. It didn't seem odd to you that the front door was open?"

"A little bit."

"I see." Tanner doesn't see. He doesn't *see* anything. Or if he does, all he sees is Matiu's rap sheet and the time he did inside. Penny straightens, pulling Cerberus to heel.

"Actually, it was lucky Matiu and I arrived when we did. We were able to pull a man out of the fire."

"He died."

"Oh."

"Yes, we'll need to confirm it—dental records and next of kin and so on—but at first glance it appears to be the doctor."

Penny nods. "I wondered. He was in there a long time. There was so much smoke, it was overwhelming."

"Oh, he didn't die of asphyxiation. Buchanan was battered. Mutilated."

Mutilated? How? By who?

Penny hadn't seen anything when she was getting him onto the gurney, but then she'd been in a hurry and the room had been full of smoke… *Oh my God, please, please don't tell me his brains had been scooped out from behind.* She covers her mouth, coughing to cover her anxiety. The explosion, the fire, must help because her act seems to satisfy Tanner, who waits for her to regain her composure.

"Had you ever met the doctor before?"

"Me? No. Although I'd heard of him. His name came up in a case when I was working for LysisCo."

Flipping back a page or two in his notebook, Tanner checks his notes, and purses his lips.

"What about your brother? Did he know the doctor?"

"Matiu? Why should he know Buchanan?"

"I don't know. I'm asking you."

"What's this about?"

"Just taking your statement, that's all." He waves his notebook in her face as if to emphasise his point. "Lucky for you, it seems to check out. Your brother just gave me the same story, and a couple of witness statements bear out your version of events, too. Plus, I have the time you called the fire service, and a witness photo posted on the net just minutes later of your dog there pulling the two men out of the building. He's quite famous already. You're in the background. I won't show it to you because it's not the most flattering photo. In any case, not enough time had elapsed for you to have inflicted those wounds on Buchanan. Someone cut the poor shit's eyes out. Did you see *that* when you were dragging him out of the fire?" He slips the pad into his pocket, pushing it down with an enormous index finger. Penny swallows. The hair on her arms stands on end.

"Someone cut his eyes out?"

Tanner examines her face, his eyes narrow. Is he checking her reaction? Her reaction is what anyone's reaction would be on hearing that. You'd have to be sick, completely sick, a total psychopath to even contemplate doing that to another human being, and if Tanner thinks, even for a second, that either she or Matiu are capable of doing something so gruesome, so horrific, then—

"It's usually symbolic," Tanner says. "See no evil. Anyway, you and your brother should go home, Ms Pandora. Get some sleep. Like you said, Officer Clark is expecting you at Hanson's farm first thing in the morning."

Penny grabs his arm, her grubby fingers smudging his shirt. "Hang on. You can't seriously think we killed Buchanan? Cut his eyes out! That's crazy. You engaged me to consult on this case!"

"Yes, that's the conclusion I've come to, too," Tanner says, staring at her hand. Penny snatches it back as if it were scalded. "Otherwise, why would you have risked your life to pull the doctor out of the fire? Any sensible murderer would have let the body incinerate. Oh, I believe this is your satchel."

Handing her the bag, the detective turns and lumbers away.

CHAPTER 22

- Matiu -

Matiu pauses when they reach the car, resting his arm on the roof with the back door open, and takes a deep breath. Penny is lowering herself with excessive care into the passenger seat, like she's hurt all over. Inside and out. Even Cerberus isn't exactly bounding as he slinks into the back seat and settles down. They're all shattered, in more ways than one. It's just been that sort of a day.

Closing the back door, Matiu drops heavily into the driver's seat and starts the engine. For a minute they sit, the engine idling, fire engine lights scrolling across the nearby buildings, a light ash drifting down to coat everything. He pulls on the windscreen washers and flicks on the lights as the wipers scrape across the glass, smearing twin rainbows through the powder.

"So," he says, coughs, his voice a harsh rasp. "You as hungry as I am?"

Penny looks straight ahead. "We just dragged a dead body with its eyes torn out from a burning building, and you're thinking about food?"

"Pretty much. How about falafels?" He puts the car in gear and cruises away from the scene, hoping to draw as little attention from the gathered crowd as possible.

"I could go for a vego option," Penny cedes. "I'm not really feeling up to meat right at the moment."

"What?" Matiu croaks. "A little blood, and suddenly you're a vegetarian?"

She glares at him. "Something cut his eyes out. I think that gives me licence to appreciate a salad instead of a burger."

Matiu turns on the aircon and relishes the artificial chill as it caresses his windpipe. They drive for a while in silence. Auckland rolls by outside the windows, looming and alien. The streets fold around them. How has this city, so familiar, suddenly become so strange? So hostile? He scoops up Penny's water bottle and takes a long pull. Normally, she'd hit the roof over something as lame-arse as sharing a drink bottle. The fact that she barely grunts her disapproval tells him just how hard she's been hit by everything that's happened. She's probably in shock. Maybe not the blood-loss kind of shock, but she might very well be sinking under layers of trauma, nonetheless. Matiu's seen it before, with boys on the streets, and it never ended well.

Trouble is, he's not exactly the sort who knows how to deal with other people's problems, unless he can fix them with a punch to the jaw or a winning grin. He doubts that either is going to help Penny. "Here's good," he croaks, and they pull over beside one of the dingy late-night Turkish places that pepper Queen Street. Pallid fluorescent light struggles to hold back the heavy night, dirty plastic orange tables and chairs receding into the depths of the place while tired, mirthless men in caricatured uniform hats and aprons drift behind the greasy metal counter, ready to take orders and cut processed meat and squirt up to two of a dozen sauces on your kebab of choice, with or without onions. Matiu lets Cerberus out, tipping the rest of the water bottle into the dog's mouth. Spluttering and lapping at the liquid, Cerberus whines low in his throat. Matiu rubs his ears as he loops his lead around a streetlight, and then he and Penny enter the shop.

"Double beef kebab, garlic yoghurt, sweet chilli, onions, thanks."

Penny punches his arm. "I thought we were having vegetarian?"

He shrugs. "No, *you* were having vegetarian. I'm *hungry*."

She shakes her head, sighing, as the man behind the counter slices slabs of meat from the barbecue skewer and dashes them across the grill. "Half a dozen falafels with tabouli and extra hummus, please."

"And any chance you could get a bowl of water for the dog?" Matiu slides another crumpled banknote across the counter to emphasise his point, sharing a nod with the chef.

Taking a seat at the back of the establishment, Matiu cracks the top on his bottle of fizz and takes a long, satisfied draught. Penny slides into the booth beside him, opening her carbonated water and sipping at it carefully, like it's the last bottle in the city and any moment now a ravening horde will pour through the doors and try to strip it from her hands.

"So," Matiu says, his voice a touch smoother for the lubrication, "bad day at the office for Buchanan, then."

"Don't be tasteless," Penny growls, dipping a falafel in hummus and biting into it. "He's dead, and the police were looking at us—both of us—as possible suspects."

Matiu takes a bite of his kebab, flinching as his mouth stings when he tries to open wide. Small bites it is, then. "That'd never stick," he says, chewing on a mouthful.

"Tanner dug up your file. I don't think he liked what he saw. If they find out that you broke in…"

"You saw that place go up at the end. They won't be finding much of *anything*."

Penny rinses her mouth again, and Matiu realises she's not trying to ease her thirst. She's trying to wash away a bad taste, not just ash and smoke, but something worse. Something he can't quite place, but which he can taste, too. The *wrongness* of it all. There's a sourness on his tongue and in the air, as if the smoke from that fire has spread across the city, driven by the bad juju he's been feeling since he stepped into a room full of blood and touched that blasted bowl.

"There's surveillance footage from around the place. And people with cameras in their pockets, and—"

"Pandora," Matiu raises a finger, slipping into his Father Dearest voice, "if you think a fellow of my capabilities would get himself caught on camera doing anything he shouldn't be doing, then you've mistaken me for being far less professional than I really am."

"Great. That's *so* reassuring. We just dragged a corpse from a burning building and nearly get ourselves killed in the process, and for what? To make the cops suspect us of arson and possibly murder? Matiu, we gained nothing from any of this. I should be back in the lab, where I belong."

Matiu takes another bite, and slides the data sliver across the table, his hand cupped over it. "Don't talk like that, sister. Not until you've looked at this. A certain doctor—now deceased—sure didn't want to let go of it, even in death." He turns his hand over, revealing the data device in his palm. There's a particularly nostalgic pleasure in the way Penny's jaw drops. He can almost hear it hit the table. "You… Matiu, please, *please*, tell me you didn't remove that from the body. Oh God, you didn't, did you?"

Matiu regards her with a slow nod. "OK," he says, forming his words very clearly. "I didn't pull this from the pocket of the dead man we dragged from the fire, the only one who seemed to know what happened to Fletcher, and who was trying to save this from the fire someone had set in his clinic. That's not what I did. But ooh, look, here's a nice random data stick I found that might be of interest in this case you're working on. You can thank me later."

Penny puts her face in her hands and doesn't take the stick. "Matiu, what have you done? How can you even know if it's of any use to us at all? Everyone carries slivers around in their pockets. You've interfered with evidence, broken chain of custody, oh God, oh God…"

Matiu waits. Soon enough she'll realise there's nothing she can do that won't make him look bad with Clark and Tanner, and then she'll come around. She looks up, her eyes red. "Matiu, you know I love you, right? Because you're my brother, and you need someone to love you."

Matiu sits back, frowning. "So?" There are moments, now and then, when he shrivels under her gaze. When he's just a little boy again, cowering in the basement, crying out at the voices that whisper in his ear. This is one of those moments. Times like this, when Pandora turns those eyes on him, and he feels like he's not the worldly-wise one of them, not the one who has seen things and done things and served his time for them. Moments like this when he wonders if he's just an ignorant little kid and Penny, his cloistered house-mouse of a big sister, is the real grown-up among them.

"Then you need to know that..." She stumbles, takes a sip from her bottle, replaces the cap with deliberate slowness, collects her thoughts, and then meets his eye again. "There's a lot I can protect you from, but some things I can't. The police are one those things, but you knew that already. You've been there. The other is yourself. How can anyone else look out for you, if everything you do has to spiral into self-destruction?"

Matiu looks away, his gut suddenly burning. He isn't hungry anymore. "I thought that doctor was alive. I didn't go in there trying to kill myself. I thought I was saving him. This?" He holds up the stick. "This was just a bonus. I thought it was what you wanted? Another clue, so we can figure out what the hell is going on and wrap up this mess. Put an end to it before it gets worse."

Penny shakes her head. "But you don't get it, do you? Everything we do that we shouldn't, someone will eventually figure out. We can't make a case based on breaking and entering and stealing evidence. And when they connect the dots, they're going to put you right back inside, and probably me too, and not even Dad's favours and connections will get us out of it. That's not how this works."

Matiu lets this sink in for a moment, her words pounding against the blackened leather that wraps up his soul, the taniwha inked into his skin snapping and frothing in defiance. She's right, in a way. In her world, she's dead right, no argument. How does he tell her, then, that they're not really in her world anymore? That whatever Fletcher and Buchanan were up to, whatever Hanson had to do with it, this isn't her realm anymore. At some point, it became his, at least in part. Like there's a shadow of the voices he's always heard now layered across everything, and even though Makere is gone, the echo of screams in his ears is growing louder, more insistent. Hungrier.

He holds the stick out to her to emphasise his point. "We need to know what's on here. So we can stop it before anyone else dies."

Penny sucks in a deep breath and grits her teeth. Finally, she takes the sliver from his outstretched hand. "At this rate, *we're* going to be the next ones who turn up dead."

Matiu forces a grin and savages his kebab with a histrionic bite. "Not if I can help it, sister. You watch my back, I'll watch yours."

Penny eyes him warily, pocketing the data sliver, and chews thoughtfully on her falafel.

CHAPTER 23

- Pandora -

Pulling her dressing gown around her, Penny reties the cord at her waist. She takes the data sliver from the bench, her hand hovering, about to slip it into the computer.

No. She shouldn't be doing this.

She shouldn't be examining the contents of this stick. Instead, she should pick up the phone right now and call Tanner. She should tell him that after struggling to haul Buchanan's body from the flames, Matiu found the data sliver caught up in his clothes. Or that she found it on the roadway, blown out of the building in the explosion.

Frowning, Penny replaces the sliver on the kitchen island. She glares at it. There's no question of her phoning the detective. She can't. Even if her explanations were halfway plausible—which they're not—Tanner would see through her lies in a second and the ugly accusations about Matiu would start again.

Giving the sliver a wide berth, Penny rounds the island and switches on the kettle.

Still, Tanner wasn't kidding when he said the bodies were piling up. Four cadavers, all of them mutilated, and Fletcher's own death looking ever more likely.

Taking down a couple of mugs, she sets them on the bench as Matiu emerges from the bathroom, one of Penny's white towels around his hips, and another being used to dry his hair. Penny notes the bluish smudge under his ribs on the left. Ouch. That's going to hurt tomorrow.

"Find anything?" he says, slinging the towel over his shoulder.

Penny shakes her head. "I haven't looked yet. But I've been thinking: maybe Buchanan wasn't involved at all. Maybe, like us, the arsonist went there looking for information, and Buchanan accidentally got in the way."

"Yep, that's good thinking, Penny," Matiu says, one hand still grasping the towel. "So how do you explain his eyes? Wouldn't it make sense to bash him over the head, set fire to the medical centre, and leave it at that? Why bother with all the unnecessary blood and gore?"

"Could be the mutilation was intended as a message for someone. A deterrent."

"It hardly seems worth going to all the effort to make a statement like that, only to obliterate it immediately afterwards by burning the body. Besides, you're assuming that the person sending the message and the person doing the killing are one and the same."

Matiu's comment gives Penny pause. She hadn't thought of that. Sandi Kerr is implicated somehow, Penny's sure of it. And Hanson's gang. But someone else involved? Who? Penny's brain is too tired. She can hardly think.

The kettle pings. Penny pours the water and hands Matiu a mug of green tea, the string of the tea bag dangling over the side. Matiu winces as his fingers curl around the handle. He hangs the wet towel over a door handle.

"Hey, there's a basket in the bathroom for those."

Matiu shrugs. "It's not doing any harm there."

"Matiu, I'm happy for you to stay over, but there are some basic rules."

"Tell me about it. No dogs on the furniture. Use the blue razor, not the pink one. Rinse the sink after you use it. No wet towels lying about. Lighten up, Pen. There are more rules here than at Mount Eden."

Penny glowers at the mention of the resurrected gaol. How dare Matiu insinuate her place is like a prison?

Matiu picks up the discarded towel and wraps it around his shoulders. "There," he says. "Happy now?"

Penny thumps him on the arm. "You have to have an answer for everything, don't you—?"

But, sitting down at a kitchen stool, Matiu slips the stick into the computer, the machine's hum blending with the ebb and flow of Cerberus' gentle snores. Quiet moments pass while Matiu flicks through the files, Penny reading over his shoulder, her mug clasped in her hands.

"Stop. What's that? See there. That folder called Osiris."

"Osiris." Matiu twists to look at her. "Egyptian god of the underworld. Responsible for resurrection…"

"Matiu, please. Don't start with that mumbo-jumbo again. Researchers often give their trials names in order to distinguish one from another, and usually on a theme. A pharmaceutical company I know of, working on contraceptives, uses a new Disney heroine for each successive trial."

"But Osiris?"

"You said it yourself: Osiris was the god of resurrection and renewal. Buchanan was hoping to give his patients another chance at life. It's just a file name. You're reading too much into it."

"Penny," Matiu whispers. "You need to open your eyes."

Penny shakes her head. "Nuh-uh. Don't start."

"You can be so blinkered, you know that, sis? So wrapped up in your formulas and your rules that you can't see your hand in front of your face. You need to wake up and see what's going on here. Science and logic don't always apply. Admit it, you don't have all the answers."

"I never said I had all the answers," Penny blusters.

Matiu snorts.

"I'm prepared to believe that someone dying from cancer might get it in their head to try an untested alternative treatment."

A sigh this time.

"They might even go so far as to undergo some kind of ceremonial cleansing—"

"Sacrifice," Matiu interjects.

"Yes, all right, they might even offer up a poor dog as a sacrifice with the misguided idea that some all-powerful being will cure their cancer and offer them a new life. I'm sure there are people out there sick enough and desperate enough to believe that. But there are no *actual* demons. No bogey monsters. No portals into dark and twisted netherworlds. Because they do not exist."

"Pen—"

"Just open the damn folder."

Shaking his head, Matiu clicks on the folder. A list of file names appears. Matiu scrolls down the list. Anne Hillsden. Plato Potaka. Darius Fletcher.

Buchanan's private patients.

"Click on that one."

"Which one?"

Penny points her mug over his shoulder in the direction of the screen. "That one at the bottom, labelled Metadata."

Matiu opens the file.

"Scroll down." The numbers whizz past in a blur. "Not so fast. Slower."

Finally, he gets it right.

"Interesting."

"What?"

"Well, it's not my field, of course, but looking at these numbers, Buchanan's protocol appears to be reasonably successful for certain types of isolated cancers, providing those cancers are detected early. This table shows that, in the main, tumours treated using his protocol either regressed or were eliminated. See here, patients' bloodwork came back clean of cancer cells. But in patients with systemic cancers, blood cancers for example, Buchanan's results were spurious." She peers over Matiu's shoulder, straining to see the footnotes in smaller print at the bottom of the screen. "The nanobots don't always behave the way they're expected to."

Matiu turns to Penny, waiting for an explanation.

She takes a moment to circle the bench and top up her mug from the kettle.

"I'd have to pull up Buchanan's papers to get a fuller picture, but from what I read at the medical centre, Buchanan uses nanobots in a specialised form of chemotherapy. Nanobots are teeny, tiny robots. About a micrometre across."

Matiu rolls his eyes. "I know what a nanobot is."

"OK, good." Penny bobs the teabag in her mug. "So anyway, Buchanan has developed a way of pre-programming nanobots to recognise certain cancer cells, and these are infused into a patient to eradicate, or at least slow down, cancers. Effectively, the bots digest cancer cells, leaving the patients' own cells intact. Unfortunately, as a treatment, it can be extremely painful with all the symptoms of traditional chemotherapy—nausea, weight loss, cramps, lethargy—only those symptoms are exaggerated. A bit of a living hell, really."

"But if it means surviving cancer, then it's worth attempting, surely?"

"I imagine some patients might wonder about that once they've started the treatment," Penny says wistfully. "In certain circumstances, death can be a kinder option."

Matiu picks up his tea, but puts it down again without taking so much as a sip.

He says, "We should check out Darius' file." Pulling up the document, he reads from Buchanan's handwritten notes: "Leukaemia. It's followed by some sort of code." Matiu reads it aloud.

"That's the TNM classification. It indicates where the primary tumour occurred, if it's reached the nodes, and the extent of metastasis—it gives an idea of how advanced the cancer is."

"So was Fletcher's cancer advanced?"

Penny nods.

Matiu goes on: "First treatment in the last week of August. Reported significant pain. Prescribed painkillers. Pain increased. Patient developed depression. Referred to a counsellor specialising in terminal illness… Bingo. There's a number here."

Matiu scoots into the bathroom and returns with his jeans. Pulling his tablet from the back pocket, he drops the jeans on the floor and punches the number into the device. After just a few seconds, he hangs up.

Penny steps over the slumbering Lab, picks up the jeans and hangs them on the door handle. "Well?"

"That number is no longer attributed," Matiu says, mimicking the standardised operator voice on the end of the line. "I'll get Scour to chase it up. See what he can find." Head down, he bangs out a quick text. That done, he slips back onto the kitchen stool and takes a swig from his mug.

He pulls a face. "Yick. Cold." He hands the mug to Penny. "Make me another one, will you?" Then, turning to the screen, he says, "So, what else have we got here?"

While Matiu mutters to himself, Penny empties the mug of cold tea in the sink, refills the kettle and turns it on.

"Hillsden. Looks like she was suffering from depression, too," Matiu says, engrossed. "She was talking about pulling herself from the trial. Buchanan referred her to the same counsellor." There's more clicking, and he resumes his reading. "Potaka: another mention of depression. Do you reckon depression could be the link?"

"I hardly think so. Terminal illness is a pretty depressing business."

Matiu nods. "Treating them must have been depressing, too. Buchanan's doodled his supermarket list on Potaka's patient notes. Bitter almonds, ten."

"What? Let me look at that." Abandoning the kettle, Penny crosses the kitchen. "Move over." She pushes her brother off the stool, slipping into the space he's just vacated to scrutinise the notes on the screen.

"This is bad."

"Why?"

"Because it's illegal to sell bitter almonds in this country."

"That's rubbish. Mum and Dad always have almonds. Bituin gets them at the supermarket."

"Those are *sweet* almonds. The notation here is for ten *bitter* almonds."

Matiu shrugs. "So it's a serving size. I don't get it."

"Eaten raw, ten bitter almonds will provide a lethal dose of cyanide."

"Ah." Matiu swings away. He sits on a sofa, leaning forward and stroking the dog with his fingers. Cerberus rolls over in his sleep.

Penny stares at the notation. Could Buchanan have been helping his patients to kill themselves? He wouldn't be the first doctor to help a patient hasten the process. They were in pain. Dying. No, it's too much risk. He could have lost his licence. But there was that case she worked for LysisCo, the one Buchanan was involved in, his patient so depressed that he took his own life.

Closing the computer, Penny moves to the sofa opposite Matiu, sitting down and tucking her feet under her.

"The doctor is involved, Penny," Matiu says.

"He's dead, though."

"Doesn't change anything."

She twiddles with the tie on her dressing gown. "By the time those patients got to Buchanan—Hillsden, Potaka, Fletcher—there really wasn't much hope for any of them. Riddled with cancer, they would've died eventually. Perhaps Buchanan was trying to be humane. If it turns out he helped them to kill themselves, then at least they were able to end their lives the way they wanted. With dignity. We might not agree, but we should respect their right to choose how, and when they die."

"You know you're sounding like a shave foam commercial, don't you? Euthanasia's against the law."

Penny sighs. "Homosexuality was against the law once."

Matiu's voice is quiet. "Buchanan isn't just some innocent victim here. He was involved."

Penny hugs her knees, nods.

Matiu stops patting Cerberus. He wipes his chin with the edge of the towel. "Whatever it is we're dealing with, I think Buchanan saw it. I think he saw it, and what he saw terrified him—"

Penny jumps up, her face hot. "That's enough, Matiu! No more talk of other worlds."

"People don't strike out their own eyes to make a point, Penny. *His own eyes.* To do that he had to go without anaesthetic. There had to be something he couldn't bear to see."

"Stop. Stop it right now. This isn't funny. I've been scared shitless as it is these past couple of days. Dead bodies. Explosions. Packs of marauding dogs. That's plenty enough to give me nightmares without you telling me ghost stories, too."

Matiu opens his mouth, then closes it again. He takes a slow breath.

"You forgot Craig Tong," he says, cracking a tiny smile. "You know, seeing as we're making a list of nightmares."

Penny stares at him. Suddenly, she can't help herself. She breaks into exhausted, hysterical laughter.

CHAPTER 24

- Matiu -

The buzz of his phone jolts Matiu awake. He barely remembers falling asleep. He shut his eyes here on the couch and then, just like that, it's morning. He shakes his head and realises he's covered with a duvet, and he has a cushion under his head. Penny must've done that.

And he hurts. Goddamn, he hurts all over. Wincing, he feels about for his phone, finds it lying on the floor beside him. Swipes it unlocked.

BURN PHONE

Matiu frowns, and the movement makes his head hurt. It's like he was in the biggest whiskey-drinking, drunk-fighting, car-crashing bender ever, but with none of the hilarious reminiscing to make it worthwhile. What the hell does Scour mean? He wants him to burn his phone?

Aching, Matiu sits up, finds a glass of water and a small saucer holding four little white pills and one brown one on the table beside him. Ibuprofen, paracetamol and B-vitamins. For all her foibles, Penny's a good sister. He knocks back the pills with the water and finds his clothes from the night before. They've been folded carefully and laid on the floor by the end of the couch. They still smell rather powerfully of smoke. Shrugging, he tugs them on and stumbles towards Penny's kitchenette to make coffee. Back on the side table, his phone buzzes again.

"What the fuck, Scour?" he mutters to himself, his voice ragged as an ashtray full of broken glass. "Don't you know what time it is?"

According to the clock on Penny's microwave, it's nearly 9:30 am. He raises an eyebrow as he fills the kettle. "OK, maybe this isn't such a bad time to message me, then."

9:30. So he was asleep for almost ten hours. That might be some kind of record. His memories of the night before are hazy, full of dust and smoke and pain. Somewhere, another phone is ringing.

Shaking his head, he tips coffee grounds into the plunger and swills it with cold water. Penny has her little rituals, he has his own. And one thing he can't stand is the taste of burnt coffee. He finds cups and sugar, checks the fridge for milk while the kettle grumbles and bubbles on the bench, and in fairly short order is sitting back down on the couch balancing the full coffee pot and two cups. The smell of the hot brew permeates the fug of his brain, and even before the first taste of it is on his lips, the world is looking sharper.

BURN PHONE

He nods and pours the second cup for Penny. He can hear her moving about in her room. Knocking things over. *Oh great, she's in a panic already.* Why is she in a panic? Were they meant to be somewhere this morning? It'll come to him.

He looks back at the next message. Scour again.

NO USERID BUT GPS TAGS LOGGED. YOU WANT EM?

Ah. Burn Phone, of course. See, everything is better with coffee. The world makes more sense.

CHUR, he replies, also in all caps, because that's how Scour rolls. Don't message him in all caps, and it's like the fucker can't even hear you. He be all like *WOT? YOU TALKIN TO ME? I CANT HEAR YOU BEEATCH. SPEAK UP!!!1!*

A moment later a file drops into Matiu's inbox, but before he can open it, Penny bursts from her room, hopping as she pulls on her socks. "Christ Matiu, have you seen the time? We're meant to be going up to Hanson's farm to collect evidence. We should've been there by now. I just had Clark on the phone, screaming at me. Get dressed!"

Matiu slowly stands, muscles howling in protest, and presents her with the steaming mug of coffee. "See," he says, more to himself than to her. "I knew it'd come to me."

Penny doesn't bother engaging his cryptic wit but nor does she refuse the proffered cup. "Hurry up."

He sips his coffee. "First thing, darling sister, I *am* dressed, though fuck knows I could do with a change of boxer shorts. Second thing is, I don't think we're going to make it to the farm, not straight away anyway."

Penny is in the kitchen, hunting through the cupboards for, he presumes, something she can eat on the run. "Don't piss around, Matiu. We need to hit the road."

"Scour tracked the phone number. He just sent me a list of GPS tag points. So we'll know where it was used."

"No time, Matiu," she says, ripping open what appears to be a healthy nut bar of some kind. "We can check it out after we get back from the farm. Put your shoes on."

Matiu nods, shrugging, and scopes out his shoes, while his thumb travels across the screen of his phone. "Got another one of those?"

Penny throws him a cereal bar and shoves one in her pocket.

"Ta. Just need to take a leak. Won't be a minute," he says, and vanishes into the bathroom.

"Hurry up," she yells. "And you shouldn't take food into the toilet. It's unhygienic."

"Why don't you take the dog out for a pee?" he yells, and grins to himself as something heavy, maybe a shoe, hits the wall. She is *so easy* to wind up.

"I can't believe I slept through my alarm," Penny grouses as she opens her tablet and begins checking her inbox, while Matiu brings up the GPS screen and pulls out of the parking garage. "You shouldn't've had so many vodkas last night," he reprimands her, his face straight.

She glares at him over the top of her tablet, but doesn't justify him with a response.

He watches the road. "Anything from your boyfriend in there?"

"I'm going to presume from your thoroughly witty tone of voice that you mean Beaker, and the answer is yes, but nothing declaring his undying love."

"Not yet? No topless selfies? That's a shame. Just boring old reports, eh?"

"They're not *that* boring. Now shut up and drive so I can read."

Matiu holds a hand up to protect his face. "Yes, ma'am. Don't whip me, ma'am. I be a good driver, I promise." Cerberus lifts his head and whines.

"Shut up."

"Don't start giving the dog a hard time too."

"I was talking to *you*. Just shut up and drive."

"Yes, Ma'am."

Matiu glances at the GPS as he weaves through the Auckland streets in the morning sun. For a while, he's almost peaceful. He still can't believe he slept for ten hours!

He turns the car into another parking lot and rolls to a stop. "Here we are."

Penny glances up from her tablet. "What are we...? We're meant to be going to the farm. Or did you miss that memo?" She's just this side of sputtering rage.

Matiu swings the GPS screen around. "This is where that phone was used most often. I thought that was pretty interesting, given where we are."

Penny is staring at him. She checks her watch, "You want me to go bankrupt, don't you? You want me to lose this job so I have to marry Craig Tong, just so you can laugh at me at the wedding and get drunk on the free booze." She puts her tablet down and cradles her head in her hands. "Why do you hate me so much?"

"Don't you want to know where we are?"

Penny doesn't look up from her moment of self-imposed misery. "Where?"

"It's an underground storage facility, out the back of the Museum of Auckland."

"And?"

"And? Well, apart from museums being all about spooky old stuff, I think if you look up you'll see what else is of interest to us."

Goaded at last, Penny gazes out the windscreen at the building and the adjacent staff car park. "Oh," she says.

"Yip," Matiu agrees. "That's more than coincidence, right?"

Penny nods slowly. "Yes. Yes it is."

The silver Falcon sits across the lot from them.

"Shall we see if the door's open?"

- Pandora -

Penny tries the door, pushing it gently with her palm. It opens. That's weird. But then she sees the corner of the door mat has curled back and stuck in the gap, preventing the door from closing properly after the last person passed through.

Still, she hesitates, her hand on the latch, the door open just a crack.

Cerberus nudges at her knees, his nose in the gap, impatient to get inside.

"Matiu, this feels wrong—sneaking into Tamaki Paenga Hira. Why not go just through the front door and ask for her?"

"Excellent idea," Matiu says, ignoring her. His own hand above her head, he grasps the edge of the door and pulls it open. "Let's do that, shall we, Pen? Let's just march under the colonnades, jump the queue of tourists, bowl up to the front desk, and demand to speak to Kerr."

"Well, what's wrong with that? The museum can't deny she works here: Scour found her name in the HR files, and her car is there," she waves a hand backwards, "in the car park. I put my palm on it. The hood was still warm."

Matiu sighs. "Penny, let's not look a gift horse in the mouth. Clark's waiting for you at the farm, remember? We haven't got time for niceties. The door's open. Kerr's up to her neck in all this."

Penny drops her head. "I know. It just seems wrong. New Zealand's first museum—we should pay."

"For Christ's sake," Matiu says. "For one thing, Cerberus won't be allowed in." He steps forward, revealing the shotgun. "And I can hardly go through the front doors with this, can I? Tell you what, I promise to pay twice next time, OK?"

Penny raises her palm. "No way. Forget it. I won't allow you to take that—"

But a couple and their children are coming along the path. Using his body to hide the weapon, Matiu hustles Penny and Cerberus though the door.

Immediately, the temperature drop gives Penny goose bumps. They're in a stairwell, on a small landing, one staircase leading up to the museum's main galleries and reception rooms, and the other leading down to the storage levels on the lower floors. The hum of chatter and a flood of light filters from the upper decks, punctuated by a staccato burst of laughter. The lower floors, on the other hand, are quiet and dark.

Penny glances at Matiu. "Which way?

Frowning, Matiu squares his shoulders and tilts his head, indicating the basement. The muscle under his eye jumps.

Why's he so twitchy all of a sudden? He's the one who insisted they come here in the first place. Could it be Makere's doing? No, not Makere. As far as Penny can tell, Matiu quit his mumbling the day before yesterday. Which is odd, because other times when Makere's shown up, he's tended to linger, fucking about with Matiu's head, teasing him, twisting him in knots until Matiu, unable to take any more, has curled up inside himself.

Either that, or he lashes out.

They start down the stairs, Penny hoping that her brother's childhood friend makes himself scarce because, imaginary or not, under his influence, Matiu can be dangerous.

Pulling Cerberus to her, Penny winds his lead about the fingers of one hand and, sliding the other along the cool steel railing, keeps her eyes on her feet. It's like descending into the blimmin' underworld, it's so dark on these stairs. Has to be less than 40 lux. Someone should write it up on a hazard sheet, bring it to the attention of the museum safety committee.

The next landing down, Matiu pushes open the fire doors and finds the lights, revealing a floor which must surely cover the entire footprint of the museum. Her mouth open, Penny stares. Books. There are thousands of them, stored in rows and rows of stackable mobile shelving. Penny has never seen so many volumes in one place, although of course they'd be stored here, on the first underground level. Occasionally, museum librarians would need to get to them, when a researcher obtains the Chief Archivist's permission, for example, and is allowed, under strict supervision, to view an original source.

"Oh my God, Matiu," Penny breathes, tingling with a desire to dash down an aisle and run her fingers along the books' spines. "So this is where they keep them— the museum's first editions and original sources. Look at them all. The colours! And that wonderful smell. It's true what they say about old books." Penny breathes in deeply. "Glorious."

Matiu's fingers tighten on the rifle. "I can smell almonds," he says, his voice tight.

Almonds? Is that what the smell is?

Penny can't concentrate, not so near to all these beautiful books. She closes her eyes and does her best to focus her olfactory receptors. Matiu's right. It does kind of smell like almonds, in spite of the filtered air conditioning.

She opens her eyes and gives him a nod.

"Right then, we should check the aisles," he declares. "And remember, Kerr's here somewhere, so be careful."

"Matiu, she's a grief counsellor."

"She's involved."

"Yes, but a murderer? I find it hard to believe."

"Just be careful, OK? Take Cerberus and start at that end, and I'll go this way."

He's about to head off when Penny pulls him back. Like a warrior, Matiu goes into an instant crouch, the firearm raised. "What? Did you see something?" he whispers.

Man, he's jittery.

"As much as I'd like to spend a few hours here, I think we'd be wasting our time," says Penny.

Matiu stands up. "But you just said you could smell almonds."

"Yes, but a lot of plants give off an almond odour: peaches, apples, cassava, even certain varieties of butter beans. It's an evolutionary adaptation to discourage herbivores from guzzling them."

Matiu throws up his hands. "You see any plants, sis?"

Penny runs her index finger along the edge of the nearest shelf, taking care not to touch the books: older tomes could be damaged by the oils in her fingers. Already the leather covers on some of these titles are showing signs of red rot.

"It's the *books*, Matiu. All this paper. Even stored under the best conditions, the cellulose and lignin in paper breaks down over time, and in the process they give off benzaldehyde, which has an almond odour. There are other breakdown products: vanillin, toluene, and 2-ethyl hexanol—which smells kind of flowery, too—and of course with books, there are the added breakdown compounds from the ink and the adhesives used in the printing and binding…" Penny breaks off. Matiu is glaring at her. "What? There are heaps of studies into that old book smell. Breakdown compounds can be helpful markers in determining the age of a document."

Switching off the lights, Matiu leaves her standing in the dark with Cerberus.

Sighing, Penny yanks open the door. "Touchy this morning, isn't he?" she mutters to the dog.

She catches up with him at the next landing, just as he's opening the fire doors. He flicks the lights on and sniffs at the air. "I can't smell it on this floor."

"Well, we're not bloodhounds," says Penny, using her bottom to hold the door open for Cerberus. "We're never going to find Kerr this way. We're being too random. We need some sort of process. What's on this floor, anyway?"

Matiu moves past her into the landing and checks the placard to the right of the door.

"B-2: Military history, land wars, armaments…" he reads.

Penny pulls a face. "I can't imagine why she'd be in here. She was consulting for Buchanan's patients as a sort of spiritual expert: a guidance counsellor for the terminally ill."

Matiu has vanished.

Hurrying out onto the landing, Penny leans over the rail. "Where are you going?"

Stopping at a turn, Matiu pokes his head into the central stairwell and looks up. "Look for early civilisations, Penny. Somewhere in the Pacific, maybe. Possibly the early Americas. Anywhere that little bowl at the warehouse might have come from…" Then, suddenly, he's off again, Penny only catching sight of his hand on the balustrade.

"Matiu," she hisses into the hollow.

His voice, raspy from running, carries back to her. "Don't bother. I know exactly where the bowl came from."

"Where?" Penny's voice echoes in the stairwell.

"Buchanan—he gave us the clue."

Penny screws up her face. Buchanan told them? But how can he have—

The file name. Osiris.

When she checks the placard for its location, Penny's heart skips a beat. B-6. Egyptology is in the basement.

CHAPTER 25

- Pandora -

Whining softly, Cerberus brushes against Penny's thighs, the warmth of his body a comfort in the cool of the museum's basement.

"Shh," Penny soothes, stooping to give him a quick pat. She can understand the dog's anxiety. It's mega-creepy down here in the bowels of the building. Row upon row of wooden shelves stacked to the ceiling and crammed with crates and artefacts—mostly the remains of dead people. It's hardly surprising everything here feels lost and forgotten. Not like the lively galleries of the upper levels, where kids will be mushing their faces into the glass cabinets for a better look at the stuffed moa or clamouring to be next in line at the interactive exhibits. Even the three heritage libraries set aside for quiet study will be more vibrant.

Under her hands, Cerberus' muscles tense. He growls in the back of his throat. Perhaps she should nip him back to the car?

Yes, that's right, Penny, just leave your brother to do your job while you climb six flights of stairs to see to the dog.

Cerberus will just have to manage his anxiety. Penny hasn't seen or heard Matiu since the fire door shut behind him a couple of minutes ago, but he'll be down here somewhere looking for Kerr.

And he's carrying a gun.

Tugging at the lead, Penny makes her way along the basement's central aisle, wishing she didn't feel quite so like the hapless first victim in a murder mystery. At least the lights were on when she got down here, but slow-moving dust motes circulating in the aircon make the basement feel eerie.

Cerberus' nails clicking on the concrete, they pass a couple of sarcophagi—one empty and open in its wooden crate at the side of the aisle, a fresh packing label on the side. They must be getting ready to transfer them to some other museum, or perhaps to storage elsewhere. Odd that the sarcophagi should be out here in the open though. Ordinarily, artefacts like these are kept in nitrogen-filled display cases to prevent deterioration. Penny glances into the crate with the closed casket. Already, the sarcophagus shows signs of flaking. She leans in for a closer look. A young woman in her twenties or thirties, her face modelled in mud and plaster on the front of the casket, stares out as she has done for close to three millennia.

Creepy.

Shifting her gaze from that soulless stare, Penny leans even farther into the crate to examine the dark base of the sarcophagus. The paintwork is worn and damaged, the design having been almost obliterated over the centuries, yet Penny can still make out the sleek snout of Anubis the Jackal, the Greek name for the Egyptian god Osiris.

Osiris.

God of the afterlife, the underworld, the dead.

She shudders. Even Cerberus is spooked. Cringing, he tows Penny back the way they came, his nails slipping on the concrete floor.

"Come on, boy," Penny mumbles, urging him to heel. She holds his doggy face in her hands and gives him a stern talking-to. "I know it's spooky down here, Cerberus-honey, but we can't go until we've interviewed Kerr. And we need to find Matiu, since he's our driver. So, chin up, fellow."

Cerberus isn't convinced. He whines softly, pulling hard on the lead, dragging Penny away from the sarcophagi and back towards the stairwell. Perhaps it would be wiser to leave him here? He hadn't reacted well when they saw Kerr outside the warehouse.

Penny loops Cerberus' lead over a shelf upright and gives him a reassuring scratch in that hard-to-reach place on the top of his head. "Back soon."

She creeps forward, less confident without Cerberus. The shelves peter out a bit farther on. An open space with tables for cataloguing perhaps? Still no sign of Matiu. Has he found Kerr? Penny can hear music or talking coming from there. Matiu must be down that way.

The lights flicker, and the sound ahead gets louder. Is that chanting? A chill seeps into her spine. Something is *definitely* going on back there. She hurries to the end of the stacking shelves and into the cleared area. Her jaw drops.

Fuck.

Quick as she can, she ducks behind the shelves, out of sight, peeking between the artefacts to try and make sense of the drama being enacted on the other side.

It's Kerr, wearing some sort of white overalls.

What's she up to? Kneeling with her back to Penny, one hand holding the collar of a Boxer dog, Kerr raises the other to the ceiling while she chants. Is this what happened at the warehouse? Some sort of weird ritual? No, it can't have, not like this, because the room in the warehouse had been locked and sealed.

Over the sound of Kerr's chanting, Penny catches a strangled mewling. The dog, trying to scrabble away, choking on its collar in Kerr's grasp? Except, it isn't the dog making the noise: it's a woman. Penny hadn't seen her before. Fairly close to the stacks and propped up against a wooden crate, she looks familiar. Penny scans the woman's face and searches her brain.

Annie Hillsden.

The woman in Buchanan's file. Although when the holo in the file had been taken Annie had been animated and plump. Now, her skin is yellowed and slack. It hangs off her bones as if she's been addicted to methamphetamines for the past year. Her eyes hooded, Annie's head lolls back. Shit. It might not be only her cancer making Annie look ill. Penny's pulse races. Has she already been poisoned? The woman can hardly hold her head up, so it would seem so. But how long ago? And why? So Kerr can kill her? Penny's all for a person's right to choose the moment and manner of their death, but not under these circumstances; not at this woman's hand.

She has to do something! Even if she can't be sure what Kerr's up to, she can't just hide here behind this stack of shelves while a woman dies. Shifting her body to the right, Penny risks poking her head around the end of the shelving for a better look.

Kerr is still chanting, her head thrown back to the ceiling, her blonde hair swaying as her body undulates. Confident that she's incapacitated Annie, Kerr's not paying the woman any attention. That's when Penny sees the bowl sitting on the floor at Kerr's feet. It's an artefact, covered in primitive drawings that resemble the ones on the bowl at the warehouse. Only that had been a cheap knock-off. This one looks real. Still, no time to dwell on it. She needs to move Annie while Kerr is distracted.

It's now or never.

Penny creeps into the cleared area and scuttles across the space to Annie. Crouching so as to hide herself behind the crate as much as possible, she drapes Annie's arm around her neck. Annie's breath smells of almonds. She's been poisoned. Was the dose lethal? Even a tiny amount can be dangerous. She'll need treatment. And soon.

Bending her knees, Penny pushes upwards, heaving Annie to her feet, for the second time in two days calling on every muscle fibre she possesses. A tall woman,

Annie's not heavy, possibly doesn't weigh much more than Penny, but the dose of cyanide has made her as floppy as four-day-old spinach, one of her feet dragging. Using a classic one-man fireman's lift, Penny shuffles Annie away to the relative safety of the stacks of shelves. Perhaps she can hide her from Kerr until help comes.

If she doesn't die first.

"Come on Annie, sweetie, you gotta help me out here," Penny whispers. A bad mistake because Annie groans. Penny's heart leaps, terrified the noise has alerted Kerr.

Please, please don't turn around.

Encumbered, Penny glances over her shoulder, relieved to see the woman is still preoccupied with her ceremony. But then, Penny catches the flash of silver in her hand and realises with horror that the ritual is coming to a climax. It's a stiletto. Or perhaps a bayonet from upstairs in the military collection. Either way, the blade is sharp and deadly. Kerr raises it above her head and brings it down on the dog's throat.

The dog lets out a strangled yelp.

Still shuffling with Annie, Penny turns away, her blood chilling as Cerberus—and Matiu—begin to howl.

CHAPTER 26

- Matiu -

Matiu strides from the shadows, the M4 butted against his shoulder and a scream of rage on his lips. There should be words, but he's past words. All the time he'd been creeping closer, ever closer, he could feel what was going to happen, but he didn't want to believe it. He knew Kerr was going to kill the dog; knew he had to stop it; knew he'd be too late. But time fell heavy on his shoulders, dragging at his limbs, weighing on his soul. This is why he's here. This is the tipping point. This is the precipice he's been treading, one foot over the void, ever since he stooped and picked up that goddamned bowl in the factory. Once he steps from the shadows, there's no going back.

Kerr spins at the sound of his voice, but her face isn't the mask of shock he expects it to be. She's smiling, a thin hard line on her sandstone features. She comes to her feet, the bayonet in her hand dripping scarlet. The dog, drizzling blood, she keeps tight to her chest. She's wearing an industrial white PVC coverall, and the blood cascades down her legs in bright rivulets. Matiu scans the floor and there it is, hidden until she had stood to face him.

A bowl.

Not the same as the one from the factory, but a bowl nonetheless, filled with the dog's vital fluids. It's stone or maybe ceramic, and there are symbols scribed across its surface, though he only has a moment to glimpse these, not long enough to decipher them. In spite of this cursory glance, he senses that the bowl is old, much older than the tacky one at the factory. It didn't come from a Manukau flea market on a Saturday morning, but from an exhibit. That's why she's here, at the museum. Whatever went wrong last time, Kerr has no intention of fucking it up again with cheap imitations.

Matiu could take her head off with the shotgun at this range. It won't matter if he hits the dog, it'll be dead anyway, nor if he takes out anything behind her. The discharge of the rifle will bring security running, and the Armed Offenders Squad, and he'll be back in prison before he knows what's happened. He's willing to live with that, if it means putting an end to whatever this is. Because he feels it, in his blood, in his bones, and he knows how *wrong* it is. This is more than just some psycho killing stray dogs for shits and giggles. He can taste the toxic winds of other times, other worlds in the back of his throat, mingled with the hot rush of fear.

Matiu stops, sighting along the barrel at Kerr. "Down!" he yells, managing to extract a word from the inarticulate rage which burns through him.

"I don't think so," Kerr replies. "But I have to say, I'm awfully pleased you could make it."

Matiu keeps the gun trained on her. The air is growing thicker around him. Static electricity coruscates across his skin, lifting the hair on his arms. Maybe that mat stuck in the door was a little too good to be true after all. "The fuck is that supposed to mean?"

"They don't like being cheated. But you'll do."

A shiver runs down Matiu's spine. The air crackles around him, hot and dry, as blood continues to sluice into the bowl from the dog's slashed throat, bubbling and slopping onto the floor. "Who don't?"

"Fletcher cheated them, and they made him pay for it."

"The fuck are you talking about?" Matiu coughs, his tongue suddenly dry, gritty, like he's been chewing on sand. He can feel the walls falling away, burning shadow pouring between the shelves to swallow them both. The gun is hot in his hands, and he hasn't even fired it.

Kerr kneels, laying the still form of the murdered dog on the bowl, where he continues to bleed weakly. Wispy tendrils rise from it, white like steam, black like smoke, and curl across the floor. "When they get here, give my regards to the other side."

She steps back, that same thin smile on her face. It's a look Matiu's seen before. It's the face of a death mask, the unflinching, impassive rictus of a sarcophagus, like something pulled from one of the exhibits around them. Staring at death and the underworld, not with fear, but with longing. Like some sort of perfect insanity. "On your fucking knees," he grates through clenched teeth. His arms are trembling, and he takes a step closer to the crazy bitch with the bloody bayonet, and the bowl with its looping, swirling streamers of mist. He dares not take his eyes off Kerr, afraid that if he does she'll suddenly be gone, melting back into the shadows, and he'll be left here alone with whatever the hell it is she's summoning. He can no longer see the walls, and a hot wind rushes over them both, tossing her hair about, stinging his eyes. The wind whips the mist into a frenzy, coiling and writhing around his legs, assuming the illusion of life. The blood in the bowl boils and thick veins of red rise into the air, twisting inside the curling tongues of vapour and giving them shape, substance.

Tentacles.

A phantasmal touch brushes Matiu's leg and he jumps back with a startled yelp, kicking at the floor, at nothing. He sweeps the gun through an arc, looking for a target, flickers of bloodstained mist snapping back and forth between this reality and another. Recovering his wits, he brings the gun back up but, as he'd feared, Kerr is gone. "Fuck!" he shouts, and breaks into a run, leaping over the bowl in the direction she must've gone.

Something wraps around his ankle and he jerks to a stop, then he's falling, landing painfully on the soft, dead dog. The bowl spills, blood sizzling over the gore-slicked floor. Matiu rolls, scrambling forward, but the grip on his ankle tightens, tugging at him. He glances back, sees the pulsing appendage, coils of looping mist and blood, looking more real with every passing breath. He chokes back a terrified cry and hurls himself forward, kicking out to break the insubstantial grasp.

He slides, but it isn't the hard concrete of the museum floor beneath him. He's in sand, soft and shifting under his hands, his feet. He can't waste time thinking about the impossibility of that. If he does, he'll be lost to madness. If he hadn't spent most of his life with one foot in this other world, he no doubt would've cracked long before now. He staggers to his knees, brings the shotgun butt to his shoulder, and swings around.

The world is a haze of shifting shadows, the storage shelves swollen to towering stony canyons, the roof a black vault of untold depth, seething with dark energy. Like how it felt in the house at the farm, with the storm brewing overhead, only more vast and utterly more horrifying. Lightning flashes, and Matiu swears there's an outline of pyramids against the horizon. Then his eyes are full of blowing sand, the universe is collapsing around him, opening its lungs and screaming, its voice silent and deafening and cosmic, everything and nothing, and Matiu no more than a mote of dust falling through the abyss. He screams back, grips the shotgun tighter, and when the tentacle of smoke and blood flashes for him out of the darkness, he fires.

CHAPTER 27

- Pandora -

Penny jumps at the shot. It's OK: Matiu has the shotgun. He'll have fired it as a warning to Kerr, or in an act of humanity to spare the dog further suffering. Either way Penny doesn't blame him. Kerr was about to butcher the dog. And somehow she'd forced, cajoled or conned Annie into ingesting a poisonous substance. *Something* had to be done to stop her. She might not have liked the idea of bringing it, but if *she* had been the one holding the gun, if she weren't pulling Annie away, Penny would've reacted in exactly the same way. For the moment though, all her energy is focused on getting Annie out of here. The woman is dying. She needs help. Still dragging her, Penny navigates the labyrinth of shelves, looking back and forth along the cross aisles for a glimpse of a service elevator. There has to be one down here somewhere. It's a fight to support her charge, because the woman is as floppy as a cotton sun hat. Annie slouches heavily to one side, forcing Penny to swerve sideways, the pair only held up by the shelving, which rocks precariously. Artefacts wobble, and dust rises.

"He's a good dog, Benson," Annie murmurs, as they lurch forward, a gob of drool glistening on her lip. "Esshhhloyal."

Benson? Could that be the Boxer? So, that was Hillsden's dog back there under Kerr's blade? Her own dog, and not one of Hanson's horde? Penny tries not to shudder. Loyal Benson may just have paid the ultimate sacrifice, allowing Penny the time she needed to pull his mistress away. But they've only just made it past the first of the sarcophagi when, pale and shaking, Annie crumples, her legs slipping out from under her as she sinks, taking Penny with her.

"Won't hurt. Promised."

"Sandi gave you something to stop you hurting? What did she give you, Annie?" Penny asks softly, as she eases the woman to a sitting position, squeezing her into the angle between the empty sarcophagus and shelving.

"Not me. Benson."

"Yes, but what did she give you?"

Annie's eyes roll back in her head. It takes her a few seconds to get them under control.

"Cancer," she gurgles.

"I know you have cancer, Annie. You're one of Dr Buchanan's patients." Annie's eyes rolls again. Bringing her face to the other woman's, Penny gives her a shake. "Annie, I need to know what Sandi gave you."

"Hurts." Annie's eyes glaze. Penny's wasting time. She's losing her. It doesn't matter what Kerr gave her. Whatever the hell it was, it was toxic. Penny needs a first aid kit. *Annie* needs the first aid kit. There's got to be one somewhere around here.

Somewhere obvious.

Abandoning Annie where she is, Penny runs back the way she came in, to the stairwell. Beside the door, where staff can find it, is the floor's first aid kit, a metal cabinet fixed to the wall, the solid red cross proclaiming its purpose. Penny slips the latch and drops the cover. It hits the wall with a clang.

Activated charcoal... activated charcoal...

There *has* to be some in here. Penny runs her fingers over the items, flinging aside the bandages and sticking plasters, eventually finding a box of charcoal pushed to the back of the cabinet.

Nooo!

It's solid. The box has been opened once before—perhaps to check the contents—and the container hasn't been sealed properly afterwards. No, here's the problem: a bottle of saline—for rinsing bits of dust and fibre out of a person's eyes—has tipped over, leaking down the wall inside the cabinet and saturating the box of charcoal on the lower shelf. Which is why the charcoal is like a sack of cement: rock-solid and as black as West Coast iron sand.

Fuck.

It's completely useless. And she can't use the saline to make Annie vomit either, because only a thimbleful remains in the bottom of the bottle. Penny swears again. If she were the boss here, the person responsible for replenishing this kit—no, the person who *failed* to replenish this kit—would be in for a right bollicking. A day in stocks wouldn't be too excessive. First aid kits have to be checked regularly! But no amount of shouting, no punishment, is going to save Annie's life. She'd need to be Rasputin to survive a lethal dose of cyanide.

Rasputin! Oh my God, Rasputin survived a lethal dose of cyanide.

Leaving the cabinet door swinging, Penny races back to Annie, digging in her jeans' pocket as she runs. Grigory Rasputin was given a lethal dose of cyanide, but he didn't die, because Prince What's-his-name made the mistake of administering the dose in a pile of sticky pastries, which Rasputin supposedly washed down with sweet wine. It didn't work because the assassin administered the dose *along with its antidote*, the glucose in the pastries binding with the poison to create less toxic forms. Not an FDA certified antidote, but unfortunately Penny doesn't happen to have a dose of hydroxocobalamin on her. What she *does* have, though, is the muesli bar she shoved in her jeans' pocket before she and Matiu left the apartment this morning. A muesli bar full of sugar and fruit. Still running down the central aisle, she slides the bar out of her pocket, unwrapping the cellophane as she closes the last steps to Annie.

Sliding in on her knees, Penny pushes the bar to Annie's lips. "Annie, honey, eat this, come on."

But Annie is too far gone to chew. The crumbs fall out of her mouth, tumbling down the front of her blouse. No matter. Breaking a new piece off the bar, Penny shoves it in her own mouth, chewing it quickly. If she can make a paste of it with her own saliva, maybe she can force it down her. Penny spits the bolus into her hand.

God, that looks disgusting.

But it doesn't stop her pressing it into the corner of Annie's mouth, pushing it in with her index finger, feeding the gluey mixture to her as if she were a helpless chick.

"Come on, Annie. Please, open up, sweetie. It could save your life."

Annie shakes her head. "I don't want to live," she croaks, her slack tongue slurring on the words. "Not like this." Her breathing is laboured, coming in short wheezes. The sound rattles Penny's nerves. She stops trying to push the food in, frightened she'll choke her.

"Sandi promised I'd be healed. If I could give up Benson..." Annie's eyes widen, her gaze far away, before her head drops to one side as she loses consciousness.

Penny checks her pulse. Nothing. Damn it, Penny, you're palpating the wrong place. She adjusts her fingertips, but still can't find even the tiniest beat.

Annie Hillsden is dead.

And yet, just seconds ago, she'd been lucid. A spike in brain wave activity? Penny has no electroencephalograph to prove it, but if anecdotal reports are true, then a person's last words uttered in those final moments of clarity are often significant.

Poor Annie. So let down by the medical options, and yet so desperate to live that she was willing try anything: even putting her trust in a charlatan like Kerr.

Sacrificing a best friend. She pushes the hair off Annie's face and, leaning close, whispers: "Thank you for your confidence, Annie. You're not to worry. Matiu and I will catch her. Trust me, we won't stop until we have the evidence to put her away for what she's done to you and Benson." Gently closing the woman's eyes, Penny hopes she finds her dog again somewhere.

Stepping back from Annie, Penny is suddenly aware of the commotion at the far end of the basement. How long has that been going on? Didn't Matiu have everything under control? Turning, she starts running along the aisle to where she last saw Kerr, but she hasn't gone more than a few steps before she's bowled from behind by a fast moving projectile. Slammed forward, the air is knocked out of her lungs.

Ooof!

Penny hears Cerberus' yowl as she goes down, plunging headlong into the second sarcophagus, her hands spread to break her fall, and catching a glimpse of the dog as he scampers past. Landing hard, Penny rolls once, pain blossoming in her thigh. Finally, the momentum spent, she comes to a stop. She holds her eyes closed an instant, hoping to deny the fact that she's sprawled in the middle of the aisle, having toppled, and no doubt destroyed, an irreplaceable museum artefact. A priceless relic dating back several thousand years.

She opens her eyes, and sighs. For the second time in two days, she's lying face-to-face with a cadaver.

CHAPTER 28

- Matiu -

The blast shatters the black and throws Matiu backwards, something warm searing his face as he hits the ground hard, flat on his back. The air explodes from his lungs, and for a second he's gasping, gagging, fighting to breathe, his skin burning cold as the void. Through the haze, a figure looms over him, its face lost in shadow, and he knows, *knows,* who it is, but he can't even find the breath to speak his name.

Makere.

See you soon, bro.

The voice rattles inside his head, and then he's stepping away, out of sight. Matiu rolls, still breathless, bringing up the gun, sweeping it around. He finds his balance, searches for a target, but sees nothing except the walls of the storage facility, cases and packing crates and shelves, the overhead lights mysteriously dark. Finally, he manages to catch a heaving breath, but the taint of wrongness doesn't leave him. If anything, he's stricken by the knowledge that this isn't the end, but only the beginning. Rising slowly, moving away from the centre of the circle where the bowl has spilled its contents and where the dog lies, a limp mass, he listens for footsteps. All he can hear is a slow, wet scraping behind him. Heart racing, he turns, the shotgun braced, trying to ignore the heat still burning at his face and hands.

From the middle of the pool of spilled blood, something disturbs the dog's corpse. The dead animal slides sideways, pushed aside by a sinuous shape which quests upwards through the blood and rises, blind and serpentine, twisting. Matiu stares transfixed as the thing grows higher, brushing the ceiling and setting the lights to swinging, its monstrous form waving back and forth in mesmeric curves. Where it touches the floor, the surface boils and blisters, cracks like glass, splits and crumbles into sand. Matiu takes a step back, and another, to avoid being knocked over by the rising mass.

Something brushes his leg. The bowl, riding a wave of sand. His legs will soon be swamped if he doesn't keep moving. The tentacle droops down and around, its tip splitting apart, revealing a toothless maw. *Maybe not a tentacle,* he thinks, numbed by the sight. *Maybe a worm.* The blind tip of the impossible thing probes the floor, its jaws finding the body of the dog. Dead or not, no animal deserves that sort of an end, to be ground up and vomited out.

Matiu aims the shotgun and fires.

The monster shrieks, a sound like broken glass scoring Matiu's spine, and its head snaps sideways in a burst of ichor. The dog's corpse is flung aside. The worm screws around on itself, seeking, while gouts of black gore pump across the shelves and onto the floor. Every instinct tells Matiu to run, but he holds his ground as it turns on him. He needs one more shot, right in the mouth as it closes in, to send it back into the void. If he runs, it's all over. Not just for him, but for everyone. The worm snakes closer. He stands dead still, feeling the sand piling up around his boots, around his ankles. He keeps the gun trained on the abyssal creature.

It lunges.

He pulls the trigger.

The chamber clicks. Empty.

Matiu is knocked down by the blow, his ankle twisting in the drifting sand and the gun flying from his grip. The worm coils about and rises for another strike. Matiu tugs at his ankle and pain blooms up his leg, drawing a hoarse cry of agony. He reaches for the only thing he can see, hoping desperately that it might protect him for just a moment longer, long enough to pull his foot free of the sand and crawl away.

His fingers close around the bowl.

The universe screams.

Matiu cries out, awash in the remembered pain of one death, another, many many deaths pouring through him, one on top of the next, like a deck of cards and he the joker at the bottom of the pile, red and black shattering over him with the ringing of long-dead screams in his ears. He opens his eyes, unaware he'd closed them, and sees the bowl in his hands. It's heavy, weighted with the sorrows of untold ages past. On its surface, the etched images of dog-headed soldiers writhe and twist, their spears slipping into spindle-thin victims while the unblinking eye of an uncaring god looks on. The dog's blood drips through the soldiers, soaking into them, and is gone. When the worm descends again, it crashes into the bowl, shattering it between Matiu's fingers and possibly also breaking several of his ribs. But Matiu is past counting his aches and pains. Scrambling backwards, he drags his feet from the sand, refusing to turn his back on the monster as it rears for another—probably final—blow.

The beast lashes out, falling with deadly speed towards Matiu, who lifts his hands to block out the sight of his imminent death, catching only a glimpse of the shape that leaps over him, nails outstretched, tail streaming behind.

Cerberus hits the worm with his full weight, tossing the creature's head askance, teeth gnashing its rubbery flesh. Ichor jets from the wound as the monster twists away, writhing and shuddering, but Cerberus holds tight, the nails on his back legs scraping black, seeping lines in the monster's flesh.

"Cerberus!" Matiu yells. Getting painfully to his feet, he holds himself upright against a glass containment crate, filled with ancient bronze swords and spears. Now is his chance to run—or hobble—away. He has no gun, nothing to drive the creature back. He can barely stand.

Yet a dog has the courage he does not.

Walk away, and run forever, or stand and fight.

Matiu was never one to run from a fight. Crouching, wincing against the pain in his ankle, he topples the glass box he's resting on, hopping as his support falls away, and goes down on his knees in the broken glass to wrench out a spear as tall as himself, its edge gleaming bronze. Wrapping his hands around the shaft of the ancient weapon, Matiu staggers forward, feeling a thousand emotions wash over him; fear of the looming battle, the screaming talons of killing rage, sharp lances of pain and remorse, the sweeping black tide of death. This spear has known its share of war and suffering. It may or may not be sharp, but it *was,* once. It knows its purpose. Using it as a walking stick, Matiu limps forward to where Cerberus is clinging tenaciously to his prey.

He knows, Matiu thinks. *He knows you killed his master.*

Gritting his teeth against the flaming pain in his ankle, Matiu lifts the spear in two hands and hops forward, hurling himself towards the towering bulk with a grunt. The spear slides through the monster's flesh with ease, and Matiu drives it in, his whole weight falling with him.

The worm writhes and bucks, its howl reverberating through the echoing chamber. Matiu fights to keep a grip on the spear as the beast rises up, lifting him off the floor. Black sludge boils from the wound, over his arms, burning him. Matiu cries out, clinging to the emotions cascading over him from within the spear.

Rage. Terror. Despair.

All of which, he knows, will be as nothing if the creature isn't banished. He rides the thrashing beast as Cerberus continues to maul its head, concentrating his energy on the core of those resonances trapped deep within the ancient spear, sweated and bled into its latticework, imprinted there from decades of conflict. At the core of all these things is the knowledge that the warrior is human. The warrior fears, because he is made of soft flesh and fragile bones. Yet he carries the strength of his fathers, his mothers, of the nation he fights for. Because he is not a mere dog-soldier, a cur to be kicked by the enemy, but a being of will and desire and determination, and he can fight until there is no fight left, fight for what he most values. For love. For life. For the blood in his veins, for knowing that even in battle, he is more than just spear and shield and rage and fear.

In this, there is a flame that burns brighter than any shotgun; a blade that cuts sharper than any sword. Matiu bends his will to this flame, this blade, and the spear erupts into light beneath his fingers.

The monster screeches, and collapses.

Matiu falls, bounding off rubbery flesh and crashing face-first into a shelf. He reels, landing hard on the floor. Broken ribs, twisted ankle, and burned skin blaze with fresh pain as he skids through the soup of ichor, blood, and sand on the floor. The creature breaks apart, white flesh and black blood disintegrating into fine sand as it falls.

Matiu lies still, wondering for a moment if he's dead, listening to the distant sound of sirens and of Cerberus barking, and then Penny is there, lifting him to his feet, and they stagger towards the service lift. She's talking, but he's not listening. What more could she have to say that could possibly matter?

CHAPTER 29

- Pandora -

"Mum, it's OK. It's just a burn," Penny says.

"You two were in a fire?" her mother squeaks. "I knew working for the police was a bad idea. What kind of trouble have you got your brother into now, Pandora?"

Now? Since when did Penny ever get Matiu into trouble? He's perfectly capable of raising hell all by himself.

Trying to ignore her mother's comment, Penny pulls back the cheery pink privacy curtains to allow their parents into the triage cubicle, taking some comfort from the fact that Matiu's look at the sight of their mother is more pained than when Penny pulled him from the museum basement.

"Matiu, baby," Mum fawns. "Just a little burn? His whole arm is bandaged!" Penny badly wants to roll her eyes. Talk about an exaggeration. Matiu has a burn on his forearm. It's serious—and no doubt he'll end up with a nasty scar—but it's not the end of the world. Still, Mum has to run to Matiu's bedside, picking up his hand and bringing it to her cheek. Matiu flinches, but he says: "Just a tiny scar, Mum. It's not serious." Oh yes, he sounds all jovial and nonchalant, but Penny's not fooled, nor does she miss the glare he aims at her.

Mum is not appeased. "Not serious? What do you mean, not serious? Pandora says the doctors want to keep you in overnight!"

"It's just to be sure there's no infection, Mum," Penny says, hoping any time now Dad will show some clemency and step in to placate their mother.

Penny's moving a chair for Mum to sit down closer to her baby, when she notes Tanner's big frame stalking through the triage aisle.

Shoot. How did he find them so quickly?

But, his eyes fixed ahead, Tanner doesn't appear to be looking for them. Penny glances in the direction he's headed, catches sight of the signage. She breathes out. He's not looking for Penny and Matiu, just taking a shortcut to the morgue. Those other murder investigations must be keeping him busy. He looks exhausted, his jacket dishevelled, and his shoes, the same ones he was wearing last night, are hoary and dusty. So maybe now *would be* a good time to talk to him…

"Inspector Tanner." Penny steps over the imaginary line marking the edge of the cubicle.

Tanner's bushy eyebrows shoot up. "Ms Pandora. Aren't you supposed to be with Clark this morning?"

"Yes, but something came up with the case. Could I have a quick word?"

Looking over Penny's head, Tanner tilts his chin upward. "What happened to your brother?"

"A burn."

"In last night's fire?"

Mum looks up from fussing with Matiu's bedclothes. "The fire was last night?" she erupts. "This happened to Matiu last night and you've only just called us now?"

"No, no, of course not, Mum," Penny says hurriedly. "Matiu was just fine last night. This happened today. A completely separate incident. It's a burn from an explosion caused by oxygen enrichment from a leak in the museum's air purification system…" She trails off, realising she's only made things worse.

Matiu is gritting his teeth, his spare hand clenched. That burn must hurt way more than he's letting on to Mum. He needs a stronger painkiller.

Tanner says, "I'll leave you to your family, Ms Pandora. Whatever you have to say, we'll discuss it when your family is more…" Penny can see him searching for the word. "Settled." He starts to move away.

"But this is important," Penny blurts. "I know what happened to Fletcher."

Tanner slows and looks about awkwardly. Penny understands his hesitation. Too many ears.

Thankfully, Dad knows enough to make himself scarce. "Kiri, I think now would be a good time for you and I to locate Matiu's doctor and get some firsthand information about his prognosis."

"Good idea," Mum says, as Dad guides her away by the elbow. "And let's order him a proper room while we're at it. It's like sleeping on the marae in here, everyone coming and going." She glares at Tanner pointedly. "And all this chatter. How poor Matiu is expected to rest…"

Finally, their parents disappear round the corner, her mother's voice fading. Tanner enters the cubicle, giving Matiu a salutatory nod while Penny pulls the privacy curtains closed.

The inspector leans against the chair that Penny had been moving for her mother, his bottom hooked over the back rest. "OK, so let's have it. What happened to Fletcher?"

"Penny—" Matiu says.

"It's OK, Matiu," She pats him on the knee. "I'll handle this." Then, turning to Tanner, she says, "Darius Fletcher is dead."

Tanner nods. "I figured as much. Hell of a lot of blood in that warehouse otherwise."

"None of it's Fletcher's, though. The lab analyses tells us that it belongs to a dog, most likely one of Hanson's fighting dogs. I'm not sure exactly whose dog it was originally, but I'm expecting the microchips Clark has at the farm will help us narrow it down…"

Still leaning against the chair, Tanner shifts his legs, moving his weight from one to the other. "Ms Pandora, forgive me if I seem a teeny bit callous, but with twenty fucking cadavers on my plate, I couldn't give a rat's arse about the dog. What the hell happened to Darius Fletcher?"

"Well, what we didn't know—what his sister didn't know," Penny gibbers, "was before that night at the warehouse, Darius was already dying. The thing is, he had an aggressive blood cancer, which was why he was seeing Buchanan."

"The doctor whose body you pulled from the fire yesterday? He was involved?"

"Yes, indirectly. You see, Buchanan's treatment is still experimental. It involves preprogramming nanobots to bind with and digest specific cancer cells. Once injected into the patient, the bots circulate systemically, hooking up to cancer cells and then digesting them, while leaving the patient's healthy cells intact. Only, it's a painful process, the outcome isn't guaranteed and, understandably, some patients get depressed, even suicidal. A couple of years ago I was involved in a case where one of Buchanan's patients committed suicide."

"You're telling me that Fletcher's death was a suicide? I'd like to believe that, but if it were a simple suicide, how did he manage to dispose of his own body, then? The room at the warehouse was locked from the inside. I saw it myself."

Matiu groans softly. Frowning, he lowers his head and examines his bandage.

Penny ignores him and goes on. "Buchanan referred some of his patients, Fletcher included, to a private counsellor named Sandi Kerr, a woman who specialises in the spiritual well-being of the terminally ill. There's evidence of Fletcher and Kerr being together, photos, internet messages and the like. But Kerr also works as an Egyptologist for the Tamaki Paenga Hira museum, and as such has established herself as the leader of a cult group involved in ritual sacrifice to the Egyptian god Osiris."

"Ah, now wait a minute…"

"She convinced Fletcher that she could offer him new life if he were willing to undergo a sacrifice."

"I hardly think…"

"Inspector Tanner," Matiu interrupts. "These are really sick people we're talking about. Not sick in the depraved sense, but desperately ill people who aren't expected to ever meet their grandkids. People with no hope left. If you're that vulnerable, you'll try anything. Think about it: what did Fletcher have to lose?"

Tanner scratches his chin.

Penny decides to push on. "Remember the little bowl, the blacked out walls? We think Kerr meant to carry out the sacrificial ritual for him, but being too impatient to receive what he believed would be a new life force, Fletcher decided to do it himself, jumping the gun on her, and purchasing a dog from Hanson—"

"Where Clark is at the moment. He says it's a bloodbath out there."

Matiu nods his head, gravely. "Internal gang warfare," he interjects. "A bit of money circulating and they all want a bigger cut. You see it all the time."

"Exactly," says Penny.

"Hmmm," Tanner says, pensive. "You still haven't explained why we never found Fletcher's body. Was he even at the warehouse? Maybe Hanson had him knocked off and thrown in an offal pit somewhere."

"He was at the warehouse," Penny confirms, as Matiu closes his eyes. "Some years ago, the warehouse was the site of a fruit processing plant, where a radioactive source—a standard Cobalt 60—was used to sterilise the fruit. Only there was a spill, which the company quickly cleaned up, and then hushed up. But background radioactivity at the site is still high—high enough to cause Fletcher's systemic nanobots to malfunction. They went berserk, consuming not only the target cancer cells, but also Fletcher's healthy cells, and then, when they'd exhausted that food source, they consumed the dog as well."

"You're kidding?"

"No."

"I don't believe it." Tanner picks up the scissors and twirls them in his fingers. Penny waits for him to take in what she's said. Eventually, he replaces the scissors in the trolley. "OK, then what about all the blood?"

"In order to function, nanobots must first attach to a receptor on a living cell. The blood had already been spilled, so the bots were either too remote, or the cells were dead and therefore not recognisable to them."

Tanner shakes his head, incredulous. "So you're telling me that Darius Fletcher was eaten alive from the inside? And by the very technology intended to save his life. Jesus!"

"Yes, sir. And there's more: Kerr managed to convince another one of Buchanan's patients to submit to her sacrifice ritual. Hillsden. We found her today in the museum basement. We arrived too late to save her. The body is still there."

"I did get a call about a ruckus at the museum this morning."

Penny nods. "We left as soon as the uniforms arrived."

"What about Kerr?"

"She's gone."

Matiu opens his eyes. "She had a shotgun," he says. "Fired it at me. There was nothing I could do."

"Bugger," says Tanner.

Please don't ask me about the gun. Please...

But Tanner isn't interested in the gun. Instead, he stands up and says, "Forward me links to those photographs of Kerr, Ms Pandora. I'll put out a call to look for her. You've definitely got the evidence to back all this up, right?"

"There are a few lab analyses still to complete," Penny replies, hoping Beaker's made a start on them. "But yes, I have the evidence."

Tanner thumps a fist on the equipment trolley then, rattling the scissors and making Penny jump. "I want a preliminary report on my desk this afternoon," he says. He has a hand on the curtains when he stops. Turns. "Hang on. What about motive? What's Kerr's motive in all this? To clean up Buchanan's mess? I can make the jump to her setting the doctor's office on fire to hide their connection after Fletcher's disappearance, but why would she commit murder on Buchanan's behalf? Was she in love with him?"

Grimacing, Matiu groans again. Penny flashes him a look. Now is not the time for him to be playing for sympathy.

"There'll be a money trail," she says. "The victims signing over funds in return for a cure. We have a forensic finance consultant scouring the net for that data right now."

Tanner shakes his head, impassive.

"But there are three bodies," Penny insists. "Two people she's murdered. Three, if you count Fletcher."

"And none of it is going to stand up in court if we can't show that Kerr had motive."

"Power," Matiu says softly. "That's your motivation. Kerr wants to wield the power of life and death. She's high on it, intoxicated by the idea that she's a priestess who can control people's destinies. I swear, Kerr's convinced she can hold back the afterlife."

He's trembling now, perspiration shining on his forehead. Did the doctors give him *any* pain relief?

"Matiu, we have no way of knowing—" Penny says gently.

But Matiu cuts her off, his eyes flashing. "You're forgetting that Kerr spoke to me down there in the basement, Penny. She looked me in eyes with the stiletto dripping with the dog's blood still in her hand, and she *spoke* to me. And what she said was..." He breaks off and, placing his hand over the bandage, exhales slowly. "The woman is deranged, insane. We need to find her, Tanner, because she's not going to stop there. She's going to keep practising until she gets it right. She's going to kill again."

When Tanner has left, Penny smooths the bedclothes.

"Well, that's that then. Case closed, almost. I should go and get on to those final assays."

"Yup. Can't let lover-boy do all the work."

Penny smiles. "Well, there's Cerberus, too. The poor fellow's been tied up outside a while now."

"Is he OK?"

"He's fine. A bit singed. He must've been close to you when the firearm ignited the oxygen leaking from the museum's air purification system. He has some cuts from a display case broken in the explosion, the one all that sand poured out of, but nothing too serious. He'll survive."

Matiu grins. "He's a good dog," he says. "A fucking lifesaver, actually."

"He's an awesome dog," Penny agrees. "Do you think Rose Fletcher will let us keep him?"

"Pen," says Matiu quietly. "This case..."

"You'll be pleased to know I called your probation officer," Penny blurts. "I told her you were being treated for injuries sustained in a fire—of course, I didn't specify *which* fire—and that you'd make another appointment just as soon as you were discharged."

Matiu shrugs. "Whatever. Penny," he says again, more urgent now. "You know there's more to this than what you just told Tanner, don't you?"

"I know it was you who fired the gun. I'm not angry. Kerr didn't give you any choice. I would've done the same."

Matiu clasps her forearm with his good hand, gripping hard. "I'm not talking about the gun."

She knows he isn't talking about the gun. She's not completely stupid. Obviously there are some unanswered questions. Does he think she doesn't have niggles? What if it occurs to someone else that hair and nails are dead cells too, and therefore they should have found some at the warehouse? Or that her theory doesn't hold with Lavoisier's law of conservation of mass because there were no fat nanobots left lying about. And sure, Buchanan may have been remorseful about his involvement, but enough to mutilate himself? And then there was the sample, the one that almost ruined the Breadmaker™, the one that wasn't actually DNA at all... None of that matters. Penny's already decided. This case nearly unhinged Matiu, her baby brother, who already treads so close to madness. The altercation with Hanson didn't help, nor did witnessing the agony of those poor dogs, and to make things worse there was Makere, Matiu's imaginary friend, hanging around, poking Matiu with a stick, causing him pain. No, this case is done and dusted. Penny plans to make sure of it.

"You're injured and you're tired," she says. "This isn't the time to go into all that. What's important is that you're OK, Cerberus is OK, and since we solved the case, my lab is OK. Can we please not open a can of worms? Can we just let that be enough?" Putting a hand on her brother's shoulder, she leans in and plants a kiss on his forehead. "For now, at least?"

Nodding, Matiu closes his eyes and sinks back against the pillows.

CHAPTER 30

- Matiu -

Matiu sets the teacup down and then, rather stiffly, makes his way back into the kitchen for the second cup. As ever, Mārama's house is cloying with damp heat, yet in spite of this, Matiu feels a chill across his back. It flows from inside him, from the hollow places he stepped through, in that half-reality, half-nightmare of the museum basement. Cups of tea and sunshine haven't yet managed to banish that cold from under his skin, and he's not sure it ever will.

He pauses for a moment, cup in hand, looking out the window and across the street, sunshine lying thick across the lawns and parked cars like warm honey, the world melting beneath it. Kids run back and forth, a ball bounces and there's shouting, shoving. So much focus, so much energy bound up in the physics of an inflated rubber bladder. Like there's nothing of any greater consequence in the world than the fate of that ball, its next arc, its next thwarted trajectory. Matiu won't ever know that carefree abandon again. He'll never see the sunshine without feeling the shadows pressing in around him, without knowing that the sun is a shining disc burning in that vast coldness, one tiny glimmer amongst the eternal empty spaces between, leaving him drifting, so very, very small.

Matiu sets the cup down and grips the edge of the bench with his good hand, in an effort to still the trembling. Choking down a clutch of breaths, his muscles settle enough for him to pick up his cup and return to the lounge, where Mārama is sipping her tea. Hugging his bandaged arm close—not that he has much choice, since it's still in a light cotton sling—Matiu settles in his customary place. But there's nothing customary about the moment. He's not used to being the victim. Nor is he used to being held in such keen regard by Mārama. She's looking at him, actually looking *at* him, *seeing* him with all his wounds and battle scars.

For once, it is Matiu avoiding the conversation, trying to retreat into his other world, and Mārama whose attention is focused intently on him, like he's sitting on secrets she needs to hear. He stares into the steam warping away from his tea, not wanting to answer the inevitable questions; *How did he hurt his arm? What happened to his face?* Questions that will lead to a conversation he doesn't want to have, answers he would rather remain hidden and silent. Because talking about what happened, giving it voice, will make it all real again. Matiu would rather it never becomes real, neither in his thoughts nor in his world, but he's not destined for that sort of luck. He's in this thing now, deeper than he wants to be, and the only person he can blame for that is himself.

Still, he's taken by surprise when Mārama speaks, her voice sharp, clearer than it has been in as long as Matiu remembers. "He's gone," she says.

The chill, *that* chill, flushes through him. He nods. "Gone from me, yes. But not gone. I think he's here, somewhere."

"You know who he is, don't you?" She sounds uncertain, despite the words.

Matiu frowns, shakes his head. "I just know he's Makere. He's been in my head since I was a kid. And now he's gone. I saw him walking away. He stepped out of... out of...*there.*"

Mārama looks away, her eyes drifting down, down, like ash falling from the sky, and Matiu thinks she's about to slip away again, but then her gaze snaps up, fixing him to his seat. His fingers are trembling, and he clamps them tight around the cup. "You didn't stop the tide, son. You bought some time, that's all. Time to run from the drowning. You need to run, you and Penny both, as far and as fast as you can."

Matiu shakes his head. "I can't, Mārama. I can feel it too, like you. We can't run far enough. Someone needs to stand here and fight."

"Your father has connections with the Chinese government. Get the whole family on one of those ships in the harbour, get to China, run for the mountains and live the rest of your days milking goats and growing rice. You don't want to be here when the tide comes in for good. You need to be gone."

"Tell me why," Matiu breathes, sitting forward in his chair, his intensity matched only by the fierce grip Mārama now has on the arms of her chair. "Tell me who Makere is."

She speaks through gritted teeth, her knuckles pale. "He'll be finding ways to grow strong, son. And then he'll come looking for you. Until you are dead and gone, he won't rest."

"Why? Who *is he*?"

Then the veil comes down once more, and Mārama's eyes turn pale and soft, and she leans back in her armchair, the rage and tension melting from her, like honey, dripping like water, and she turns her gaze to the window, and the sun, and the clatter of the ball as it rebounds off the fence. "So nice, when the children are all playing together, don't you think?" she says, a thin, tired smile creeping across her features. "I do so wish you'd had a brother to play with, my boy. Boys need brothers, to keep them out of trouble. But not you. You were always such a *good boy*."

Matiu stares, for as long as he can stand it, and then gets up and walks from the room, pausing only to put a hand on his mother's shoulder and kiss the top of her head. She's in her own world again now. She's lucky. Unlike Matiu, and Penny, she has a place to escape to. He doesn't bother saying he loves her. She knows that already, and in any case, he doubts she can hear him.

All she can hear, like Matiu, is the surging roar of the tide rising around them.

END OF BOOK 1

Glossary of Māori and local terms

Aotearoa	Māori name for New Zealand, meaning land of the long white cloud
amonga tapu	neighbouring tribespeople
CBD	central business district (down town)
Cooee	to be within cooee of something, is to be in calling/shouting distance, in earshot.
cow pat	cow pie, cow manure
DoC	Department of Conservation
floosie	(colloq) woman of low or loose morals, a version of floozy
full tit	(colloq) New Zealand bastardisation of the term 'full tilt'
gander, take a gander	(Brit) to take a look
hapū	kin, clan, tribe
Kapok	java cotton
kauri	gigantic podocarp tree
kia ora	Māori greeting, hello
kiri tuhi	tattoo, in this case without cultural significance
kuri	dog, four-legged friend
lino	(colloq) abbreviation of linoleum
lose one's wicket	to lose one's cool
marae	Maori communal meeting place used for religious and social purposes
moa	extinct flightless ratite native to New Zealand (larger than an ostrich)
manky	(Brit) unpleasant, dirty, scruffy, old

pīngao	orange bladed sedge grass found in coastal locations
pōhutukawa	native myrtle, commonly known as the New Zealand Christmas tree
pong, pongy	(colloq) smelly, rank
pōrangi	mad, insane, deranged
pugged	ground deeply rutted by hoof prints
radiata	species name for a northern pine
rewa-bread	Māori sour-dough bread made from fermented potato
Rēinga	The northernmost tip of New Zealand, spiritual place where departing souls depart for the afterlife
rimu	New Zealand red wood conifer, protected and highly sought after for building and cabinetry
spliff	joint, marijuana; specifically a blend of marijuana and tobacco rolled together and smoked
tap	faucet
Takahē	flightless bird, indigenous to New Zealand
taniwha	mythical monster, typically lizard or serpent like
tino pai	the best, all good
toa	warrior
Tū	abbreviation of Tūkāriri, the god of war
turps, on the turps	literally Turpentine, colloquial term for alcohol, being on the booze, getting drunk
vego	vegetarian
wacky backy	marijuana
wairua	Māori term for soul, spirit
whangai	to foster or adopt, young person/fosterling
Work and Income	New Zealand term for social security
yabber, yabbering	to talk or jabber, derived from the Australian aboriginal term yabba

About the Authors

Lee Murray is a multi award-winning writer and editor of fantasy, science fiction, and horror, including the bestselling *Into the Mist* (Cohesion Press), which World Horror Master Michael B. Collings described as "adrenalin-fueled excitement in a single, coherent, highly imaginative and ultimately impressive narrative". She is proud to have co-edited six anthologies of speculative fiction, one of which won her an Australian Shadows Award for Best Edited Work (with Dan Rabarts) in 2014. Lee lives with her family in the Land of the Long White Cloud, where she conjures up stories for readers of all ages from her office on the porch. www.leemurray.info

Dan Rabarts is an award-winning short fiction author and editor, recipient of New Zealand's Sir Julius Vogel Award for Best New Talent in 2014, and the Paul Haines Award for Long Fiction as part of the Australian Shadows Awards in 2017. His science fiction, dark fantasy and horror short stories have been published in numerous venues around the world, including *Beneath Ceaseless Skies, The Mammoth Book of Dieselpunk*, and *StarShipSofa*. Together with Lee Murray, he co-edited the anthologies *Baby Teeth - Bite-sized Tales of Terror*, winner of the 2014 SJV for Best Collected Work and the 2014 Australian Shadows Award for Best Edited Work, and *At The Edge*, a collection of Antipodean dark fiction. Find out more at dan.rabarts.com.

CPSIA information can be obtained
at www.ICGtesting.com
Printed in the USA
LVHW042227101022
730372LV00004B/189

9 781935 738961